GROTESQUE

ALLISON PAIGE

FINNEGAN PUBLISHING GROUP

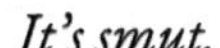

It's smut.

TRIGGER WARNINGS

Blood, Death, Dub-con, Explicit language, Gore, Graphic violence, Graphic sexual scenes, and Somnophilia.

Welcome to Glamis Manor

There are three rules which must not be broken:

1. Do not look into the mirrors for more than a moment.
2. Do not invite guests into the manor.
3. Do not leave the shelter of the manor after nightfall.

Chapter 1

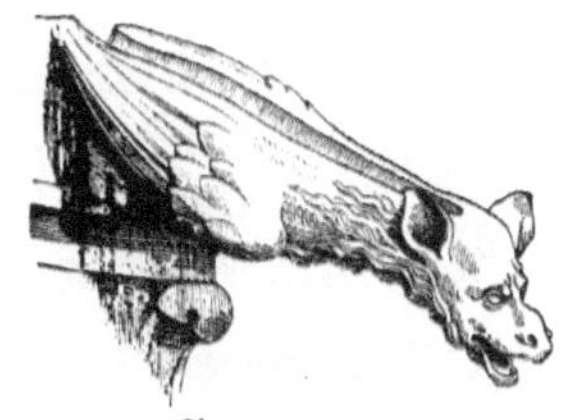

SORCHA

There were three things I knew about Grandma Macky. One, she was batshit crazy, or so my mother said at least. I never actually *met* my Grandma before she died, but it was obvious that her and mom hadn't gotten along. Any time they spoke things would quickly escalate, ending with Mom slamming the phone down with an exasperated, "She's nuts."

Number two, she was filthy rich. Money had been found stashed in all sorts of odd nooks and crannies in all of her residences. Behind picture frames, stuffed into mattresses, and even within the walls of her pantry. Calling them "residences" was being generous – all three had been rotting away. It was a sad state she had existed in when she'd clearly had the means to live comfortably.

The third thing I knew about Grandma Macky, was that she had a laundry list of secrets. One of which was staring back at me with ominous arched windows for eyes, and a sweeping entryway as a gaping mouth. Unlike the other properties, Glamis stood polished and proud. Its dark paneled walls and verandah were gleaming, looking as though they'd been freshly oiled. The manor's obvious grandeur and the quality of its intricate wooden balustrades and stone carvings were the only hints at just how old it was.

My thumb hovered over my mom's name on my phone. I should call her. I should, but...

"I leave Glamis Manor in Bristol, Massachusetts to Sorcha Eleanor Grendel."

"That hovel," my mom had scoffed. Her eyes had rolled so far back in her head I thought they'd finally get stuck.

The attorney continued, "All property within the grounds will transfer to Sorcha on the condition she lives in the home for one year. In addition, she will receive the sum of $1,000,000 upon the end of the first year, and $500,000 each subsequent year she remains in residence, to a total sum of $7,000,000. In the event she leaves prior to the year's end, Sorcha forfeits this gift and all her inheritance, including what has already been bequeathed. Should any one of the family try to interfere with this, they too shall be stripped of their inheritance. I have left each of you more than enough, a reflection of our relationship in the living world."

The will went on. As the attorney spoke, he had slid a copy of the notarized deed over to me, my name already on it in a flowing script. He'd explained Bristol was actually in Rhode Island, but that it had been a part of Massachusetts once. The rush of blood pounding in my ears drowned out anything else he said.

Not much was known about Glamis. Mom and her brothers hadn't seen it since they were kids, and all they remembered was it had been creepy and practically falling down. It had never been a manor at all, Mom argued, but Macky had insisted on calling it that anyways. My mother and uncles sure as hell hadn't known I would be written into the will, and at the mention of the amount of money I was to receive, I felt as if there'd been some horrible mistake. The way they'd all looked at me, it was like I'd stolen something out from under them. Betrayed them without even meaning to. Without even having *met* the woman. They did seem a little less vindictive about the money when they heard it was Glamis I was to inherit. As they were all quick to tell me, Glamis had withered long before Macky passed; ceased to exist. Was as good as a ruin.

The three of them had each been willed one of Macky's other remaining homes with a fair share of money. Of course, they had dug through the houses like cockroaches and pilfered her hidden stashes, gorging themselves. There had to be thousands, if not almost a million in cash for them to divide on top of what they called their "measly inheritance".

Standing in the curved gravel drive and staring up at what was to be my new home, I was inclined to agree with them. Whatever they remembered from their childhood, the place had clearly fared better than any of them imagined.

Macky hadn't just left me a house, she'd left me a mansion that looked like it had walked straight out of a gothic horror film. And it was no ruin.

It was surely an elaborate joke. A reflection of our relationship? How did not having one with her entitle me to *this?*

The hair prickling sensation that I was being watched crawled along the back of my neck. Cold, uncomfortable awareness slid down my body slow as oil, and I adjusted the heavy duffle bag on my shoulder.

It was absurd to think anyone could be watching me when I was the only one here. And yet, the unblinking stone eyes of the gargoyles glaring down at me from their perches made me uneasy. The "manor" looked more like a castle, with its stone carvings and stained-glass windows. Sure, it was old, and something felt a little not right about it, but it was most certainly anything *but* a hovel. My eyes slowly travelled down the turret that stood proudly at its center; its magnificent windows framed with their pale grey curtains. An upper balcony with a stone railing wrapped around the right side of the house, its curvature reminding me of a smirk. I didn't like that. Didn't like that the manor had the features of a living thing.

I turned my attention to the woods that crowded the eastern side of the property. All those dark trunks and tangled branches did nothing to ease the sense of foreboding that seemed to blanket the place.

I walked a little to my left so I could see around the back. From where I stood, I could just glimpse what looked to be a wild garden, or a decorative hedge, maybe? White pebbles covered the ground, winding in eccentric patterns. Paths, I guessed. The vegetation rose up behind the manor like a giant gothic frame, crowned by thorns and assorted colored flowers.

I swallowed as a chill raked a cold hand up my back and turned to look back towards the entrance. The long driveway was empty, save for a few scattered leaves across the gravel. At its end stood the massive black iron gates. They had swung open smoothly on my approach, no screech of rust, no cobwebs, no overgrown ivy as I had expected. It was perfect, almost too perfect.

Why did you keep this masterpiece hidden away Macky? And why leave it to me?

I kicked my car door shut, the sound a startling shot in the otherwise silent air. It was the auditory equivalent of a nail slamming home into the lid of a coffin.

I gave a choked laugh. It was official, this place gave me the fucking creeps.

I wasn't superstitious by any means. Despite being a lover of the horror genre, I had never believed in ghosts or demons, but approaching the front door I couldn't help but wonder if I would finally come face to face with something that went bump in the night.

I paused at the top of the steps, admiring the stonework and the handsome oak of the thick double doors. *Glamis Manor* was inscribed in iron over the arch, the cursive oddly familiar.

That odd feeling rose within me once more, and I shut my eyes.

The second Mom found out about the true state of this place she would try to strong-arm me into giving it to her. As far as she knew it was a ruin like all the others. Already she had tried to talk me into splitting the money that was "rightfully hers". My uncles would be at my throat next. It didn't matter than the will had stated they would lose everything if they interfered. Greed had a way of blinding people.

I loved my family, but they had their...quirks. Mom was a narcissist, Uncle Hank was a drunk, and Uncle Ken, the youngest of the three, was a mix of both. It was a hard thing, to love people who only loved *you* when they got their way.

"What the fuck, Macky," I breathed.

There were no cameras that I could see in the entryway and none when I first opened the door with the heavy brass key the attorney had given me, just a broad marble foyer and dark staircase leading up to the next level. Cameras or no cameras, the nagging sense of eyes on me wouldn't let up.

My attention caught on the small table in the center of the room, where a welcome basket sat proudly, a card tied to the front. Reaching for it, I peeled the envelope open with my nail and shook the small rectangle of heavy parchment free.

Welcome to Glamis Manor
There are three rules which must not be broken:
1.　*Do not look into the mirrors for more than a moment.*
2.　*Do not invite guests into the manor.*
3.　*Do not leave the shelter of the manor after nightfall.*

Ok, so there were four things I now knew about Grandma Macky. She was a stickler for rules, short as they were. And *freaky* as they were.

A fresh wave of chills trickled through my body, curling my toes. Grandma Macky clearly had a knack for spooky things, fact number five.

I flicked the card back onto the table. No matter, I could follow three simple rules and keep up my end of the inheritance bargain.

I took a deep breath and started to explore what would be my home for the next year.

I moved from room to room, vaulted corridor to sweeping staircase, in silent awe. The manor was incredible! Unlike Macky's other homes, it was in perfect condition, as pristine as the day I imagined it was built. The outside had been something, but this? Everything inside looked freshly restored, modern comforts tastefully interwoven with the Victorian furnishings and ornaments. I spun in the middle of a lushly carpeted hallway, when an abrupt laugh burst from my chest.

This is insane!

Glamis Manor had six bedrooms and eight bathrooms, a large kitchen complete with a walk-in pantry, a library, two parlors, a study, and a locked room that the brass key was no use for.

Having carefully inspected each bedroom, I picked one closest to the top of the stairs, that by all appearances, seemed to be made for me. The terracotta crushed velvet bedding and matching curtains reminded me of my favorite season.

Everything looked brand new, even the kitchen had been freshly stocked with supplies. Was this place magic?

Sorcha, I scolded. *She obviously arranged for someone to ready the place for your arrival.*

I gazed through the bedroom's broad windows, admiring the view of the black gravel driveway and long stone wall that shielded the property from the rest of the world. The tall gates didn't seem as menacing from up here. I could even describe the place as charming, with the way the sunlight glinted off the iron and caressed the manicured lawn. My reservations were fading fast as my mind spun with all the possibilities of living in this magnificent space. Something shifted in the corner of my eye but when I turned towards it...everything looked the same. I couldn't put my finger on what it was, other than I had the distinct sense that the house looked different depending on the angle you looked at it from.

Satisfied with my self-guided tour, I strode back to the car to grab the rest of my luggage. As soon as my foot hit the gravel, I felt it again. That horrible sensation of eyes boring into the back of my head.

I spun around but just as before, there was no one. I had searched every room, closet, and corner before coming outside. I scowled at the gargoyles. "You're not doing your job very well."

Gargoyles were supposed to be protectors, guarding the homes or places of worship they flanked the roofs of, warding off evil spirits. Two were crouched over the doorway, their long talons digging into the stone banister. Several more with long spindly necks hung off the second floor, their gaping mouths ready to channel a heavy rainfall. The last was a single statue coiled over the very top of the main entryway... it looked more like a dragon than the rest, with its membranous wings furled at its back. The long neck was decorated with scales, and four horns protruded from the brow above its snarling face.

Grandma Macky liked *very* spooky things.

The longer I looked at the gargoyles the worse my sense of unease became. Why was something that was supposed to be protecting me from harm so damn terrifying?

Once everything I thought I might need was out of the car, I explored outside. The forest concealed a decent amount of the property to the east but behind the house, past the garden, was a clear open field, at least another five or six acres. There was no telling what was beyond that, but I assumed it all belonged to the manor. Belonged to me. A place like this wouldn't do well with neighbors backed up against it like in the suburban sprawl a few towns over.

The garden was just as unique as the house. No, not a garden, I realized as I drew closer – it looked like a small hedge maze.

I circled the lush greenery, open-mouthed. There were four entrances, each crowned by a white lattice arch draped in lavender wisteria. A pair of small shrubs adorned with dark berries flanked each lattice. The hedge, tall, and comprised of what looked like some kind of freshly trimmed weed, connected the entrances in a perfect square. Inside, I could see plots of roses, lilies, and other florals I didn't recognize, lining the pathways between the strange, weed-like hedge walls. The flowers almost looked out of place, despite how purposefully they had clearly been planted. I bent down, reaching out to examine a pink-petaled shrub.

I hesitated before my fingers touched it. There hadn't been a rule about picking flowers, but with how particular Macky seemed to be...

I rubbed my fingers together. The nagging sense that whoever was watching me still had their eyes on me made me tug my fingers back. Best not push my luck.

I couldn't shake the swarm of emotions that hounded me. Excitement. Foreboding. Gratitude. Fear.

"Get a grip, Sorcha." I muttered to myself. I'd seen one too many horror movies and now every time something seemed a little off, I immediately assumed the worst. It didn't matter that in every horror flick the girl who went into the big scary haunted mansion got killed. That was film. *This* was real life. *This* was a dream come true. I had an entire *manor* with an entire kitchen stocked full of food, a whole forest to explore, a claw foot tub that had been calling my name since the moment I laid eyes on it, *and* I was going to be rich. One. Million. Dollars. All I had to do was remain here for one year. And every year after that I would get more. And how could I *not* love this place for all the lavish charm and mystery it offered!?

All the same, I locked the front door behind me when I reentered the manor.

This would be a piece of cake.

In fact, now was as good of a time as any to celebrate.

I walked into the kitchen and popped open a bottle of champagne.

Chapter 2

SORCHA

The sky turned molten as the sun made its descent over the treetops. Swatches of magenta were splashed against the clouds, and warm light spilled into the manor, washing me and everything in it in bright colors that felt like a dream.

I was *in* a dream.

I rested my chin on my knuckles as I stared out the bay windows of the kitchen, taking in the view of the garden and the open expanse of the field behind it.

I can't believe this is mine.

I waited until the sun disappeared behind the trees, only faint glimmers of its golden light peeking through the branches, before turning to make my way upstairs.

I paused at the bottom of the steps, unsure what had stopped me. Trailing my gaze up through the dimness, I caught sight of the mirror hanging at the top in its ornate frame, and thought back to the welcome note with its short list of rules. My heart thundered as I flipped the switch to my right.

Artificial light flooded the staircase, illuminating the landing, and the mirror. It looked like the sun had re-appeared, and was suspended, forever reflected in the glass.

I made my way up slowly, my eyes flickering to the mirror and back down to my feet. As I finally made it to the top I stopped.

I was looking back at myself.

My dark brown hair was mussed from having laid on the couch too long. One of my cheeks was tinged pink, and creased with lines from one of the pillows. My jeans and wrinkled bookish tee shirt were baggy and made me look larger than I was. (But I was comfy, so who cared?) My green eyes were wide.

I'd never seen fear on myself before. The longer I stared at my spooked expression, like a deer caught in the headlights... the more at ease I felt.

I let out a little breath. Nothing was going to happen.

I lifted a hand, the reflection doing the same. That's all it was, a reflection of myself. Ghosts weren't real. Maybe Mom was right, and Grandma Macky was just batshit crazy.

By the time darkness had settled into the house, I was curled up in the upper parlor with its pink velvet couch and floral-patterned chairs, a stack of books I'd pulled from the library at my feet. My own book collection was in the car, waiting to be hauled out, but that could wait until morning. For the moment I was content with exploring what Macky had left behind, and with discovering just what else occupied the enormous shelves downstairs.

To my surprise, Macky and I had a lot in common. We both enjoyed fantasy books. She had a broad collection of epic and high fantasy novels with a few non-fiction books sprinkled throughout. The current book I was thumbing through could be described as a tome. It had caught my eye immediately, being so large, and bound in heavy leather. There was an eccentric dragon carved into its cover. Mythical beasts were sketched on its pages in what looked like charcoal, accompanied by scribbles I couldn't discern. There was no author. No name anywhere that I had seen in the book.

I wasn't sure if this was some elaborate sketchbook Macky had crafted, or a collectible she had acquired for her library. Whatever the case, it was simply stunning.

I slid it beneath the novel I was currently reading as I tucked myself into the corner of the couch. Mine was an Irish folk horror about a woman unknowingly being toyed with and hunted by two creatures that lurked within the icy waters just offshore. The blurb had hinted at romance, but there weren't yet any orgasms building in the heroine, just a sense of creeping unease. It was just weird enough that I wanted to give it a shot. But not so weird that I thought it would spook me further.

The tableside lamp flickered, drawing my attention up. It was entirely dark now, save for the lamplight and what spilled into the room from the hallway. Outside the window, the dark seemed to deepen. To take on a life of its own, as it swallowed up the landscape. I stared, holding my breath as I waited for my eyes to adjust, but the trees never came back into view. There was nothing but a giant black void. The only thing I could see was my own reflection.

Does this count as a mirror?

I looked back to my book quickly, pushing the thought away as soon as it entered my head.

There was no harm in mirrors.

Except everything I had read or watched said they housed spirits. That they were portals to other worlds. That they showed reflections of doppelgangers. That they grew hungry.

Something moved in the corner of my vision.

I jerked my head up.

I could have sworn that I saw something dark flash through the hall-way. Like someone had sprinted past. But there was nothing. No sound of retreating footsteps.

I berated myself. *Night one and you're already losing your wits? Get. A. Grip.*

Surely it had been my eyelashes, or the lamp flickering. A shadow I'd glimpsed at the wrong angle, and my overactive imagination had done the rest.

In the large room with its massive, uncovered window, I felt suddenly exposed. Tucking the books beneath my arm, I rose to my feet.

It rose with me.

I don't know what *it* was, only that I felt *something* move when I did. But there was nothing in the hallway. Nothing lurking in the room with me, that I could tell. I turned, very slowly back to the window.

The window where I could now see the moon's light casting down over the forest. It washed over the balcony, bathing the banister and two gargoyles that looked out over the garden in silver.

There had been something there. Something before that had been blocking my view.

I'd never moved so fast in my life.

My heart was pounding, blood pumping in my ears, as I walked quickly to my room. I wanted to run, to sprint, but the idea that something would chase me if I bolted kept me in check.

I reached the safety of my room, locking the door behind me, and rushed to the windows, pulling the curtains closed with shaking hands. Before I could second-guess myself, I was pulling the bedspread free and tossing it over the mirror of the vanity, trying desperately to hook a sheet over the one in the bathroom.

All the while my mind raced.

There had been something watching me. Something obscuring my view of the property.

The rational part of my brain said that a cloud had been covering the moon and that was why I couldn't see anything. But there is always some sort of light, even if the moon's face is hidden. You can always see in the darkness, trace outlines and shapes. Through the parlor's window, there had been nothing.

I rested a trembling hand over my chest and dug a nail into the skin.

One night at a time. I could do this.

It was nothing. It had been a cloud covering the moon. It's a big house. An old house. A big, old house that had been well taken care of, and houses that are taken care of don't harbor anything sinister. Ghosts weren't real.

I went through a list of rationalities until I finally calmed myself down. I let out a breath, my chest tight from holding it. I laughed, leaning my head back against the wall. "Good one, Grandma," I said. Maybe ghosts *were* real and this was Macky's way of getting back at me for not being part of her life. I get a free home, and she gets a free haunt. It was a win-win.

I also *clearly* needed to layoff the horror movies.

The warm water of the shower was a much-needed comfort as I eased out of my anxiety. I lathered quickly, washing and rinsing my hair and body, before standing there to let the heat melt into my bones. It had been a long day. A long week. It had taken me longer than it should have to drive up from Florida. Major life changes always took it out of you, and I was exhausted. Not thinking clearly.

Maybe the house and I had gotten off on the wrong foot.

"Hello Glamis Manor, I'm Sorcha, pleased to meet you." I held my hand out expectantly.

"Nice to meet you, Sorcha," I said with a deeper voice.

"I'm sorry for barging in here like this, but you see, Maxine was my grandmother, and she left you to me. I'm going to take care of you from now on. So, I'll obey the rules, and you don't pull any pranks. Sound good?"

Of course there was no answer.

Still, it felt like the house was listening. I smiled to myself as I got out of the shower, water dripping lightly to the rug beneath my feet.

I wrung out my hair and changed. Even though I felt better about what had happened earlier, I was still too chicken to pull the sheet from the bathroom mirror. I made another pass through the room, checking all the closets and even under the bed, but as I already knew, it was just me.

I climbed under the covers with my book, but hadn't even made it another ten pages before my eyes began to droop. Placing it on the bedside table and switching off the light, I curled into a small ball beneath the throw. I was tired. So tired now that everything had finally caught up with me and the adrenaline had completely worn off.

Tomorrow would be better.

Now that the house and I were acquainted, everything would be just fine. I let a soft, rhythmic tapping –like a bare branch on a windowpane – lull me to sleep.

Chapter 3

CORBAN

How delicious.

Her brown hair had appeared dull through the windshield of her beat up car, but as soon as she'd stepped out, the sunlight had burnished it a dark copper. She had looked up at the manor and that was when my breath had caught. Bright green eyes, like two fine emerald gems. I flexed my tongue, imagining what they would feel like rolling around the inside of my mouth. She was a long-legged meal I could make several courses out of. I would have to take my time with her. Savor her.

It had been six months since the death of Maxine. Six months of waiting before the jewel-eyed beauty rolled up the drive and stepped onto the Glamis grounds. I'd been seething, a mass of fury and rage until the girl appeared.

Maxine, as dull-witted as she had appeared, had been cleverer than I had given her credit for. As she'd lain dying, her last breaths coming quick and shallow, she had spat in my face.

"You will never get what you desire," she rasped.

All this time, all the years that I had spent priming her, the luxuries I had showered upon her, fantasies I had fulfilled – meant nothing. A wasted effort.

"I will have it," I snarled.

She had smiled, a shadow of what used to be her greatest feature. "My children and their children will never know about you. It ends here, Corban. Your time has run out."

Before I could strangle her, she was gone. Just like that, all the hard work I had carefully crafted, vanished in a final exhale of breath.

I'd torn the house apart for months until I finally found where she had stashed the will. It had taken another two weeks before I found the correct names of her children, and the single offspring of the female. As the youngest, the granddaughter would be the easiest to mold. The one with the longest thread in life, that I could take my time with.

I would not make the same mistake with her that I had with Maxine. Sorcha would be different.

Sorcha.

Something in her name clawed through my blood.

The funny thing about magik, is that you can shape it into whatever you want. Of course there is always a price, but when you have lived as long as I have, that price means little. A brief intention had the letters rearranging themselves, new words appearing between them, and the will was good as new, naming little Sorcha Grendel as heir to Glamis Manor. The 'hovel' that was meant to be forgotten. That Maxine would have left to rot.

I was not someone who would be forgotten.

I'd waited patiently throughout the day, watching Sorcha as she made her rounds through the house and the grounds. I tracked her every move. Stars, my blood was alight with anticipation.

"You're not doing your job very well," she had said.

Was she talking to the guardians?

I let a feral grin fall over my face. The gargoyles no longer moved. It was a mystery to me if they lived at all or had finally truly turned to the stone that encased them. Not that I cared. They had been nothing but a nuisance with their incessant nagging – insisting that I could not eat anyone that came on the grounds. The constant lecturing, that I was to *protect* the women of the manor, not *torment* them. But I was no gargoyle, and their rules did not apply to me.

I tracked Sorcha across the grounds as she circled the hedge-shrouded garden. She reached out hesitantly to one of the pink blooms, her brow furrowing. Oh, it would do no good if she touched it. If she played with something that could kill her before I had my fun.

While the Belladonna Garden was exceptionally beautiful, it was also exceptionally deadly. Maxine had taken to planting more thrilling plants, as if they would ward me off or keep me from her. That was lethal oleander that bloomed beneath Sorcha's fingertips. A little down the path, should she dare to enter, she would find foxglove, deadly nightshade, and so on. And that was to say nothing of the danger the hedges themselves concealed.

I exhaled lightly when Sorcha withdrew her hand.

Good. If she really wanted something from the garden, I would pick it for her myself. Or depending on where her eyes fell next, slip it into her evening drink. Did she drink? Most of them did. Liquor was a poison in and of itself, but it worked too slow. The side effects would take years to surface.

Brushing her palms over her thighs, she turned back to the house.

Yes, finish your exploring. Take your time. And then we can play.

I would have pounced on her there and then had the sun not been cocked high in the sky. It would be hours before I could relieve my impatience. It did, however, allow me to remind myself that I needed to take my time with this one. That I needed her.

As the last of the light faded between the trees, I slipped out of the shadows. I slunk onto the balcony that wrapped around the second-floor parlor and peered down at the young woman. Her head was bent over a book. I couldn't see her eyes from this angle, though.

I let a flicker of my power skirt across the hallway. Her head snapped up.

"Look here," I breathed against the glass. I spread myself wide, making sure that she would see only me. "Turn around, Sorcha."

Slowly, she did.

Those eyes.

They paired with a proud, angular nose and full pouty mouth that was parted in fear. Oh, the wicked things I was going to do to that mouth. I wondered how her teeth would feel sliding against me. Biting into me.

My blood thrummed within my veins. I took a step back as she turned away, and leaned against the far side of the balcony. My heart was racing, my need burning. Before she looked back outside, I was leaping onto the roof and loping to the room I knew she had made for herself. I didn't have to wait long before she came bursting in, locking the door behind her.

I tsked. That would not keep me out.

I was leaning toward the glass when she jerked the curtains closed. With a flash of my teeth, I went to the next set of windows, but she covered those too.

Fine.

I would wait her out. I had all night. All year. All of eternity.

I waited until I heard her fingers gliding through the pages of her book to come to a halt, until the light seeping through the crack in the curtains was extinguished. I tapped against the window, inviting her to look out and find me. There was no response.

It would be risky slipping into the house now when I couldn't see if she was asleep, but by the sound of it... I cocked my head, pressing my ear against the window. It sounded like she was. Her breath deepened with the sound of dreams.

I slipped in through the front door, pausing in the foyer to cast a glance down at Maxine's silly list of rules, exactly where I'd left them for Sorcha to discover. I snorted. As if those flimsy lines had ever worked. As if they would stop me from taking what I wanted.

They hadn't before.

Well, almost.

In two bounds I was up the stairs and before her door. In the wink of an eye, I was on the other side of it, leering down at her.

Sorcha was even more attractive up close. She looked nothing like Maxine, and I supposed that was a blessing. Maxine had been short with a craggy face, and a pudgy, splotched body to match. All of Sorcha was sharp and long, while the best parts of her–I pulled back the sheet to confirm–looked deliciously soft.

Sorcha stirred, mumbling in her sleep, but didn't wake. I continued my visual feast.

A black moth was tattooed on her upper thigh. I ran my talon over the outline of the wing. Normally I detested tattoos, but this one was special. It was a bad omen.

So, my little meal liked death, did she? I wondered how at ease she would feel once she was face to face with it.

I let my hand drift over her face, but I didn't touch her the way I wanted to. Not yet. I wanted to savor this moment. How innocent and unprotected she was beneath me, a predator of lethal shadow.

She would do nicely.

Chapter 4

SORCHA

The cool breeze of the bay blew through my car window as I drove into town. Bristol was a sleepy little place, right on the water, which was dotted with an assortment of sailing and fishing boats. It was about a forty-minute drive from Glamis Manor. The red brick factories and whitewashed colonial homes were in stark contrast to the gothic abode I had moved into.

Last night had been *long*. On more than one occasion I had woken up with the eerie sensation of being watched crawling all over my body. I knew I was alone, that my bedroom door was locked, and that nothing could look back at me through the mirrors since I'd ensured they were covered. But the feeling had made for a hellish night, and even worse dreams.

Reading horror novels before bed was hardly helping.

The last thing I'd done before leaving the house this morning was cover the rest of the mirrors. I'd pulled sheets from the beds in a couple of the spare bedrooms, tucking their corners firmly to conceal the dark, still reflections. Better to be safe than sorry, I figured.

There wasn't anything I needed in town, but exploring always did my soul good. I spent the afternoon wandering antique shops and boutiques before I made my way into a small pub, *McBride's* scrawled boldly across its doorway in big gold lettering.

Revelers spilled across the patio, but I had to blink against the darkness as my eyes adjusted to the dim lighting as I walked inside. For a Thursday afternoon, the place was buzzing. There was a small crowd huddled at the bar with few people standing in the middle of the floor, laughing and hollering about something John did on Monday. I squeezed myself between two bodies and made a beeline for the last seat at the bar.

Luck was on my side today.

I had enough money saved up from my old waitressing job that I could afford a beer or two on this fine afternoon. Macky's attorney had explained that I would be receiving the initial inheritance payment within the first month of residency at Glamis. It would be enough to get me through the first year. After that, the big checks would roll in and I'd never have to worry about a thing ever again.

My phone buzzed.

Mom: How's it going?

I hadn't told her I had made it to the house yet. Part of me was still anxious about the whole 'secret mansion' thing.

Me: Fine. I should be there in another day or two. I keep pulling off to explore all the little towns along the way.

Mom: Alright. Be safe and let me know as soon as you get there.

I took a sip from my glass. I had no clue what I was going to tell her. I couldn't avoid her forever. I knew Mom, though. She would ruin this just as soon as she found out. She would make it about her. Hell, I wouldn't be surprised if she tried to get me to sell the place. Or worse, take matters into her own hands and move in with me.

"Want another?" The bartender nodded to me.

I looked down shamefully at my nearly empty glass. "Um, yeah."

"Something stronger?"

I smiled. "No, the same is fine. I have to drive back." My shot nerves protested, but I remembered seeing wine in the pantry. I could break into that once I got home. I just needed to be away from the manor for a little bit.

Someone bumped roughly against my shoulder. I turned to see a man's back as he stumbled past me, grabbing the edge of the bar to steady himself. A sharp remark starting with *how about you watch where you're going* and ending with *asshole* was on the tip of my tongue when he suddenly glanced my way.

A cocky smile turned his lips up as he made a quick head to toe assessment of me, his gaze lingering on my thighs.

"That's a cool tattoo," he said. His dark brown eyes had an odd flatness to them, like he was looking through you, or into you. When that smile deepened, there were soft crinkles in the skin around his eyes and lips.

"Thanks," I said, turning my attention back to the bartender. "I'll go ahead and close out."

"What's it for?"

It was the cringiest most annoying question in the book about tattoos. "For me. I got it because I liked it."

"Well yeah, but does it mean anything?" the guy asked.

"It means I like moths, so I got one tattooed on me."

The man frowned. He opened his mouth like he was going to say something but shut it when someone clapped a hand on his back.

"Jeremy, Katelyn is asking where you're at. Maybe stop hitting on other women and go check on your wife." He was tall with broad shoulders and a waist to match. His smile seemed pleasant enough, but the look in his eyes as they bore into Jeremy's stated in no uncertain terms that he meant business.

Jeremy looked between us before grumbling and rising. "Ass," he hissed.

The man slipped onto the stool beside me. "Sorry about that."

"I feel sorry for Katelyn."

He snorted. "Me too, that's my sister."

"Yikes." I watched him and the bartender, Jason, exchange a few words. My new bar companion worked in IT a few towns over, it seemed. Jason was asking him how the new contract was going before he turned back to me.

"Very yikes," he said. "I'm Quint, by the way. I don't think I've seen you before."

Quint was handsome, no doubt about it. He had a tan that said he worked out in the sun when he wasn't sitting behind a desk. His jawline was bare, but shaded with the barest hint of stubble.

"Sorcha. And I just moved here."

"Oh! Well, welcome. I love Bristol, but kind of an odd place to move. Where are you from?"

I took a sip of my drink. "I'm from Miami." I laughed when his eyes widened. "Yeah, big change."

"No kidding." His brown eyes sparkled. "Why the jump?"

"It's a long story." No way was I about to tell some stranger about the small fortune I had landed on.

Quint held up a hand. "No pressure."

"I just needed a change of scenery," I settled on.

"I get that. I've thought about moving myself but it's hard to get away when your roots are so far in the ground."

I nodded like I understood. I didn't really. I was thankful for the space I had now put between me and the toxicity that was my family. It was a shame you couldn't pick them the way you chose friends. That you were just stuck with them for life, good or bad.

I had a small group of friends back home that I missed already, but I could make new friends. My gaze slid back to Quint who was recommending the best spots in town for food. At the mention of a burger my stomach growled. Now that he mentioned it, I was absolutely starving. In my haste to get out of Glamis this morning I'd skipped breakfast, and it was now well after lunch.

"A burger sounds amazing," I said.

"I was going to swing by Carmel's if you're interested in joining me? It's block up from here." The hope in his question made me smirk.

I'd met guys like Quint before, but he seemed genuine.

Sure, there were a million things that could go wrong leaving with a stranger you just met, especially if you're a woman, but Quint didn't strike me as a bad guy. He had the good ol' boyish character that balanced out his gruff features.

What's the worst that could happen in a place like this?

We finished our drinks and strolled up the street. I told him about Miami, and he told me how the biggest city he had ever visited was Manhattan – a trip to visit another one of his sisters. Before I knew it, we were seated and stuffing our faces with possibly the best burger I've ever had. Whoever Carmel was, hats off to him.

It felt like I had known Quint for longer than a couple of hours. He had a familiar air about him. He was confident with a slight edge, but I caught him blushing at least once when I allowed myself to truly smile.

I'd been so spun up with the drama around Macky's death and the sudden move, and was finally feeling like I could relax a little.

I stopped mid laugh at a story he was telling about how he had stolen his friend's car as a prank when he was younger. The sun had completely vanished from the sky. I hadn't even noticed when it had started to set, but now the tangerine blush of the clouds reflected off the water. I had less than an hour to get back to the house before the light would be gone completely. Before it was dark. *Rule #3: Do not leave the shelter of the manor after nightfall.*

"Oh fuck," I hissed under my breath. I burst up from the table, fumbling a wad of cash from my pocket down. "I'm so sorry but I have to go."

Quint's entire countenance fell like I had just socked him in the gut. "Is everything ok?"

"No– yes. I'm sorry, I have to get home before dark."

He cracked a hesitant smile. "You going to turn into a pumpkin or something?"

How did I even begin to explain my grandmother's crazy rules and that I had no idea what would happen if I broke them? She was clearly superstitious, but I had already made the house a promise: that I wouldn't break any of said rules. Not on the second night at least. Not until I found out *why* she had those rules.

"Something like that."

Quint grabbed my hand before I could dart out. He let it go when I whirled around. "Sorry," he said. He handed me back the cash I'd left on the table. "I got it. Can I get your number at least? I'd like to see you again, or if you ever need someone to show you around town." Words were tumbling out of his mouth too quickly for him to keep up with.

A personal rule I have is that you never give the first nice thing that comes your way a shot. At least wait and see what your options are before diving headfirst into anything.

But clearly, I was turning into quite the rebel today.

"Yeah," I said breathlessly. I watched the color slowly leak from the sky as I rattled off my number to him. It felt like ages for him to type those ten little digits into his phone. I forced a smile as he shot me a text with his info. "I'll talk to you later." I was out the door before he could get another word in, sprinting for my car.

Dark was not far off as I rolled through the wrought iron gates and up the drive. The sky had lost most of its color, turning a sickly gray between the muddied pink clouds. I let out a sigh of relief. I had plenty of time to spare. What was I so worried about?

Before I even opened the door I felt it. The awareness of being watched. I hesitated, looking through the windshield for any sign of who might be looking back at me. As the sky darkened further, I felt a prickling sensation on the back of my neck. It took everything in me to exit the car slowly and not sprint into the house. Whatever paranoia was trying to take root inside my body would not win. Grandma Macky would *not* scare me off with her stupid rules.

I slammed the car door shut and step by step, made my way up to the shadowy entrance. By the time I had locked the front door behind me, it was completely dark outside. White fog was pooling from the forest and slowly creeping toward the house.

I let out a slow, shaky breath and flipped on the porch light. Inside, the pressure of being watched was less intense, like I was safe inside the house. *Safer*, the thought skulked in. I turned away from the window, taking in the yawning expanse of the shadowy foyer. I'd hadn't turned any of the lights on before leaving, not having planned on staying in town so late. The dark sprawl of the silent manor was overwhelming.

I flipped a lamp on in the hallway, then moved to the living room and kitchen. The warmth of electric light lifted a little of the weight from my shoulders as it chased away the shadows. I poured a glass of wine before flipping on the tv in the living room. Alcohol wouldn't fix my paranoia but it would help dull the burning of my nerves. I poured a second glass after downing the first.

I didn't remember dozing off. I couldn't say what woke me, just that I was passed out one minute and sitting bolt upright the next, straining to hear whatever sound may have stirred me. An alien chasing crew members on a spaceship flashed across the tv screen. I turned it down just as the creature jumped on one of the men, its long tongue shooting out to wrap around his throat.

At what point had horror become my comfort? There was nothing I enjoyed about the gore and violence that often came with it. Maybe it was the controlled dose of fear, the knowledge that the horror always ended when the movie or book did. Or maybe it was the adrenaline, the chill of it in my blood leaving me wide awake, ready for anything.

I flicked through the channels until a children's cartoon popped up. Now was as good of a time as any to change my demented habits. I was easing back down against the pillow when I heard a soft swish of fabric from the depths of the house.

What was that?

I padded into the kitchen and cocked my head to listen. Outside the darkness still held its ominous shape. Maybe it was the wind I had heard. Until it came again, this time from the back hallway. I headed towards the sound, stopping short as I came face to face with myself. One of the sheets I'd placed earlier in the morning had fallen from the hallway mirror. My pulse skittered as I realized where the first sound must have come from. I backtracked to the bathroom set off the living room – that mirror was uncovered too.

I tucked the corners of the material back around the frame. A mirror revealing itself wasn't the scariest thing in the world. *Wait, why would I think that? A mirror revealing itself?*

I obviously hadn't secured the coverings as well as I thought I had, and they had come loose. That was all. I was halfway through fixing the one over the mirror in the hallway when I heard the snap of a sheet from up above.

I turned slowly to face the bottom of the stairs.

My heart thumped painfully at the same moment chills burst across my skin. I hadn't been afraid until that moment, thinking it was some silly fluke that two sheets had slipped off the mirrors, but that sound of a third ripping free was no coincidence. Material doesn't snap like that when it falls. Someone would have had to yank it free for it to make that sort of noise.

If ghosts weren't real, then that meant someone very human was in the house with me. How long had the house been vacant before the attorneys reached out to us? Had it been vacant at all? Maybe there was a maid living here? It would explain why the house was so well kept. But wouldn't someone have mentioned that? Surely, they would have introduced themselves.

The greeting on the back of my tongue died as I hovered at the base of the stairs. Nothing good ever happens to the person who goes investigating strange noises. I needed to know, though. I needed to see for myself that the sheet had been taken off and that I wasn't the only person in here.

I crept up the steps until I could see the mirror cresting the landing. I let out a deep sigh of relief. It was still covered.

Encouraged, I made my way up to the top and scoured the rooms. There was nothing to see. No other mirrors uncovered. Whatever I had heard must have been a twisted joke of my imagination.

Until another sound reached me. It wasn't the same this time, rather, it was the sound of fluttering. Like wings against glass.

I carefully approached the landing mirror, my eyes locked on its covering.

It shifted slightly. Like something was trapped beneath it.

I stood frozen, transfixed. Until the sound came again. The whispering and tapping.

The sheet fluttered, the fabric reaching towards me like long fingers. Almost without thinking, I reached back, my fingers grazing the material. I kept reaching, farther, farther, until I couldn't deny it.

I was pushing the material *through* the mirror, not against it.

In my panic I snatched the fabric down. I jumped at the sight of my own reflection, then covered my mouth as I started to laugh. I was simply looking back at myself... just as I should have been.

And then I saw what had caused the disturbance behind the sheet.

Moths. Three of them perched on the surface of the mirror, their wings spread wide. Death's-head hawkmoths to be exact.

I took a cautious step closer. The vivid yellow and black of their wings stood out against the soft glow of the lamplight. The skulls decorating their backs stared back at me as if in warning as I traced my fingers in the air above them. My mouth felt as though it were filled with sawdust as I touched the fingertips of my other hand to the tattoo on my thigh.

Death's-heads were not native to the Americas. So, what the hell were three of them doing in the house? Had Macky been collecting them? Breeding them somehow?

As far as I knew my grandmother hadn't been a pet person so I found it highly unlikely she would have been a bug person.

I turned, trying to decide on how or where I would put them if I collected them. Maybe I could put them in one of the back rooms. The downstairs bathroom seemed best, it was smaller, and it would be easier to catch them again when I figured out what to do next.

Another sound pulled me reluctantly away and into a bedroom. My heartbeat quickened as I pulled the sheet covering the vanity mirror to the side. It slid slowly to the ground as I took a step back.

More death's-heads. Six. No, seven.

I was moving before I heard the next flutter of wings. I wasn't thinking. The rules didn't even cross my mind as I pulled the sheets away from the mirrors. How could I? When with each reveal there were more moths. More eyeless sockets staring back at me. It didn't dawn on me until much later, when I was facing my reflection in my bedroom, that the moths were only on the mirrors, and nowhere else in the house. I touched the glass before me, but it remained firm.

I had drunk too much. This was some drunken stupor I was currently in.

My nails dug into the ink on my thigh. Death's-heads were often associated with rebirth or the afterlife. I'd gotten the tattoo to symbolize my fresh start.

But they were also associated with, and best known for, being a sign of death. They were a bad omen.

A terrible, awful feeling slunk into the room. It was in the house, now that the mirrors were uncovered. Whatever had been watching me was here.

Chills rushed across my skin as I swallowed the unnecessary terror. I was being ridiculous. There was a perfectly good explanation for the moths. There had to be.

I reached out to the glass again. Still, it remained firm under my touch. I slid my finger down to one of the moths. Its small legs tickled my fingertip when I pulled it away.

I didn't sleep that night. Not when there were so many mirrors to uncover. So many moths to count.

I had reached fifty-two by the time the sky paled. But by then I had curled up in one of the bathrooms, one with a much smaller mirror that bore only a single moth.

I sat down on the toilet, pulling my feet up on top of the lid so I could wrap my arms around my legs. That is how I dozed off, watching the moth, wondering how many more were appearing now that no one was counting them.

As if they were multiplying all on their own. Or creating an army. As if they were preparing for something.

When I woke with a start, the moths were gone.

Every. Single. One.

Chapter 5

SORCHA

I'd finally worked up the courage to text my mom that I had made it up to Glamis. If something strange was happening, I wanted someone to know where I was.

I'd texted Quint too. He'd responded quickly, like he had been waiting for me to reach out. That had been three days ago.

Quint: Want to grab dinner this week?

My thumbs hovered over the keys. I couldn't help but feel that the incident with the moths had been some sort of warning. That I had cut it too close coming in late the other night.

Me: How about brunch?

There was a slight pause as three dots flashed up on the screen, disappeared, and then came back.

Quint: Brunch is perfect. There's a spot called Two Eggs that's excellent. Should I pick you up?

Me: Sounds great! Is today too soon?

Quint: Not at all. 11?

Me: Perfect! I'll meet you there.

Unease clogged my throat as my stomach churned. I'd been at Glamis for less than a week and already my nerves were raw and bleeding. I couldn't breathe until I was off the grounds, hauling ass down the road like a bat out of Hell. How was I going to make it an entire year?

I'd done my best to ignore the strange tapping on my window at night. The tapping that had grown ever more insistent the more I refused to acknowledge it.

I wasn't due to meet Quint for another hour, but I couldn't stand another second alone in the manor. I also couldn't continue to maneuver through its empty halls blindly. I needed to know more about its history. A place that old surely had some stories to tell. I needed to know why, of all people, Macky had left it to *me*.

A quick Google search had me punching in the address of the local Bristol library, and thirty minutes later I was standing out the front, looking up at its stately, brownstone façade. Rogers Free Library was beautiful, if a little less grand and a little more moss and lichen-covered than it had been when first constructed. I examined the photo of the original building – built in the late 1800s, apparently – proudly displayed inside the front entrance. The passage of time was so very evident between the pristine, multi-story building in the image, and the worn, single level structure before me. Not like Glamis, which had been built even earlier, yet seemed untouched by the decades. Huh.

I paused over the threshold. What a strange thought to have.

I approached the front desk hesitantly. "I was wondering if you had any records on Glamis Manor?"

Color drained from the librarian's face. She touched her pointer fingers to the back of her ears before placing them delicately over her keyboard. "Nothing in the collection, but plenty of stories to tell. The place is haunted."

"What do you mean 'haunted'?" No way I was living with a fucking ghost. Though, that would explain the overbearing presence and constant sense of having company.

The woman, *Beth,* according to her desk plate, shrugged. "No one really knows. Some people think it's the ghost of a man who was murdered there when the house was originally built." I opened my mouth to interject but she held up her hand, "Let me finish. Others think it might be a vampire. I know that sounds crazy but, whatever it is that lurks up there isn't good."

Putting the murder to one side, the town sounded as cooky as Macky.

"You shouldn't be asking about that place. It makes for terrible gossip."

"I just moved in. My grandmother, Maxine Harris, left it to me."

Beth whistled. "That's quite the legacy to leave to just one person. Was Hampton not able to answer your questions?"

"Hampton? Who is that?"

"He's the groundskeeper. He started working for Maxine a couple of years ago. Nice fellow, doesn't talk much, but as far as I know he's still employed. I'd heard Maxine passed, but I didn't know she had any family. Never mentioned them. We sort of expected the place would finally fade away."

I nodded, tucking that information away for later. That explained why the manor had been fully stocked when I arrived. Possibly. Groundskeepers typically took care of everything *outside* of the house.

"Thanks," I mumbled. For nothing, I added mentally.

"If I were you, I'd sell the place. That or put a match to it."

My stomach flipped. "That bad?"

Beth nodded. "Too many strange happenings around Glamis. The people that go in either wind up mad or dead. Not trying to scare you, but it's true. Maxine seemed sweet enough, and forgive me for saying this, may she rest in peace, but there was always something off about her."

This was the first person that wasn't a family member to say she was a little off. Maybe Mom hadn't been overreaching with her tall tales.

"I can't sell it. Not yet." I waved my hand in the air. "There's too many legalities behind it."

Beth's finger traced over the space bar of her keyboard. Her large dark eyes narrowed with concern. "Just be careful. Stories' gotta start from somewhere, right?"

I nodded. "Speaking of... the murder?"

"Oh, right. That," she released a breath, her cheeks puffing out. "Glamis Manor was built by Gerald Thatcher and Rosaline O'Connor – maybe, in the early 1800s? You can do a quick search on the internet, but I'll save you the trouble. Anyways, something wasn't quite right with Rosaline, just as soon as they'd moved in. She started talking about how a monster lived within the walls. Everyone thought she was crazy, of course, I mean, Gerald had built the house himself so he knew there weren't monsters living anywhere inside. Not that he would have believed in them if there were."

I blinked slowly, trying to keep up with the random tangents of Beth's story. Just get to the point, I wanted to say.

"But then Rosaline started getting attacked at night. She would wake up covered in scratches and bite marks. Mmhm, actual teeth marks if you can believe it. At first everyone thought she was doing it to herself, but then, how does one bite their own neck? There was talk about institutionalizing her until one day everything just stopped.

"No more strange marks. No more raving about a monster."

My brows furrowed so tight together I knew they were touching. "What happened?"

Beth threw out her hands. "She killed him. Took an axe to poor old Gerald and then hung herself from the balcony right after."

What. The. Fuck.

"Yeah," she said slowly. "Went from being normal, to mental, to that."

I let out a long breath. If anyone had mentioned this story to me prior to moving in I don't think I would have uprooted my life to take on the challenge. Millions of dollars to live in a haunted mansion where someone was murdered and a woman had hung herself? Fuck that.

Except...I couldn't go home now. Not when I was already here. I had to see it through. It's just a story...a horrible, awful, terrifying story.

"And the vampire?"

Beth looked over her shoulder, but we were still the only two people in this section. "People get curious, you know. Couple of folks, teenagers and such, have gone up there and there's been sightings of a creature with horns and big wings. It's the devil, if you ask me." She crossed herself and sat back.

The thought crept in unbidden: *is that what's been watching me?* I pushed it away, but the prickle of unease spread across my skin anyway.

Beth threaded her fingers together. "Glamis changed hands a couple times before Maxine bought it. As far as I know, she never had any trouble with monsters or ghosts. But it's true something was different about her once she moved in. I could never put my finger on it, but it always felt like she had some secret the rest of us weren't allowed to know."

"Like what?" I pressed.

Beth shrugged. "Hell if I know. Maybe Rosaline's monster was real, and she met it after all. Anytime anyone asked her about living in Glamis she always had this secret smile and would say it's been nice. Other times she'd nearly bite your head off for asking at all."

I audibly gulped as I backed away from the desk. "Was it lead poisoning maybe? Something in the ground, or the water up there?"

Once again Beth shrugged. "I don't know if anyone has ever tested the place. They're too afraid. Too superstitious. Once people started getting hurt while snooping around, everyone stopped trying to get answers."

Had Macky gone crazy before or after she moved into Glamis? And if the house had something wrong with it, why did she choose to stay there instead of moving into one of her other properties?

"Um, thanks," I said halfheartedly.

"Listen..."

"Sorcha," I said.

"Listen, Sorcha. If anything strange starts to happen, don't wait around to find out what it'll do to you. You're too young to be dealing with curses."

I left before she could see how bad my hands were shaking. How could I admit that things had been strange since the moment I arrived? Who was I going to tell?

By the time I sat down across from Quint I was a nervous wreck.

His pleasant smile faltered. "You ok? You look like you've seen a ghost."

A hysterical laugh bubbled up my throat. I rubbed at my neck and smiled instead, trying my damnedest to suppress it. "It's been a long couple of days, what with moving into a new area. I haven't been getting much sleep."

Quint frowned. "Do you want to talk about it?"

The way he was looking at me, I wanted to. I wanted so badly to tell someone the truth of what was going on. "You're going to think I'm crazy," I said.

"Try me."

It wasn't like me to spill everything to a stranger, but I couldn't keep it in anymore. My restraint had gone out the window with the sleepless nights and before I could think twice about the effect my words might have, I was spilling them on the table, laying everything bare to Quint.

I pressed my fingers against my temples as I told him about the moths. "They're native to Africa and some parts of Europe. I know how crazy this sounds, but there is no way that many death's-head moths could have been there."

"And it wasn't a dream?" It didn't sound condescending when he asked, but I couldn't stop myself from bristling.

"It wasn't. I touched one. I just," I shook my head, "I don't know. I went to the library today to try and find any history on the house but all the lady told me was ghost stories."

Quint took a sip of his coffee. "Not gonna lie, when you said you moved here, I didn't expect you to be living in Glamis Manor. Hell, anywhere but that place. I know the stories she's talking about, most of Bristol does. But," he paused, leaning forward until I met his gaze, "I don't think you're crazy."

I huffed. "You're just saying that."

"I'm not. A few years back me and some of my buddies went up there. I guess it would have been your grandmother I saw, Maxine, you look a lot like her from what I remember of her. She was sitting on the front porch reading a book."

I watched syrup drip off the chicken on my plate, pooling on the waffles stacked beneath. I wasn't sure what to make of that comment.

"A man, or what I thought was a man, walked out of the house. I don't know if what I saw was real, your mind plays tricks on you when you're scared, but he had big horns coming out of his head. He walked right over to her and kissed her on top of the head."

My fork clattered across my plate as I fought the urge to roll my eyes. Great, he was making fun of me.

"I swear, the five of us were hiding in the woods, but when he looked up, I could *feel* him looking at us. I'm not saying this to try and spook you further, but we saw that and ran. I've never been back."

"Don't play with me."

Quint held up his hands. "Honest to God."

"You're telling me the vampire story is real?"

Quint shrugged. "I don't know what he was, but it wasn't Halloween, you feel me? Everyone that's been to Glamis and survived has a different story. Three of the other guys saw it, but Jeremy swears he never saw a thing. I think he tells us that as much as himself though, to try and forget."

I swallowed and asked the question that had been at the back of my mind since the library. "How many people have died at Glamis?"

Quint winced. "At least one or two a year go missing from the town. Sometimes there's a body, other times," he trailed off and took a sip of his coffee.

I stared at him. I slowly shut my jaw, which had dropped open at his response. "And no one has ever investigated that?" This was insane. Glamis, Macky, Rosaline, the town. It was all sheer madness. I couldn't wrap my mind around any of it.

He shrugged. "This town has been around long enough to believe in curses. People that believe in curses don't want anything to do with them."

We ate in silence after that. No doubt he was trying to process what I'd said as much as I was trying to untangle everything I'd learned today.

Maybe I should tell mom what was going on. She would know her own mother better than anyone else. Wait, wouldn't Mom have lived in the house at some point?

I'd get to *that* later.

I stuffed the last bite of chicken into my mouth. "It's gotta be the land. Some sort of toxin buried in the ground."

"Maybe. Your best bet would be to get someone from out of town to come in and test it, because no one local will. I know you just moved but, do you have anywhere else you can stay in the meantime?"

"No. And I have to live there for a year anyways."

"Why?"

"Because otherwise I don't get to keep the house." I wasn't fool enough to tell him about the money I'd come into. People were killed for less, though Quint didn't peg me as the murdering type. Ted Bundy was a real gentleman too, though.

"Sheesh," he mumbled.

"I know." I leaned back in the booth. "Thanks for listening. Again, I know I sound nuts, but...thanks."

"You don't sound nuts. Ok, maybe a little, but seeing a bunch of moths is the least scary story I've heard coming out of that place." Quint reached across the table and nudged my hand. His smile was infectious, and I couldn't stop my own when my eyes met his.

I wondered if everyone else's experiences had started off small. "I guess you're right."

We walked back to my car. It was chilly by the water. I wasn't used to the crisp air and would need to buy warmer clothes for the winter months to come. I stuffed my hands in my pockets to try and retain the little bit of heat I had left in them.

I looked up into Quint's honey brown eyes.

"If you need anything, I'm a phone call away," he said.

I ducked my head, suddenly feeling shy with the way he was looking at me. "Thanks." I chewed the inside of my lip. "For listening, and for believing me."

"Of course." He held out his arm. I propelled myself forward into the side hug and allowed myself to hold onto him a little longer than necessary. "Text me when you get in?"

"Sure thing." I smiled, turning back to my car. As soon as it was running, I cranked the heat all the way up.

I was still smiling as I drove away, but it faded as I caught sight of Quint in the mirror. His own smile was gone, replaced with a grimace. Worried. He looked worried.

Chapter 6

SORCHA

Scopaesthesia: the fear of being watched. I scrolled down the search engine's homepage. All other definitions said I had paranoia. Was that why grandma Macky had left the house to me? Did some sort of twisted paranoia run in the family? Surely the haunted house and vampire stories couldn't be real.

Night had settled about an hour ago. The fog that came with it wrapped the house in a cool embrace.

I settled onto the couch downstairs and clicked my phone off. I needed to relax.

By relax I meant put on a movie to distract myself. I silently thanked Macky or whoever had paid the electric and cable bills to ensure I would be taken care of until I fulfilled my end of the bargain.

I settled on a classic horror I'd somehow never seen, my mind wandering as the credits rolled and the film got underway. I'd always liked scary movies, probably because they helped desensitize me. If I watched them enough, they stopped being scary. And if I was ever faced with a situation in real life, then I'd already know what *not* to do in order to survive. Well, in theory anyway.

My attention floated back to the screen. The lead actress was relaxing in the bathtub, her eyes closed, completely unaware of the stalker in her home.

The shot flashed to the intruder, the camera panning slowly up the length of a hunting knife in his leather-gloved grip. It crawled up his black-clad form to a masked face.

There was something strangely erotic about the way he watched the woman, and how she stretched and slid deeper into the water. She kicked one of her legs over the rim of the tub. He pushed the door open a little wider with two fingers, but still her eyes remained closed.

Heat wound down my throat, slinking into the pit of my stomach. I knew this was supposed to be a horror movie, but the way he was watching her was hot. It was even hotter when he strode into the bathroom, confident and menacing.

I ran my hand over my chest as the camera panned over her breasts, peeking through the soap suds. The next shot was of her red man-icured toes and that dangerously sharp knife grazing the air around them, following the arch of her foot and across her calf. How could she not feel him looming over her?

"Open your eyes," I hissed as I let my touch trail further down my body, beneath the top of my shorts.

As if she heard me her eyes slowly opened, then widened, but before she could scream the stalker had grabbed her ankle with one hand and pressed the knife against her throat with the other.

"Not a single sound," he said; his voice gravelly beneath the mask. Blood trickled into the water that lapped at her throat.

My fingers slid through the wetness leaking from my slit. I knew it was wrong to be so turned on, but fuck. There is something undeniably sexy about a man in control.

I missed whatever he said next but now the woman was standing up in the bathtub. Her stalker was looking her over, appraising her like a lamb ready for slaughter. He traced the knife over the curve of her thigh.

"Maybe we should have a little fun before I kill you," he purred.

My legs were thrown apart shamelessly, my fingers moving in and out of my pussy while I rubbed my clit.

The stalker held the knife in front of the woman's face. "Lick it," he commanded.

I threw my head back and stroked myself faster.

Knock.

Knock.

Knock.

My eyes fluttered open. I hadn't remembered closing them, but I snapped my attention back to the screen, my fingers slowing but not stopping, waiting to see who the new character would be.

Knock.

Knock.

Knock.

Ice cold shot through my entire body, burning my nerves and heating my face all at once. I jerked my hands from between my thighs and whirled to face the sound as it echoed down the hallway. Someone wasn't knocking in the movie, they were knocking on *my* front door.

My heart slammed painfully against my ribs as I realized how exposed I was next to the window. How I must have looked if the person on the porch had looked in as they walked up.

Had they seen me?

Who *was* knocking at this hour? I paused, my ears straining. Maybe it was one of Macky's friends come to check on the house? As far as I knew, no one knew that I was here. The only people that knew I was on my way up to Bristol were hundreds of miles away.

Quint knew.

Is he playing some sick prank on me?

Dread leeched into my stomach. Would he have looked inside first? If he didn't think I was crazy before, surely, he would now. Embarrassment heated my cheeks, flooded my entire body as I rose from the couch.

Knock.

Knock.

Knock.

I flicked off the table lamp. The only light spilling into the room was from the film as the girl on the screen mimicked my movements and slowly crept down a hallway. Clearly, she'd escaped the stalker for the moment, but I didn't like her chances. My skin prickled uncomfortably as I darted past the window beside the entrance, hoping whoever it was hadn't seen me.

The double doors were solid oak save for a patch of glasswork at the top, too tall for me to peek over. I was thankful I had turned off all the lights and that whoever stood outside couldn't see my shadow hovering on the other side of the door. I pressed my ear against the cool wood.

Knock.

I stumbled back, my heart lurching out of my chest.

Knock.

This one was harder, more forceful.

Knock.

My hand hovered over the doorknob. "Who is it?"

Rule #2: Do not invite guests into the manor.

I didn't plan on letting whoever it was in, let's get that straight. Rules or no rules, I had a feeling that whoever was banging on my door wasn't here for idle chit chat. My gut twisted in agreement.

Something shifted on the other side. "Is Maxine in?" The voice was deep and male. It wasn't Quint. He had a nice voice, but this...this one sounded smoother. Like honey melting into tea. I should have felt relief but somehow it only made me more anxious. Who the hell just strolls up to someone's house at night?

And this house of all of them?

Then it hit me, whoever it was maybe didn't know Grandma Macky had passed. My stomach flipped as I wondered again if they had seen me pleasuring myself to a woman about to be murdered.

"She's not," I said.

A shadow slipped past me as the man stepped in front of the window. I tensed, pressing closer to the door. Was he looking in? Looking for me?

"I have something for her. Could I leave it with you?"

"You can just set it down out front." No way in hell was I going to open the front door.

"I'd prefer to leave it with you. I'd hate for someone to steal it."

Typical for a man to refuse when you told them no. It didn't matter which way you formed the words, they never listened.

"I think it'll be safe out there."

There was a slight pause and though it made no sense I swear I could hear an intake of breath, like a hiss, before he said, "But are you?"

I looked at the door blankly. Surely, I had misheard him.

"Are you safe in there?"

It felt like someone had knocked all the air out of my lungs, as if something dark and menacing had reached right through the barrier between us and yanked it out. This had to be some sort of fucked up joke, a local who knew about Macky's will and wanted me to fail. Whoever it was wanted to scare me, and they were doing a hell of a good job. Maybe it *was* Quint and one of the *buddies* he had mentioned.

"Get the fuck off my porch or I'm calling the cops," I snapped.

My stomach sank as I realized I had left my phone in the other room.

The shadow flitted to the window flanking the other side of the door. They tapped their finger on the glass. The sound was quiet, barely a whisper of noise, and yet I knew it was the same tapping I'd heard the last couple of nights outside my bedroom window. All the way on the second floor. "You're not going to call the cops. Not when you seem so eager for a stranger to come in and surprise you." I didn't even have time to register the taunt – what it meant – when the doorknob suddenly turned and the door swung inward.

I slammed my shoulder against the wood, forcing it closed, and turned the bolt. I hadn't noticed it unlock, hadn't even heard it slide free from its sheath. There must be a key hidden somewhere out front. A key that this obviously dangerous man now had. He could come in whenever he wanted.

"That's right," he said, as if in answer. A low, musical chuckle filtered through the cracks around the door. "It would be more polite if you just invited me in."

"What do you want?"

"I want to give something to Maxine," he said.

"Maxine's dead!"

His footsteps paced back and forth and then gradually, they faded. A shadow moved in the corner of my eye. I kept my hands braced against the door as I leaned back, looking down the hallway. A tall silhouette slipped across the floor, making its way toward the living room.

He was heading to the kitchen, to the French doors. I didn't consider that it could be a trap, that he was possibly leading me away from the front door so he could double back and get in. I bolted to the doors, my blood rushing in my ears.

I skidded to a halt right as he reached them.

Whoever he was, he was tall, lanky even, but broad-shouldered. Dark hair framed his face but that was all that I could see. Even without light casting directly onto him, I should have been able to discern some features. Instead, there was total blackness.

"We can do this all night." Malice lurked behind the laughter in his voice.

My heart galloped. My arms had gone numb, my mouth dry. All at once it felt like my chest was seizing. I couldn't breathe.

Why couldn't I see his face? Not even the glint of his eyes. It was as if a black hole stared back at me instead of a man.

The weight of his gaze was too familiar. It was the same over-whelming awareness that had fallen on me the moment I stepped onto the property. I knew that this was the man I had felt watching me. As we continued to stare at one another, a profound, inexplicable sense of evil pooled at my feet. I felt it clawing at my legs, threatening to drag me under if I so much as blinked.

"What do you want?" It was barely a whisper. I hated that despite how much I thought I would be prepared for a murderer or stalker to come after me one day, I was entirely frozen with fear. No number of movies or books could have prepared me for the utter terror that pounded through my veins.

Somewhere in the background the woman screamed on the television. Holy fuck, I was going to end up just like her.

The stranger extended an arm, revealing one pale, grey-tinged hand. The hand opened, a silver chain tumbling from it. He wriggled his long fingers, so that the charm on the end danced.

It was a locket necklace. A heart locket.

"I was saving it for Maxine, but I think it would be prettier around your neck."

The threat in this voice was obvious. I could practically feel the venom behind his words dripping onto the porch.

I dragged my eyes up to his empty face. "Will you leave if I take it?"

The sick feeling around my legs pulsed. The stranger cocked his head slightly to the side, enough so that light cut across the edge of his chin. "For tonight," he said.

Anything. Anything to get this freak off my property and on his merry way.

"Leave it on the handle and step back," I said.

The man tilted his head the other way and though I couldn't see his expression I felt he might have been scowling at me. He let the chain glide down his fingers onto the doorknob. It clacked twice against the door before he finally stepped back.

I shook my head. "All the way off the porch."

He let out a heavy sigh and walked backwards, not once turning his face away from me. I unlocked the door slowly, watching him until his feet hit the grass beyond the decking. I opened the door and jerked at the chain. It fought against me as I tried to free it. With a final yank, it snapped and I pulled it inside, locking the door once more.

The stranger hadn't moved. I could feel him laughing at me, though he made no sound.

"Aren't you going to open it?" His voice was crystal clear. As if he were standing right in front of me still, rather than eight feet away.

I looked down at my hands. The locket was silver, finely made. My hands were shaking so badly it was a wonder I managed to open it on the first try, but somehow I did. Inside was a mirror.

I looked closer. A ripple spread across the glass, and in the space of a blink there was a moth sitting on its face. The familiar skull pressed into its delicate wings stared back at me.

A shadow fell across my hands, obscuring the locket and its contents.

"You must be soaking wet by now."

A tingling sensation prickled along my skin. He had seen me. Had been watching me for who knew hold long as I pleasured myself to a woman being attacked.

I knew what I would see when I looked up, but nothing prepared me for the shock when my eyes travelled upwards to find him looming over me once more. Dread was not a strong enough word to describe the sheer force of him. Looking into nothing, into the blackness where a face should be, I knew what true fear was for the first time. And there was nothing sexy or inviting about the realization that he was about to hurt me.

Shrieking, I hurled the locket against the window.

"You don't like the face of death now that you've met him?"

Time seemed to slow.

The stranger reached for the doors, and with the barest of touches, they drifted open. With my heart in my throat, I stood transfixed as fear himself crossed the threshold.

The locket clattered to the floor, breaking the spell. By the time he had fully stepped inside, I had already turned to run.

I didn't have time to grab my phone, knowing he was hot on my heels. I sprinted up the steps, my blood pounding, every sense screaming that death was right behind me.

As I turned and slammed my bedroom door in his face, I finally caught a glimpse of what stalked me.

His skin was pale, almost luminescent. Any chance I had of committing his other features to memory faded as I caught sight of his eyes. They were *red*. Glowing, fucking, *red*. His lips were peeled back in a sneer, exposing... were those *fangs?*

The vampire was real. Rosaline's monster was real, and it was in the house!

A chuckle came from the other side of the door as I struggled to slide the dresser in front of it. It felt like my heart was going to erupt from my chest. Fuck, I couldn't breathe!

"I won't come in. Not tonight," he purred. "This is just a taste. So you know how easy it is for me to get to you."

"What do you want?" My throat felt raw.

"Isn't it obvious?" There was a loud thump of something hitting the floor.

I flinched, looking frantically around the room. What else could I put in front of the door? What was I going to do now that he had successfully trapped me in here with no phone?

"It's alright," he said softly, gently even, as if he were trying to sooth me. "Get your rest. I'll be back another night to play."

I listened as his footsteps retreated down the stairs. Finally, the sound of the front door opening and then closing echoed through the house. I crept to the windows overlooking the front yard.

A dark silhouette stood in the fog; his face tilted up to my room. Even from this distance I could see the red glow of his eyes. He lifted his hand in a silent, mocking goodbye, and then he was gone.

Chapter 7

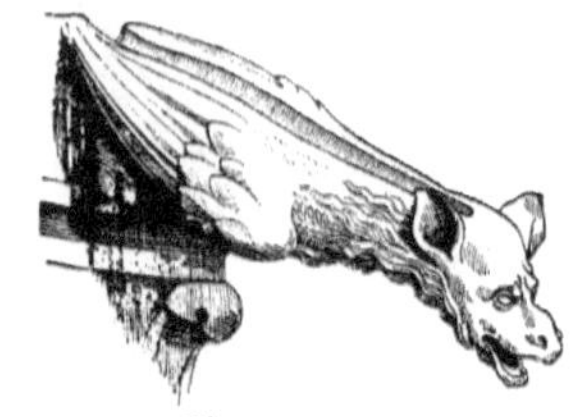

SORCHA

It took until dawn for me to work up the courage to unlock my bedroom door. Peeking into the hallway, I was surprised to see my phone lying on the carpet. The thump I'd heard last night, it must have been him dropping it there. Another reminder of just how powerless I was against him. I grabbed it and made straight for my car, hightailing it down the driveway. I slammed my thumb against Quint's name.

"Hey!" His voice was bright over the line despite the early hour.

"Quint." I took a deep breath. Tears burned the back of my eyes. I slowed to a stop at the end of the drive as I started to cry.

"What? What is it? Sorcha are you ok?"

"I don't know. I think the vampire is real, or maybe it's just some freak. Someone broke into the house last night." I was blubbering my words, gasping in between as I tried to calm myself down.

"Did you call the cops?"

"Do you really think the cops are going to believe Maxine's grand-daughter?"

There was a faint pause before he let out a long breath. He didn't need to say anything to confirm my suspicions. I would be lumped in with the rest of the women that had gone mad at Glamis Manor.

"Listen, give me about ten minutes and I can head your way. Is that ok?"

I nodded.

"Sorcha?"

"Yeah," I choked. "Yes, please."

"Alright, just stay put. Don't go back inside until I get there. And hey, I don't think you're crazy. Ok?"

"Ok," I said quietly. The line went dead, the silence cutting through the shock that had kept me numb all night, and I burst into tears.

An hour had passed when Quint finally pulled up, finding me in exactly the same place as I'd made the call. My car doors were locked as I stared rigidly at the forest. My only comfort was that it was daylight. If it *was* a vampire that had visited me last night, at least I'd be safe from him during the day.

Or I hoped so, at least.

Quint followed my car slowly back up the drive. By the time he stepped out onto the gravel alongside me, I had pulled myself together enough to recount the events of the previous night without crying. As we approached the looming front door, I couldn't help but think that Glamis seemed somehow even more foreboding now that I knew inside was no safer than outside.

We stepped into the manor's shadow, a sick feeling sharp as lightning struck me, and I faltered. Struck us both, by the way Quint stopped as well. I considered Macky's second rule – *do not invite guests into the manor* – but if those rules were meant to protect me, they hadn't done jack shit last night. Silently, I steeled myself, and motioned for Quint to follow me inside. We stood in the foyer as if we were waiting for something to happen.

Quint broke the spell first. "Let's start upstairs and work our way down," he practically shouted. I almost laughed – he might have been playing the tough guy, but I could see the sweat beading on his brow, and knew I wasn't the only one thoroughly spooked by the feeling that seemed to stalk us as we made our way to the top floor.

Searching the house was even more agonizing than I expected. Every little sound made me jump. At one point, Quint brushed against my back when he was leaning over to inspect one of the closets. I squeaked, making him jump too.

"This place gives me the creeps," Quint said, then winced. "I'm sorry. That doesn't really help."

"Do you feel it, though? Like you're being watched?" I led the way downstairs, pausing briefly to look at the giant mirror where I'd first found the moths.

"Yeah. I haven't seen any cameras either."

"No, I looked when I first moved in. There aren't any."

I was looking right at Quint, at the smooth, ornate wallpaper behind him, but once again the feeling rose that just outside my vision the house was not as it seemed. "Quint," I started hesitantly. "Does the house look different to you when you're not looking directly at it?"

"Huh?"

"Like when you look at it, do the parts you're not looking at seem different?" How else did I explain the way there seemed to constantly be a mirage shimmering in the corner of my vision, like heat rising from a sunbaked road. That the manor seemed pristine up close but seemed to wilt or discolor as the eye travelled away.

Quint's arm brushed against mine as a visible shudder ran through him. "Now that you mention it…"

I pursed my lips together and nodded. "Just making sure."

We didn't say anything after that. I felt a little better having Quint with me, and by the time we had scoured Glamis from top to bottom some of the tension had released from my shoulders. There were no signs of anyone else having been in the house.

We ended our search in the kitchen, leaning against the center island. He looked over his shoulder at the French doors. "Chances are the guy found out you're living here alone and is playing some kind of prank. I'd call the cops, so they have the report on record. I know a couple of the guys at the station. I just wouldn't mention anything about vampires."

I chewed on my thumbnail. He was right, it was the only reasonable explanation. Vampires weren't real. Ghost weren't real. None of that superstitious crap was real.

"It's better to be safe," he encouraged.

"Maybe it was a one-time thing." That didn't sound convincing even to my own ears. The stranger had said he would return. Fuck it. I dialed the non-emergency line before I could doubt myself.

The officer that showed up was in fact someone Quint knew, Officer Tyler Davies. They'd gone to high school together and slapped each other's backs in greeting. I watched as Quint dipped his head, whispering something I couldn't hear as they walked up the front steps. I stayed on the porch, my eyes straying to the tree line where I imagined the stranger had darted off to last night. I never did see any headlights, and I'd watched out the window for a long time before sleep overtook me.

"Ms. Grendel."

I blinked, turning back to the men.

"There's not much I can do. By all accounts there was no forced entry, and you're unharmed."

Fuck no– he wasn't going down this road. I didn't deign to listen to the rest of his patronizing speech before I barreled over him.

"A strange man came into my home, *threatened* me, *promised* he'd be back, and you're telling me there's 'nothing you can do about it'?"

"Ma'am–"

"Tyler, you know how things go around here. Can you leave a car overnight or something?"

Officer Davies rested his hand over the top of his holster. "Our team's short at the moment, there's no one available." Turning to me he said, "The best I can do is have someone patrol the area later this evening."

"And the evenings after that?" I wasn't scared anymore, I was furious.

"Not unless something else happens," he started.

"Unless something *worse* happens, you mean." Unless I wound up harmed or dead. By which point it would be too late. I opened my mouth to tell him exactly what I thought of his *team*, then snapped it shut. Cops didn't respond well to anger, and I could already tell from the look in his eyes he didn't believe a single word I'd said. It didn't matter that I had left out how fast the man had been and that his eyes had glowed red. I might as well have told him it was the vampire of Glamis Manor that paid a visit.

Quint was urging him to reconsider. "Will you at least file the report?"

Officer Davies sighed. "Yeah. I can file it, but like I said, my hands are tied. I'm sorry, but it's likely just a dumb prank. There's a lot of rumors that circle this place and it was probably some kid."

"Do you know any kids that are six foot five?" I arched a brow. As expected, neither one of them had anything to say to that.

The manor sank back into silence once the officer left. I looked out at the yard to the spot I had last seen the stranger. I knew he was out there somewhere, waiting. Would he come back tonight? Or would he make me wait? Slinking back from the shadows just when I'd had the audacity to relax my guard?

"You okay?" Quint asked.

I rubbed my arm to hide the way his voice had made me flinch. "I'm fine," I lied. The whole interaction had gone as well as I had expected it to.

Quint leaned against the wall separating the living room from the kitchen. There was a tight smile on his face that made me realize that perhaps he didn't believe me. He hadn't tried very hard to back up my story to his *buddy*. But he was here, so that meant he didn't think I was totally insane. He'd told me his story of the horned man after all. My stranger didn't have horns.

"I can stay, at least for tonight to give you some extra peace of mind. That couch looks comfy." He nodded to the couch in front of me. A smile played at the corner of his mouth.

Part of me wanted to refuse. On the other hand, it would be nice to share the big empty space with someone else. For a night.

I nodded, before a smile of my own pulled free. "You know how to fight a vampire?"

He snorted out his nose. "No, but I do know how to make a mean pasta sauce. I'll load it up with extra garlic to be safe." He winked before turning to the kitchen to scour the pantry.

In the back of my mind, I wondered whether I was putting myself or Quint in danger by breaking one of Macky's rules. But what danger could a guest bring compared to an intruder?

Quint had downplayed just how good his cooking was. The entire house smelled like an Italian restaurant, making my mouth water. The food itself, garlic and all, had been to die for. There had been enough for lunch and dinner and I'd happily stuffed my stomach full both times.

After dinner we sat curled on the couch, the TV murmuring something about an unsolved murder. My mind had been hyper focused on the stranger as the sun began to set, but now that I was warm, full, and cozy beneath a blanket next to Quint, *he* was all I could focus on. His heat was an antidote to the chilling dread that still clung to me.

A shadow of rougher stubble grew across his cheeks and chin, giving him a more roguish look. There was a white scar tucked in the corner of his mouth. Was that new? Or maybe it had already been there. Maybe the cut of his jaw had always been that sharp, and I was only just now paying attention to how handsome he was.

I bit the inside of my lip when his fingers brushed against mine under the blanket. Quint hadn't taken his eyes off the TV but I could feel his attention zero in as the electric shock sparked between us. The spark ignited when he slid his hand over my knee, his thumb working in slow circles.

I should have pushed his hand away. Instead, an invisible force turned my face to his. His hand slid higher as I tipped my face up–

BANG!

We jerked apart. I worked to untangle my legs as I lurched up from the couch, spinning to the window. Quint was already moving, jerking the front door open and sprinting down the porch.

"Quint," I hissed. *What if he's out there and we're running into a trap?* The thought chilled me as I ran after him.

Quint was standing with his back to me, staring at something on the decking. Peering around him I saw what he did, a crow, wings spread limply on the wooden boards, its neck twisted at an awkward angle. My fingers flew to my lips as I looked down at it.

"Fuck," Quint breathed.

"What is it doing out at night?" I dragged my eyes up to his face and turned.

The quiet pressed down on me as I looked across the lawn. Fog spilled from the forest, making its languid advance toward the house. I was an idiot. There was a stalker or crazed monster on the loose and I'd allowed my guard to drop, *literally* the next night, and nearly kissed Quint.

Heat bloomed up the side of my neck as I dropped my fingers to it. "Let's get back inside."

Quint made a slow turn of the porch, looking into the darkness as I had. "Yeah," he agreed. I let him lead me with a touch to the small of my back.

"Lock the door," I said as soon as we were back in the foyer. I took long strides to the kitchen and tested the handles, locking, unlocking, and relocking the French doors. If there had been a key out front that the stranger had, I doubted that he would have been kind enough to put it back, but the ritual made me feel a tiny bit better regardless.

Quint was returning from the back of the house when I rounded the corner. "Everything's locked up."

I wrapped my arms around myself. "There are plenty of bedrooms if you'd like to sleep somewhere more comfortable."

He shook his head. "I'd rather be down here so I can hear if anyone tries to get in."

"Alright," I breathed. I rubbed what was going to turn into a permanent crease in my forehead if I didn't stop pinching my brow. "I think I'm going to go ahead and try to sleep. My nerves are shot."

"I'll come get you if anything happens."

I was already at the foot of the staircase. "Thank you."

"Sure thing, Sorcha." He gave me a mock salute. "Welcome to Bristol."

I about choked on my laugh, but with each step, some of the tension eased from my neck.

It was fine, I was *fine*.

Here's hoping there were no more guests planning to stop by tonight.

Chapter 8

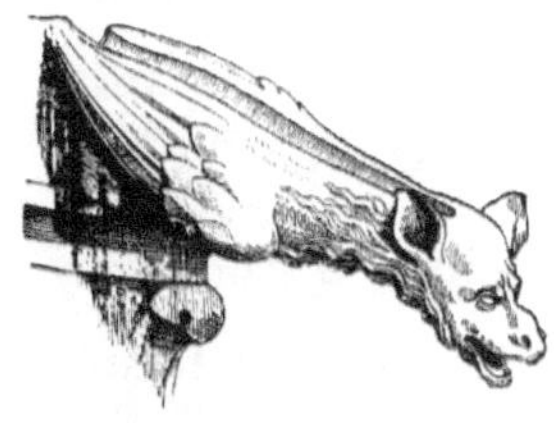

CORBAN

The scent of Sorcha's fear was a rare delicacy I wanted to dine on. I'd been watching her carefully since she'd moved in, and her love for the macabre, her obvious dark streak, drew a tingle down my spine. Wooing the lady of the house hadn't worked for me on the last four occasions, so I wouldn't waste my time on hearts and flowers, but I knew Sorcha and I would have *such* fun together as I tested just how deep that darkness within her ran.

And *deep* it ran. The film she had chosen piqued my interest, but when I tore my eyes away from the screen to see her hands down her pants it struck a sinful chord within me. One that shot straight to my cock.

She was wicked, and wicked things deserved to be punished. I had watched her breath hitch and the slide of her fingers through her wetness. I couldn't smell her through the glass, but my mouth watered in anticipation. I couldn't let her cum alone and unaware. If she wanted release, then I would be the one to give it to her.

I was disappointed she hadn't let me fulfil her little fantasy and had barricaded herself from me instead. Not that I minded too much. It had allowed me to draw out our game a while longer. To prepare her for what was to come.

What *had* peeved me was the sight of another male, one whose arrogance I could smell from across the yard. The man was practically preening over the fact that Sorcha needed help. I wasn't at my full strength in the daylight, but I'd still let my power flood down the front steps, making them both come to an abrupt halt.

He was sorely mistaken if he thought he was going to have Sorcha before I had a taste of her. He wouldn't be sampling her at all.

My blood simmered as the day dragged on, and the man didn't leave.

Oh Sorcha, you naughty girl. As silly as I found Macky's rules to be, they were proving to be useful in that they gave me reason to discipline Sorcha. I might have let it slide that she'd invited the man in for the day, but once night fell and he remained inside, my generosity went out the window. She thought she could break the *rules* of the manor and go unpunished? Not in my house.

I watched the man from the shadowed corridor as he made himself comfortable on the couch. I cocked my head, listening to Sorcha's feet pad across the upper floor before the sound of her bed creaking filtered down to me.

I didn't need to enter by door or window, but to prove that locks wouldn't stop me, I turned the deadbolt of the back door with the flick of my wrist.

I slipped into the hallway adjacent to the living room where Sorcha's guest was sprawled on the couch. His back was to me, his eyes glued to his phone.

It never ceased to amaze me how dull most humans' senses were. The male was utterly ignorant as I slunk through the shadows, even as my shadowy silhouette loomed in the light reflecting off the TV.

It took everything in me not to grab the man by his throat, rip it out, and toss him at the foot of Sorcha's bed. A little gift for her upon waking. She clearly hadn't liked my first gift, perhaps she would appreciate something more sentimental.

Alas, I couldn't do that without drawing unwanted attention to Sorcha, and thereby, myself. For as savvy as she looked, she wasn't very bright. Now that she had called the cops, they'd likely return. Adding the mutilated body of her *new squeeze* to the mix was not something that would help me win her over.

But she needed to learn her lesson.

I clenched my fists until my knuckles paled and made for her bedroom. I wouldn't kill the man yet, but she was going to learn that I was not someone to fuck with.

Ah, there you are.

Her hair obscured her face, like she had been tossing and turning. Just the sight of her, even like this, stilled the churning waters of my rage.

A flick of its remnants darted out in time with my tongue across my lips. I couldn't be patient when it came to her. There was no time, when need burned through my veins and demanded to be fed.

I crept to the other side of the bed, watching for any signs of her waking. Couldn't she feel death in the room with her?

I slipped into the bed behind her, my jaw aching with hunger, claws begging to sink into her. I slid right up against her and nearly came undone.

She was so small and warm. Oh so fucking warm that I could not contain the shudder that had me pulling her closer.

I brushed the hair from her face and peered down at her. Poor Sorcha, meant to be forgotten down in Florida but found, and here in my arms because of a demon's hunger. A hunger that knew no bounds.

The other women had been beautiful in their own right. Each crafted by the careful hands of whoever they deemed their creator to be. But none of them had made my blood sing the way Sorcha did. I'd tasted them all, gorged myself on their blood and their bodies. The bodies of their husbands and guests too. None of them made me salivate so. They had not tempted me in the way Sorcha's soft, pouty mouth and luscious curves did.

I traced my finger over those lips that I knew hid a straight-toothed, sharp smile. Her small oval face reminded me of the porcelain doll collection Maxine had stashed away in the attic. Her eyes moved faintly behind her closed lids, her thick lashes brushing her arched cheeks.

I licked my lips, sliding my palm down her body, to the curve of her hip and swell of her thick thigh. She fit against me perfectly, like she was made for me. Plush and malleable against my strength.

The hard length of my cock strained against my trousers, begging to be released, to slip inside of her. I pushed against her ass, but I knew it would take much more than that to appease my hunger.

Not yet. My patience was paper thin but that could wait. Just a little longer.

Her body tensed and she pushed back. My heart fluttered that she responded to me so readily. Perhaps I would be able to fulfil her fantasy sooner than I expected. I'd be able to slide inside of her and feel her wetness for myself. Feel how warm and ready she was for me.

Would she take me easily or would she be a tight fit? Would she moan when I grabbed her hips and pounded into her, or would her head be thrown back in a soundless scream? I had to know.

I rolled my hips forward, my breath catching as she pushed back again and a sudden exhale left her lips.

I dipped my nose into the hollow between her shoulder and neck, inhaling the soft scent of the soap she'd washed with. She didn't need to clean herself for me. Not when I was going to make her sweat, so I could lick it from her skin.

Languidly, purposefully, I licked up the side of her neck, savoring the smoothness of it.

"Sorcha," I hissed, my lips grazing her ear. "Wake up, wake up."

My grip bit into her hip, a gentle nudge to pull her from whatever dream encased her. Sorcha was mine. The darkness could have her when I was done with her.

Chapter 9

SORCHA

I grew up with nightmares. It was a rare surprise for me to have a pleasant dream, or wake without having dreamt at all. Maybe that was why I was drawn to horror stories– they were rarely worse than what greeted me every time I closed my eyes.

I'd heard of sleep paralysis but was fortunate to have never experienced that torment.

Until now, apparently.

As my eyes adjusted to the darkness around me, I was acutely aware that something had changed. The silence was so complete, the only sound I could hear was the breath moving in and out of my lungs. I felt my body straining to coil in on itself as I realized what had woken me.

There was someone in my bed.

It was the dip of the mattress at my back that had woken me, as they slid beneath the sheets. I could feel their chest against my back and their hand on the back of my thigh.

How long had they actually been there? Was it Quint?

Something in their utter stillness, in the menace I felt misting in the air like smoke, told me it wasn't Quint paying me an unsolicited visit in the dead of the night.

My fight or flight sense seemed to have abandoned me entirely. I was frozen, unable to move as the hand on my thigh started to move. The touch was gentle at first, but then the fingers splayed over my skin, grazing it with the edges of razor sharp nails... claws?!

"There she is." The rumbling voice was male. Its pitch was low, and scratchy, like he was parched.

A silent scream died in the back of my throat as my entire body remained rigid. Something pressed against my hair, his nose I imagined, as he inhaled and let out a groan.

Why the fuck couldn't I move?

He slid his hand over the top of mine and moved it down between my legs. "How about we have a bit of fun? Last night was cut so short," he hissed. His fingers curled over my own, the tips of his long nails biting into my sensitive flesh.

The man in the shadows. It had to be.

Somehow, he had gotten into the house again, and past Quint.

And now, the stranger was in my bed.

Get up. *Get up Sorcha!*

A spark ignited in my blood, cracking the ice holding me in place. I jerked forward. Not fast enough, before a clawed hand encircled the entirety of my throat and pinned me back to the man's – creature's – cold body. Humans didn't have claws.

Dreams couldn't hurt you. Not even nightmares had the power to come to life. Which meant... my stomach dropped as a wave of nausea hit me. This was real.

"Sorcha," he growled. "If you don't play my game, I'm going to wake your guest downstairs, and slit his throat. A guest you're not supposed to have."

I stilled, my breath coming short and fast. He smoothed the flat of his hand over my chest as if he meant to soothe me.

"That's right, I know the rules. And you've broken every single one, which gives me the right to punish you. Now, are you going to play with me?"

A garbled sound came out of me before I found my voice. "Don't hurt Quint." He was innocent in all this. And the stranger was right, I knew the rules but had brought him in anyway. I'd subjected him to this psycho's whims.

"Don't make me," he purred.

I nodded. "Ok," I whispered.

When I tried to crane my head back the creature hissed. "Not yet, little dove. You may not look upon me yet." His nose pressed to the side of my head as he nuzzled my hair again. "They always send me sparrows, little birds that do not satisfy my hunger. But you, my dove, I think will fill me up."

My stomach flipped and roiled. I was going to be sick. I could feel my gut churning violently. Burning erupted across the back of my throat and I heaved, gulping in air like it was the last time I'd ever get a taste of it.

"Shh," he crooned. His fingers worked over my throat, easing their grip as he rubbed the tension from it.

I shut my mouth when I realized I was gasping. It was near impossible to breathe through my nose but I focused on each exhale, trying to calm my nerves. Freaking out wasn't going to help me.

He slid his hand from mine, trailing those sharp nails over my stomach and up my chest. The press of his fingertips over my beating heart intensified the pressure building within me.

I exhaled slowly. "What's the game?"

"Close your eyes," he said. "And then sit up. If at any point you open your eyes, the game is done, and I kill your boyfriend."

This guy was fucking psychotic.

Warmth flooded my body when he rolled away from me. I hadn't realized how cold I had been, or that he was the source of it. His sudden absence ran shivers down my spine. I sat up slowly, my hands trembling as I placed them on either side of my hips.

Reluctantly, I closed my eyes, letting darkness shroud me.

I flinched when I felt his cool presence move in front of me. It was all I could do to not shrink back when he took my hands and pulled me to my feet.

"I've already seen you." As soon as the words left my mouth, I slammed it shut. My teeth clacked together so hard I felt the impact in my jaw. I shouldn't have told him that. He would kill me now that I had admitted to catching a glimpse of him last night before the door slammed in his face.

A spiteful chuckle rumbled from his throat. "No, you haven't."

He led me away from the bed. Once satisfied with my position he began to turn me, moving his hands from shoulder to shoulder. I could feel the room shifting around me as I lost my bearings. Round and round I went until both of his hands slid down my biceps to still me.

"So you don't cheat." Something soft banded across my eyes. I opened them instinctually, but only blackness stared back. He had blindfolded me. Tightness clawed its way back up my chest. I wouldn't say I was claustrophobic, but it suddenly felt like the walls were closing in around me.

"The rules are simple." His voice circled me. "Figure out where I am, and if you can touch me, then you win."

Wait...what? That didn't sound that hard. The room wasn't that large and there were only so many places he could go before I found him. It was too easy, which meant something was terribly wrong with his proposition.

"How do I lose?"

I could practically hear the smile in his voice when he said, "You have two minutes to find me. If within that time you have not caught me, then I win."

I clenched my fists at my side.

Teasingly he asked, "Don't you want to know what happens if I win?"

The fear simmering beneath my skin twisted as my blood began to heat. My instincts sharpened as I tracked his slow circles around me. He paused somewhere on my right, by the way the hairs on that arm tingled.

"What?" I spat between gritted teeth.

"I get to taste you."

Heat bloomed over my face. Curling my hands into tighter fists. I scoffed. "Absolutely not. You've had plenty."

He chuckled again, a deep thrum within his chest. "Not near enough," he breathed against my left ear. I'd been so certain he was on my other side.

Stay focused.

"Two out of three," I said.

I felt the hair on the right side of my face stir. "You're not really in a position to bargain." He hummed quietly. "I suppose it is only fair to agree. It is your body, but with three tastes of you I might not be able to stop."

"Prick," I snapped. It should go without saying that you should never antagonize someone willing to hurt you.

His breath ghosted my lips. "The game starts now."

I lunged forward, my hands diving through empty air as my momentum carried me forward into the wall. Something heavy and sharp-cornered dug into the side of my hip as I slammed to a stop.

I swallowed hard as I lifted trembling hands, turning away from the wall. I couldn't hear anything over the sound of blood rushing in my ears, waves crashing against the shore. Every rustle of my t-shirt as I moved my arms, or scuff of my foot on the ground sounded too loud. Too loud! I couldn't hear him.

I could feel him, though. That terrible feeling of being circled, of him pressing right behind me–

"You agreed to play," he murmured, his breath whispering against the back of my head. The touch of his fingers slid up the inside of my thigh.

I whirled, fingers clawing into nothing. "I am playing!" I bit my lip. "Fuck, this isn't fair," I whispered.

He laughed, a deep, menacing sound that clenched my heart. "It's not supposed to be fair."

I followed the hum of his laughter, staggering forward into another impenetrable object. My fingers brushed over something soft– the bed! I ran my hand along its edge, my other still waving in front of me.

"Thirty seconds."

Fuckfuckfuck!

I wasn't going to find him in time. I spun, turning back in the direction I had just come from. Aching cold brushed against my side, a finger across my back. I spun around, reaching for him. He was right there!

I stilled, listening, my blood raging. There wasn't time, but I had two more rounds to win. Two more and then...and then what? I hadn't thought to ask what I would win.

"Times up," he whispered against the shell of my ear.

I wanted to punch him. I was so angry I could scream. He was like a shadow, swirling around me, as uncatchable as smoke.

"Each round gets a prize," he said against my neck.

My knees buckled. If his hands hadn't grasped me beneath my elbows I might have dropped to the floor. I flinched when his nose brushed against mine. The gesture only caused me to tremble more, my breath coming out in ragged bursts.

His nose trailed over the top of my cheek. Even though I knew what he was about to do, I still tensed. Cold lips ghosted against mine. His fingers curled into my arms, holding me steady. He kissed me. My mouth parted as I jolted back. He followed, kissing me softly until I was backed against a wall, where his mouth grew more insistent.

I don't know if it was his kiss or the rush of the game, but my head felt foggy. Everything else was heightened, and the taste of him, the feel of his tongue against mine shot a heated line to my core.

"Just as delicious as I imagined you would be," he said. The pad of his thumb ran over my lower lip and dragged down to my chin. "I could eat you right up."

Warmth seeped into my lips and a heady rush of desire flooded my system. A defense mechanism. There was nothing sensual about the way he was toying with me, and yet I found my tongue flicking against his as he withdrew.

"Are you ready for the next round?" A hiss of anticipation filled the air.

I swiped a hand over my mouth. I hadn't meant to kiss him back. This was some side effect of the game or his vampire powers. Was he a vampire? He moved like one, his form spilling across the floor with the grace of water.

"Fuck you," I whispered.

He chuckled. "You keep losing and I just might."

This time I was more confident. Not that I had a choice; I couldn't lose again. I stayed stock still, cocking my head and listening for any sign of movement. I breathed slowly, calming my racing blood.

Creak.

I turned slowly in the direction of the loose floorboard. One step at a time. I kept my hands lifted; my head turned in the direction of the sound.

"Warmer," he said.

I lunged forward and brushed...something. He was turning from me. I heard his footsteps round behind me and I turned with him, following him back across the room in a blind dance.

"Much warmer." The silk of his voice was closer, wrapping around me, leading me to him.

I bared my teeth when I bumped into something. A dresser, or the bed again, I didn't take the time to assess.

"You're on fire," he purred.

I dove, my nails curling like talons as I aimed and struck true. My fingers latched onto the fabric of a shirt, the thrum of a wildly beating heart beneath it. "Got you!" I said, triumphantly.

The stranger slid his hands over mine. "That you do." The weight of his gaze caressed me. My fingers flexed beneath his. "You win a question"

"A... a question? You kissed me and all I get is a question?"

"Rules are rules," he purred.

"You're making the rules up as you go." I had the vague idea that he was shrugging.

"So? Are you going to ask?"

I pulled my hands away slowly. "Are you going to kill me?"

The stranger sucked the back of his teeth. "How boring. Of course not." He sounded annoyed that of everything I could have asked of him, *that* was what I'd settled on.

A trickle of something slid down my spine. I wouldn't call it relief but at least I could take comfort in knowing Quint wouldn't find my strangled body lying on the floor in the morning.

Was Quint alright? Was he fast asleep downstairs? Or had the stranger lied and killed him already to toy with me freely?

No, don't think that. One thing at a time. For now, I had to trust that the stranger was being honest. If I let my mind stray, I'd panic.

"Who are you?"

The stranger hummed. "You have to win the next round for that answer. You better try very hard this time, Sorcha, but you should know." His hands slid up my arms, as his face pressed against mine. "I don't like to lose."

Chapter 10

SORCHA

The room felt hot and airless despite the chills that spread over my arms as I searched for him. I had to win. He had taken a kiss as his first prize, and I hardly believed he would settle for only a second kiss, if the greed in his voice was any evidence.

"Work for it." His voice whispered and echoed from every corner of the room. It was disorienting, the way he moved around me, taunting me. In the darkness the room had expanded, with seemingly infinite hiding places for him, while I was blind.

"Give me a hint," I said.

A single knock came from my left, in the direction of the bedroom door...I think? I moved to it, one foot in front of the other.

A louder knock sounded on my right. I twisted only to hear a third ricochet above me. I flinched, moving into a half crouch as I pictured him crawling across the ceiling.

Screw not panicking. Now that the image was carved in my head, I couldn't get it out. I staggered backward, following the sound of scuffling that trailed after me somewhere high above.

With a shaking hand I reached up to the ceiling. I rose up on my toes.

A hand gripped the top of my shoulder. "Time's up," he hissed.

I yelped in surprise, my arms flailing as I spun to push him away.

"Stop! Give me another round."

"The game is over, little dove."

Cool hands guided me back onto a plush surface. He had me against the bed. I reached for the blindfold, my fingers digging into the underside of the fabric when he caught my wrist.

"The blindfold stays on," he growled.

"Please," I whispered. I'd pulled the material up just enough that I could see the shine of his boots framing my bare feet.

He pulled my hand firmly, forcing the blindfold back in place and me into darkness.

His icy touch slid over the curve of my waist, steadying the tremors that now wracked my body. One remained planted while his other slid languidly up my front. He brushed my hair over my shoulder, exposing that side of my neck to the warm air.

Lips to skin. Teeth on my neck.

He was a vampire. He was a *vampire*, and he was going to rip my throat out.

Twin needles sank into my skin. The prick was sharp and thrilling, followed by a lush blanket of warmth that swam over my body; head to toe. I hadn't realized I'd latched hold to the front of his shirt until my grip weakened. That line to my center intensified. It was throbbing now, and my breath was coming in ragged gasps as something akin to desire dripped between my thighs.

The hand on my hip turned, and he slid his fingers beneath the band of my underwear, pushing them down.

A flutter of panic blazed white-hot in my mind, then was gone as the sensation at my neck intensified, pulling me into a lavish embrace.

Eventually the pressure eased, giving way to something warm and wet. He was licking me, but it felt odd. Like his tongue was split in two. My head was full of fog, knees weak as I slumped against the bed, falling onto my back.

He followed me down. "Consider this a consolation prize," he murmured against my lips.

What was he talking about?

His cold hands slid down either side of my waist, down until he gripped my knees and forced them apart. The elastic of my underwear kept my ankles trapped. Wait–

The delicious flick of a warm tongue swept across my pussy. Except I was already slick, the strain of his game unspooling all the tension in my body. A strangled sound came from my throat in surprise. I bucked against him when he did it a second time and remained there, his tongue working slowly over my slit.

"Oh fuck," I gasped.

"You are even more delicious here. Sweet Sorcha, you are a feast," he hissed. Another lash of his tongue had me seeing stars.

I slammed my palm into the top of his head and tensed when his lips fastened over my clit. A stranger was eating out my pussy and instead of trying to fight him off I was holding onto him. Holding him right there– Oh fuck. Yes. *Right* there.

He hummed against me, sending thrilling vibrations straight to my core. He worked his mouth lower, back over my folds and then slipped his tongue inside me. A tongue that shouldn't be that thick or that long and...who fucking cared? I'd never felt anything so divine. I dug my nails into the top of his head.

Soft caresses made their way across my thighs. His fingers took the place of his tongue as he withdrew, stroking the outside of my pussy slowly.

"Should I stop?" His voice was low and indulgent.

The taste of copper burst across my tongue when I bit my lip too hard. He should. Of course he should, but I was so close to the edge that I didn't want him to.

I shook my head.

"Tell me," he said, those two words coated with desire. The same twin pricks I'd felt against my neck fastened to the inside of the thigh he lifted over his shoulder.

I winced, leaning into the pain, seeking it out.

He slipped a finger inside of me, working it slowly until a second joined it. I tensed, expecting to feel the sharp claws I had felt previously, but there was only the soft pad of his fingers gliding in and out of me.

"You're sick. You're a devil," I gritted even as I leaned into his delicious touch.

"That I am," he said with a laugh. He twisted his fingers, angling them up as he started rubbing.

I shifted up on my toes, trying to get his mouth back on my center. My hand slipped across his scalp, knocking into something cool and hard on the top of his head. My heart slammed against my chest.

"A man, or what I thought was a man, walked out of the house.... he had big horns coming out of his head."

Quint's words came echoing back and were snatched away when the stranger fastened his lips once more over my clit and sucked. Simultaneously he worked his fingers inside of me, moving too fast for my mind to break down that there was possibly a monster between my legs. He sucked and pulled, drawing my soul out with every harsh breath that burst out of my lungs.

I was going to come.

His tongue worked wildly over my clit, his fingers moving faster, until bright white light exploded behind my eyes, squeezed tightly shut beneath the blindfold, and I was screaming as I came apart for him.

He pulled his head back, his fingers still working furiously. "Fuck," he growled. He jerked his fingers free and rubbed them over my clit, jolting my orgasm to an impossible new height as I continued to come. Pleasure twisted into pain when he worked me harder.

"Fuck. Please. Stop," I panted.

His only response was to pull my other leg over his other shoulder.

His wicked mouth returned with a vengeance, his tongue delving back inside of me. He worked me again and again until I was a shaking, sopping mess.

When at last he was sated, I felt the pressure of his arms around my neck and behind my knees as he carried me back to the top of the bed. Electricity buzzed through every nerve in my body. A piercing ringing sang in my ears.

He slapped my pussy. Was he going to fuck me now?

I swallowed, my fingers gripping the sheets beneath me. I wasn't ready for that. Just because he had given me the best oral of my life didn't mean I wanted his cock inside of me. Fear pitched in my gut.

A dark chuckle fanned through the air. His damp fingers ran over my throat, sliding between my breasts, over my erratic heartbeat. He paused before sliding his hand back down to my thigh. Something sharp cut into my skin and I winced, pulling my leg free.

"Something to remember me by," he purred. "Stay in your room tonight. If you go out and wake him, I'll know. Neither can you tell him that I was here." When I didn't respond he laced his fingers around my throat. "Do you understand?"

"Yes," I said, still panting. "I won't say anything."

"Good girl. I want you to count to ten and then you can remove your blindfold." He kissed me. I could taste my flavor against his tongue when he swept it across mine. "We are going to have so much fun, you and I."

The force of his presence left the room slowly. I waited a few extra seconds before I started to count.

When I lifted the blindfold, the stranger was gone.

Chapter 11

SORCHA

My reflection moved with me as I skimmed my hands over my legs. Bruises in the shape of bite marks peppered the inside of my thighs. And there, just under the tattoo, was the shape he had carved into my skin. A crescent moon, or "C".

I'd hoped it had all been an elaborate dream, but the proof was undeniable. Rosaline's monster was haunting me.

I'd barely been able to meet Quint's eye when I'd finally worked up the nerve to go downstairs the next morning. I'd feigned that I had nightmares, which wasn't *technically* lying, last night had been terrifying.

And delicious.

The stranger hadn't needed to threaten me not to tell Quint about him. There was no way in hell I was going to tell anyone how I'd become a willing partner in the midst of being attacked.

"Do you want me to come back tonight?" Quint ran a hand through his hair.

I hated the way he tried to catch my eye. I felt as if he could see through my jeans and sweatshirt to the bruises and bite marks the stranger had left behind. "No. Hopefully you being here last night scared him off." I tapped the screen of my phone. "I'll call you?"

"I'll be over as soon as you do. Even if it's just another bird." He jerked his chin.

That reminded me that I needed to dispose of the crow. I didn't want to leave the thing rotting on my front porch. No telling what other unwanted guests it might attract.

I let out a deep sigh. "Thanks, Quint. You're a hero, you know that?"

"Just call me Clark," he said with a smile. He rose from the table. "I've gotta run to work, but seriously. If you need anything, don't hesitate."

I pulled a smile from where it was buried deep within. "I'll text you later to check in."

He gave my shoulder a gentle squeeze on his way out.

I took my coffee into the next room to watch him drive away. Once his car was out of sight, I turned around to face the house.

I cupped my hands over my mouth. "Come out! Come out!"

The lack of response unnerved me. Mysteries shouldn't be so scary during the day.

I made a quick online search for nanny cams and ordered four. Three for each of the main entrances that would catch anyone coming into the house, and a fourth for my bedroom. They would be here in a couple of days. I was dipping into my savings to order them, but it would be worth it once I had the proof I needed for the cops to take me seriously.

And then what? How did one get rid of a vampire? It's not like the police would be able to do anything about it. It's not like staking vampires was a part of their job description.

I did another search on how to ward off vampires. There wasn't anything new to uncover from what I already knew about them. Stake to the heart, obviously. Not all vampires were inhibited by sunlight. (This one I didn't think was true. So far, the monster had only visited me in the evenings. If that was any indication of his limitations, I suspected that he couldn't come out while the sun was shining.) Silver burned them. (I also didn't think this was true based on the locket he had tried to give me that had magically disappeared.) They didn't have reflections–

I walked to the mirror in the foyer and pulled off the sheet. Why was there a rule to be wary of the mirrors if they would help me determine what was real and what wasn't? What did the moths have to do with all of this? I wrapped the sheet around my arm absentmindedly.

There was something important about the mirrors I needed to figure out. I remembered how my hand had pushed through the glass. I reached out tentatively, my fingers hovering over the surface, but when I pressed against it, nothing happened.

Relief flooded through me. At least that part could be explained away. I'd just had too much to drink. My hand couldn't have gone through the mirror because that's not how they worked.

Grumbling, I snatched a trash bag out from under the kitchen sink. I needed to get rid of the dead crow. Doing two things at once wasn't my strong suit, but I only had so many hours of daylight left before my stalker would return. It wasn't fair that I had to clean up the monster's mess. My room had been a wreck too, everything askew from where I had bumped into every available surface.

I grabbed the crow through the trash bag and flipped it inside out, tying a knot at the end. Now to find a shovel.

There was a small shed at the backside of the manor, its door hung crooked on rusted hinges. The wood was grey and brittle with age. It looked out of place when the rest of Glamis Manor was shining and new. The door tipped farther forward, threatening to fall off completely when I pulled it open.

I frowned.

The floors were completely rotten through, cobwebs galore lining nearly every nook and cranny. I wondered vaguely about the groundskeeper Beth had mentioned at the library. *What was his name again?* Surely this wasn't where he kept his tools... everything was rusted.

I grabbed a shovel with a broken handle and made my way to the back field where an oak tree stood alone. It seemed like a decent enough place to be buried. It was better than chucking the bird into the woods or a garbage can at any rate.

The broken handle made the work awkward. I had to crouch every time I dug the blade into the dirt. All the while trying not to tear up my hand with splinters.

A cool breeze fanned the sweat building at the back of my neck. I glanced toward the house when the familiar twinge hit me. It was nothing. The creature was a vampire, and he couldn't get me right now. I could almost feel him laughing at me, though.

Thunk.

I pulled the shovel free. A broken root looked up at me forlornly. I muttered a quiet apology before angling in a new direction. The soil was softer on this side, and made the progress faster. Just another foot and I would be happy with the size of the hole.

Clink.

I struck the ground again and the distinct scrape of metal came as I hit something that definitely wasn't a root. I worked the shovel around the flash of silver until four sides of a rectangle were revealed. I reached down, digging through the grit until I'd pried it free.

It was a small metal box, unremarkable and streaked with dirt and rust. I raised an eyebrow, and popped off the lid.

Inside lay a small leatherbound book and a collection of photographs. I wiped my hands on my pants before flipping through them. The photographs captured a young woman with dark hair coiled about her head and a sharply mustached gentleman a few years older, standing stiffly at her side. In the back sprawled Glamis Manor in all its glory. There was nothing written on the back. The other photographs were much the same. Smiling couples who remained nameless, photographed in what I recognized to be various parts of the manor.

The last picture was a charcoal drawing that was slightly smudged. It depicted a young woman standing in a garden, holding a thin stem covered in small white flowers. I'd seen the same ones in the garden out back. I flipped the picture over.

Rosaline, 1812

It was her.

I sat back on the ground, the bird momentarily forgotten as I raised the small notebook.

A tremor ran through my hand as I opened it. Rosaline O'Connor was scrawled across the upper corner of the first page.

"Holy shit," I said. It was a diary. My heart thumped in my chest. It felt like I had found a long-lost treasure. I turned the pages gently, not sure how they'd welcome being handled after being forgotten for so long.

The first few entries were without event. She wrote briefly about moving North, how the journey had been long and cold. They'd come from a settlement in Virginia. A difference in beliefs had driven Rosaline and her fiancé, Gerald, up north. They'd left as soon as the ground had thawed, unaware that it would take longer for the North to defrost than where they were coming from.

I skimmed through the next couple of pages until I got to a piece that said they were constructing a new home.

June 13, 1812

They say the land is cursed here and that this is why we were able to attain such a large acreage for such a low sum. But how can something so beautiful be cursed? There is a large field in which Gerald has started construction of our new home. New builders come every day from Bristol to help. It's going rather quickly, I dare say we'll be in by the end of summer.

August 19, 1812

A gentleman came by this afternoon to view the property. He is a merchant of sorts. He was selling these hideous stone creatures from his cart. Gargoyles he called them. They're supposed to protect the property they're set to guard. I hate them, but Gerald has bought eleven. The one that looks like a dragon is being set over the front door, while the others will go on the balcony. I hate having them where I can see them from my bedroom.

September 4, 1812

There is a strangeness to the house that chills me. Maybe this is the curse everyone was talking about. In the daylight it feels as if I am being watched. The sensation follows me from room to room. Once I even felt its presence in the garden. But it is when night falls that it becomes more insistent, this constant weight, the knowledge that I am not alone. What scares me most is how keenly I sense its hunger. *Gerald says it is because I am still adjusting to our new home. He doesn't feel the weight of it as I do.*

Once I felt something grab me while I was sleeping. Gerald works long hours, and he was not in bed when this happened. How can a house be haunted when no one has yet to die in it? I know how morbid that sounds but there is something very wrong here.

Gerald has named the house Glamis Manor. He says it came to him in a dream.

I turned, scooting my back against the tree so I could face Glamis as I continued to read. I knew the feeling she was talking about. I could feel it crawling over my skin at that very moment.

September 30, 1812

I was right. There has been someone watching me, and last night, I met him. He's beautiful. Lord, forgive me for saying this because I do love Gerald, but this man is the most beautiful I have ever seen. I know I should have been afraid of him but when I saw him standing at the end of my bed, I thought him to be an angel.

When I asked him if that's what he was, he laughed at me. His voice was as beautiful as he was. He said he is of a divine power, something greater than an angel. I didn't know there was anything above the angels, but I believe him. If you saw him, you would understand.

November 29, 1812

I'm sorry I have not written in some weeks. In truth, I have been too ashamed to pen these words. The angel – even though that's not what he is, it is what I call him – has been visiting me every night. It started as a kiss upon our first meeting, when I was so awed by his beauty. Since then, his kisses have become more abundant, leaving decadent marks in the most indecent places. I'm blushing as I write this, but he kissed me between my legs. I've never felt anything like it. I didn't know one could put their mouth there and feel such bliss. I am certain it's a sin, but oh the feeling is so wonderful.

The angel tells me not to have guilt for what we do and so I try not to. But I can't help feeling that I am betraying Gerald in some way. I can't allow this to go on any further. Gerald and I are married, and marriage is sacred. I'll tell him the next time I see him that this has to stop.

December 9, 1812

My angel hasn't returned. Have I offended him in some way? Did he know I was going to tell him to stop? Now that he is no longer here, I feel like I am going mad without him. I want to feel his lips on mine again. If he returned, I think I'd like to put my mouth on him the way he did to me. Between his thighs.

January 2, 1812

It has been some time since I've written but so much has been happening–

A chill skittered across my skin, dragging my attention up. The sky was darkening. I lurched to my feet, kicking the box and its contents across the ground. Had I been reading all day? I looked down at the book clutched in my hand, my finger between the pages. I was already halfway through it.

I scooped up the photographs and journal and set them back in the box. I turned back to the bird laying in its plastic bag. The beady outline of its eye was pressed against the film.

"I'm sorry little guy." I slid the bag into the hole. I hadn't meant to forget about it, but finding Rosaline's diary felt like I had already won the million dollars owed to me. No, not owed, gifted to me. Finding this felt like a gift.

I shoveled the dirt into the hole and gave it a solid pat. There wasn't time for a prayer (do you pray for animals? I don't think they have souls, so it probably doesn't matter) and scooped up my new treasure before jogging back to the manor.

It wasn't until I was safely back in the house that dread hit me. I looked down at the box I held. I shouldn't have taken it. Yet I found myself gripping it tighter. The journal was proof – even if it would only be proof to *me* – that what I was experiencing was real.

As much as I was aching to keep reading Rosaline's story, I knew I didn't have much time. The sun would sink and then my stranger would return. I knew whatever Rosaline had to say was true, and so I could not let him get his hands on this precious diary. As the last bit of light faded from the sky, I tucked the silver box beneath the mattress of one of the back bedrooms. The diary I planted in plain sight in the library, between *The Divine Comedy* by Dante and another nameless spine. I'd be back to finish Rosaline's account of her time with the 'angel'. And though my stomach churned with the knowledge of how her life had ended, a small part of me hoped the diary would contain the secret I needed to rid myself of the stranger, before I met the same fate.

Chapter 12

SORCHA

Two days later and the nanny cams were installed and running. There had been no trace of the vampire since his last visit. A wave of disappointment hit me when four days rolled by without any sign of him, in person or on the footage. The only thing I learned was that I tossed in my sleep a lot, but there was no strange man creeping into my home, much less my bed, at night.

The more time he spent away the more anxious I grew. Perhaps the cameras were enough to deter him.

It wasn't that I wanted him to come back: I was on edge, flinching at every sound. Yet a darker part of me was slick with anticipation. Fear did not outweigh the memory of how hard he had made me come. The sweep of his tongue between my legs was a visceral memory that had haunted me every night since the event.

By day five I was at my wits end, so I drove into town to get some distance. It was a *good* thing that he hadn't returned. It wasn't normal to crave the attention of a stalker. It wasn't sane.

As I pulled into a parking space by the water my stomach dropped. This was the early stages of the Macky madness. It had to be. I lowered my forehead to the steering wheel, banging it gently a few times in an attempt to knock some sense into myself.

Absentmindedly I made my way through a couple of Bristol's boutiques. I didn't wear the type of clothes they sold here. They were too modest and dull-colored, covered in ruffles and bows, much more traditional than what we wore in Miami. Then again, I supposed my style would need a complete overall from flashy bikinis and shorts. I looked down at myself, the jeans I was currently wearing were one of only two pairs that I owned.

I made mental notes of a few pieces that weren't totally hideous and planned to come back for them when my allowance came in at the end of the month. I did, however, allow myself the purchase of a book from *Wicks and Pages*, a candle shop and bookstore in one, that even offered wine while you shopped. The blurb promised a dark romance about a vampire hunting a woman on the streets of New Orleans, whose obsession with her begins to override his thirst for her blood. A quick search of reviews online varied from "Keep a vibrator on hand" to "This book and its author are seriously messed up".

I had my priorities straight obviously. Maybe it could even give me a little insight into my current situation.

Ha, I really was losing it.

I nestled in a leather chair in the back of the store to finish my glass of wine. The book was shockingly good, and I only made it through five pages before realizing it was going to be an instant favorite.

Somewhere at the front of the shop the bell rang, and gruff voices broke through the cozy silence.

"Come on, it'll be real quick. Books fix everything," one of the guys said.

"You don't even know what it's called." My ears perked up. That one sounded vaguely familiar.

"So? I know it has a castle on the front and that it's some new fairy smut or whatever. Fuck man, I don't know how women get away with reading this shit, but men get thrown under the bus for watching porn. The double standard bullshit gets to me."

A low chuckle came from the second man as they moved in my direction. That laugh I definitely recognized. *Quint.*

We had traded a few texts here and there but truthfully, I wasn't invested in keeping the conversation going when I had so many other things occupying my mind.

"Yeah, it's bullshit." Quint sounded disinterested.

I was putting my book away to greet him when I heard the first guy say my name. "So how's it going with that Sorcha chick? You fuck her yet?"

I froze, holding the book suspended between my lap and the bag I was sliding it into.

"Uh, not yet." It sounded like Quint said something else, but it was muffled.

"Why not? She's fucking hot."

"And you're with my sister," Quint said, his tone gaining an edge of annoyance. "You shouldn't be calling anyone hot."

"Whatever. Where the fuck... ah, fantasy section's over there. So, why haven't you closed the deal yet, bro?"

My heart was pounding, that they were right behind me. I pulled my book out casually and shifted so that my back would be to them if they came around the corner.

"She's new and still getting adjusted to the area. I'm taking my time getting to know her."

"Since when have you ever taken the time to get to know someone?" There was a slight pause and the thump of books as they were pulled off the shelf and slid back into place. "There's something else. What is it?"

Quint sighed and with it my heart dropped. "I think she's crazy."

It was like all the saliva in my mouth dried up with those four words. Nausea twisted in my stomach at the same time as my hands dampened.

"Oh, she's a freak?" The first guy snickered.

Quint chuckled too. "I don't know, maybe. She's Maxine's granddaughter."

"Oh shit. You serious?"

"Yeah. She had me stay over the other night because she thinks a monster broke into her house. She called me crying and everything."

The audacity! I didn't make him stay over; the asshole offered. He told me his own story of the horned man. My stomach twisted again. It had been a ploy to get close to me, and I'd been an idiot for not realizing. I didn't catch whatever they said next because my blood was roaring in my ears, drowning out all other sound. I'd gone from being embarrassed to fuming.

I knew for a fact I wasn't crazy, I had the marks to prove it. I hadn't imagined anyone coming into my house, it had been real.

The sound of a book being slapped snapped my attention back into place. "Yes! This is it!"

"Cool. Now let's get to Henry's, we're going to be late," Quint said.

Their footsteps started to recede. I stuffed the book in my bag and downed the rest of my wine. I followed them down the aisle. I had no idea what I was going to say if I confronted Quint, but I knew for *damn sure* I was going to let him know I had heard every single word he said.

"The crazy ones are always the best in bed. Just fuck her once and then drop her. Might as well." The man, it was the same one I had met at the bar my second night in town who'd commented on my tattoo. Jeremy! "Text her. See if she wants to come to Henry's party." Jeremy nudged Quint's denim clad shoulder. "I know she's your sister, but Katelyn–"

"That's enough," Quint snapped. "This chick is actually crazy, and I don't want to hear you talk like that about my sister."

The saleswoman flashed a big smile at the men when Jeremy tossed the book on the counter.

Everything I wanted to say died on my tongue. I twisted the wine glass in my hand and walked up next to them, pausing next to Quint and sliding my glass across to her. "Thank you," I said sweetly.

The air took on a charged quality the moment I felt Quint's attention fall on me. I didn't deign to look at him. He saw me, and it was enough. It was enough to know that he knew I had heard him and that I was pissed.

"Oh shit," Jeremy half whispered half laughed.

"Sorcha," Quint stammered, but I was already walking out the door.

The bell clanged a second time as someone rushed out behind me. I lengthened my stride when I heard Quint running to catch up.

"Sorcha," he said and reached for my elbow.

I turned on my heel. "Yes?" Remain aloof and disinterested. Don't let him see that you're hurt or angry. Indifference, I found, was an effective trigger that pissed most men off.

"Hey, um—" he looked from me to somewhere over my head and back again, "—you just walked right out without saying anything."

I cocked my head. "Was I supposed to?"

Quint's brow furrowed, the lines around his mouth tightening.

"I heard everything you said about me, so I don't think there's anything left for us to talk about," I clarified. I turned away abruptly, planning on making a beeline for my car, which was six blocks up.

He cursed under his breath before following. "I didn't mean any of that."

I laughed. "You're right, I probably imagined that whole conversation. *Crazy Sorcha.*" I made a mocking gesture with my hands.

"I was trying to get Jeremy off my back," he pleaded. "You know I don't think you're crazy."

"I just caught you talking shit about me. Ever heard of integrity? I uprooted my entire life to come out here and I've had nothing but problems since. You seemed like a good thing, but I was wrong." I walked faster, trying to outpace him, but his legs were much longer than mine.

Quint rounded in front of me, effectively taking up every inch of the sidewalk with his broad stance. "I'm sorry, Sorcha. I swear I didn't mean it. Some friends of mine are having a party tonight, why don't you come with me and I can make it up to you? Let me prove I didn't mean any of it."

"So I can continue to be the butt of your jokes? I don't think so."

"If you knew Jeremy you would understand. Sometimes you just have to say whatever to make him happy, so he'll shut up."

"And that makes it ok?"

"No, it doesn't and that's why I'm trying to apologize."

I was so full of rage at this point I was seeing red. I bent down and rolled up the cuff my pants and thrust my ankle out, revealing where bruising in the clear shape of a handprint marked me. I jerked the collar of my shirt to the side in another quick motion, flashing the bite mark, that was healing slowly. "Proof that I'm not crazy, you asshole."

Quint's eyes widened. "What is that? Who did that?"

I stomped my foot back on the concrete. A sharp pain radiated up my shin, making me clench my jaw. "Who do you think?"

He lowered his voice. "He attacked you? When? Why didn't you call me? Did you call the cops?"

I scoffed in an attempt to force back the tears burning behind my eyes. "Don't look so concerned, Quint. Lying doesn't look good on you."

A slow breath escaped his flared nostrils and he ran a hand through his hair. His tongue darted between his lips as he mulled over what to say next, but eventually, he just settled on looking into my eyes, his expression defeated.

This time when I walked away from him, he didn't try to stop me. I tried to ignore the fact that he was still standing in the place I'd left him on the sidewalk when I drove past. I didn't dare look at my phone in case he'd texted me as a last-ditch effort.

By the time the iron gates of Glamis Manor rose before me, I was awash with so many emotions I didn't know which to tackle first. Anger had wedged itself in my side like an iron poker, stoking the heat of my indignation as Quint and Jeremy's conversation replayed in my head. Guilt was next to wound me, when I thought of what I had allowed the stranger to do to my body.

Maybe I *was* a little crazy. No one in their right mind would have permitted that. I told myself I hadn't fought back because I was worried for Quint (fuck him) but truthfully, I hadn't wanted to fight. The monster in the shadows had called to me and I had answered willingly.

Somewhere beneath the flurry of emotion, fear still lurked. I was terrified of being alone. But I wasn't sure what scared me more: that the monster would pay me another visit, or that he was gone for good.

I grabbed a glass and bottle of wine to join me and my new book in bed for the evening. Whatever came from tonight, I wouldn't be awake to deal with it for much longer.

Chapter 13

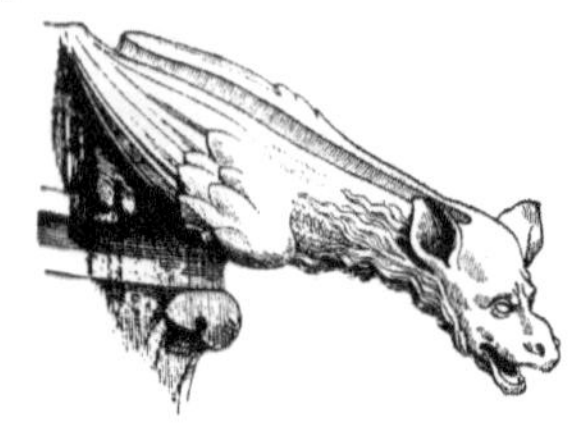

CORBAN

I didn't intend to leave Sorcha alone for as long as I had, but our night together had drained me more than I expected. I'd retained some of her energy through the blood I'd consumed, but it had not been enough to ground me in the mortal world.

I'd been irked that she had been gone most of the day, but when her car pulled up the long drive, my pulse fluttered with anticipation. Something like relief washed over me – relief that she had returned at all. Fear was a foreign feeling to me, but I pondered whether that is what I felt skittering in my blood as I worried that she had left Glamis Manor, me, and the glamour I had built behind.

There were a few hours of daylight left but I felt stronger than I had in a long while when she opened the front door and then slammed it, hard. I wanted to leap down to her, have my fill of her – but then I saw the sparkle in her eyes and the firm press of her lips.

What is this? I loomed over the banister to get a better look as she walked into the foyer, her breath coming up short and ragged. Was Sorcha crying?

I lapped at the air as she passed beneath me. Those were not tears of sadness.

Anger simmered in my belly. I was the only one that had the right to Sorcha's anger, to the tears that welled behind her eyes but never fell. My claws dug into the wood-paneled walls of the house as I forced my way inside them, moving along the manor's bones as I trailed her.

She didn't even notice when I slunk up the stairs right on her tail. I cocked my head as she turned into her bedroom. Could she not feel a predator stalking her? I doubted she would notice me in this form, but I was still peeved she hadn't even *looked* for me.

That wouldn't do. Surely Sorcha had not forgotten me so easily.

I coiled myself around the banister and perched atop the railing, where I waited impatiently for night to fall. Each tick of the second hand was agony.

As the splash of wine hit the bottom of her wine glass for a fourth time, my jaw clenched. At this rate, she would be passed out by the time I got my hands on her. I flicked my gaze to the window where the sky had paled to a soft pink. She took a large gulp before setting the glass on her bedside table, where it sloshed over the rim.

The sheets rustled as she sank lower into them, her eyes fluttering as she turned a page in her book.

Patience was a virtue, but I had no virtues. I'd likely have to return earlier in the night to my post, anyway, so I couldn't wait a moment longer. I needed her. Needed to touch and kiss her and chase away whatever was bothering her.

The curse that bound me lashed like lightning across my skin as I pulled myself free from the house. My claws ripped through wood and stone, one limb, and then another, and another, until finally I jerked free and fell into a heap on the floor. I rose quickly, shaking off the dust in case she came out to investigate the heavy thump.

I paused indulgently and frowned when she did no such thing.

Sorcha's head was tipped back on her pillow, her flushed face relaxed with the first signs of sleep. I leaned forward until my lips were just over her ear.

"Sorcha," I said. "Wake up, my dove."

A little moan came from her lips.

"That's right," I encouraged.

"Nmm...what," she slurred.

"I've come to lick up your tears and eat your anger." I kept my face next to hers and gently stroked the side of her cheek with my thumb. "Will you let me give you pleasure?"

The quickening pitter-patter of her heart was music to my ears. I squeezed her bicep gently, trying to coax her back to the edge of awareness. She was so soft. Her skin smooth like healing flesh. I pressed my lips to her temple and let my fingers on her cheek drift down to stroke the hollow of her throat.

In that same moment I smelled the change in her scent. It had turned hot and sweet with need. I could not keep the smile, nor the feral beast within me at bay as I silently gloated. *She wants me,* craves *my darkness. Well, let her have it.*

"I'm tired," she moaned. She tried to sit up, but her arm slipped out from under her.

"Hush," I crooned. "It's okay. You can sleep. Allow me to please you in your dreams."

She turned to look at me, but I knew at this angle, being so close to her, that she couldn't see me fully. I slipped my fingers farther down her chest until my claws were skimming across her nipple beneath the cotton fabric.

Her scent was getting stronger while her eyes were getting heavier. "Kay," she mumbled and rubbed her face against mine.

That simple gesture, her skin brushing against mine, her lips grazing the corner of my mouth, made my cock stone hard. I caught her lips against mine and kissed her fully, but she was already dozing again, sleep had pulled her to him swiftly.

My stomach flipped with anticipation.

The marks I had left on her legs were already fading. I would need to leave more; deeper wounds that would take longer to heal.

"Just a little sting," I whispered, gripping her below the knee as I carved a new crescent into her flesh. She liked being marked. If she didn't, she wouldn't have the tattoos inked into her permanently. I made sure my second cut was deep enough that it would scar once healed, marking her as mine, lest she forget in the coming days.

I brushed my nose across her face again. Her breath coaxed me to return to her mouth – so soft and inviting – where I kissed her gently. I slid my tongue over the edge of her teeth. What I wouldn't give for her to bite down on me.

Her lips were luscious. I found myself pushing my tongue deeper. The spice of the merlot coating her throat added another layer to her flavor. Her lips tightened around my retreating tongue.

Perhaps she wasn't totally asleep after all.

It was better this way, though. I wanted to make her feel things only I could before she finally saw me. Before she laid eyes on the beast that would make her scream in pleasure, in fear, and then devour her later.

A little sigh escaped her, making my cock twitch. What sort of sounds would she make if I put that in her mouth?

Not yet. For that, I would wait for her to be fully conscious.

I turned her body, dragging her hips to the edge of the bed as I slid to my knees before her. She was so soft, so malleable to my touch as I positioned her where I needed her. The cotton panties glided off her hips with ease. I folded them neatly beside her before easing my focus back to her center.

I'd had plenty of offerings before, plenty of sparrows to keep my hunger sated, but none were as perfect as Sorcha sprawled out before me like my own personal feast. I was going to dine on her like she was my last supper.

I leaned forward and pressed my nose against her slit. She smelled of musk and faintly of her lavender body wash. A purr of satisfaction rumbled through me when I leaned back, resting my cheek against her soft thigh. She was a pretty pink between her legs, the folds unfurling like rose petals when I slipped my finger inside. I took my time savoring how beautiful she looked parting for me before I reached down to free my cock. I gave it a firm squeeze as I continued to explore her with just my finger, tracing the outline of her lips and then spreading her apart again to reveal that small channel I would soon be in.

I leaned forward and swiped my tongue between her folds.

Sweet as a dark cherry, her flavor came to life in my mouth. The taste of her was carved into my very being. I had not known the effect she would have on me the first time I tasted her, and it took every grain of my will to restrain myself from taking her this time around. Forcing myself upon her wouldn't be as pleasurable, not when I knew that deep down, she wanted me.

I withdrew my finger, replacing it with my lips and tongue, which switched between kissing and licking the outer part of her sex. I grabbed the outside of her thigh, pulling her legs wider as I forced my tongue inside her.

Her pussy flexed around my tongue, encouraging me to push it deeper. Her heat was exquisite and her taste as delicious as the first time. I worked my cock in time with my tongue, thrusting and pulling out, curling the forked tip over the ridges that lined the top of her cunt. It wasn't long before her wetness coated me, proof that even in sleep she loved what I was doing to her.

I knew she would. It pleased me that she trusted me enough to satisfy her while she slept. To chase away whatever had tormented her before she came home to me.

I slipped my free hand beneath her shirt to grip one of her breasts. Her nipple standing erect beneath my palm only further confirmed that she was turned on. I pinched it, twisting it between my thumb and forefinger. A short intake of breath snapped my eyes up to her face. Her eyelids were fluttering, brows knit together as I pinched her again, but it was when I thrust my tongue deeper that she let out a moan.

The sound sent a jolt straight to my cock. I held it at the base, trying desperately not to come. I twisted my hand, fisting the entirety of her breast and squeezing while pumping my tongue faster inside of her. I buried it as deep as I could, until I hit a spot that made her hips buck. Her breathing hitched, her body flaming red as I heard her heartbeat pounding for me.

My hand stroked my cock of its own accord, my body stiffening in time with hers as I felt her getting closer. There is nothing more satisfying than fucking someone to climax without the inhibitions of their mind restraining them. I ground my face into her when her thighs tightened around my head.

I rubbed my tongue against that spot again and in a breathy moan she came. I drank what I could, licking and sucking, but it was too much. Lightning crackled behind my eyes, and I surged up from the ground.

I rubbed the head of my cock over her now sopping pussy. White-hot fire shot through me and then I was coming too. Ropes and ropes of steaming cum splattered across her pussy. I kept stroking my cock, making sure I drained every drop on her. My hips jerked against my hand and the tip of my cock slid inside her slick warmth.

I threw my head back as her heat encased me.

"Fuck," I hissed and pulled out. I hadn't meant to do that. Not yet. I took a staggering step back before I did something I might regret.

Glistening cum dripped onto the sheets, staining them in pools of wetness beneath her thighs. I scooped up the excess and pushed it inside her pussy. I might not be able to fuck her yet, but there was no sense in letting good cum go to waste.

When I was sure she was good and full I slid her panties back on and repositioned her at the top of the bed.

The night was silent save for her soft whimpers and the erratic thumping of her pulse as sleep held her captive. Knowing she was full of my cum made her even more beautiful. Desire's heat flared once more, tempting me to take her fully, or perhaps that pretty mouth of hers that parted as she relaxed and started to snore.

A wicked part of me hoped she wouldn't remember this. I wanted fear to grip her when she woke full of cum, before it lost out against her desire. That dark, alluring desire that I could see, taste, and smell. Pulsing like a bleeding heart.

Chapter 14

SORCHA

The shadow expanded as it eased into the manor, looming far larger than any man had the right to be. Whatever it was didn't walk, but slunk through the house, pooling from one patch of darkness to the next. My stomach curled as the image on the screen fluttered, before the shadow spilled up the stairs, disappearing from view.

The bright light of the computer screen wasn't doing my raging headache any favors. It felt like I'd been hit by a truck when I woke up this morning. But as the hours ticked by, bits and pieces of the previous evening had trickled to the forefront of my mind.

The shadow on the screen wrapped around the banister, coiling and writhing like a snake. That's when the screen froze, right before it leeched out of frame.

"Got you," I breathed.

I finally had something. It had to be him. Unless there was another dark entity in the house.

Chills burst across my skin. "One thing at a time," I muttered to myself, clicking on the next file, the one belonging to the camera in my bedroom. I skipped the feed forward to a few seconds after the shadow in the hallway had disappeared.

There was a jump in the feed and then the shadow (I assumed it was the same shadow) was looming over me in the shape of a man. Dread leeched into my stomach as I finally saw just how large the thing was. I'd described the stranger as being six foot five, but looking at whatever it was on the screen, he had to be bigger than that.

The light on my nightstand highlighted his silhouette, the lanky form and broad shoulders. But there were no obvious features. I knew his hair was dark, but not if it was black or brown. And his skin, that I *swore* had been pale, was as dark as the rest of him. As if he wasn't a vampire at all, but a phantom made entirely of shadow.

I felt the ghost of claws trailing down my cheek, my neck. A memory?

He was saying something, but the camera hadn't been rated highly for its audio quality. I turned the volume up and pressed my ear to the speaker.

"Will you let me give you pleasure?" His voice came across as clear as day despite how muffled it had been previously.

There was another sound, more words exchanged, and then: "You can sleep. Allow me to please you in your dreams."

Holy fuck.

The image blurred before freezing. The timer ticked another five seconds before the picture moved again. My stomach twisted into a thousand knots as the shadow repositioned my body near the edge of the bed, slid down my thighs and very clearly pulled off my underwear.

I could do nothing but watch as he knelt before me while my body writhed lazily beneath him. The image of a dark-haired man looking up at me with glowing red eyes flashed across my mind.

Even with his distorted image I could tell he was eating me out, fucking me with his mouth the way he had the other night. Slick, wet sounds slipped through the crackled audio every now and then. I must have moaned because the sound he made was deeper, almost a growl, when his shadowy hand moved beneath my shirt.

That's where it froze again. The image remained the same until it skipped, to reveal him standing between my legs. And that's when the distorted memory revealed itself, of what he had asked me.

"Will you let me give you pleasure?" The words spoken last night came back clear as day. I'd thought I was dreaming, drunk and needy when I'd answered him. That knowledge did not alleviate the chill rushing down my arms, however, when I watched his body jerk between my legs. Nor did it quiet my racing heart when he moved his fingers inside of me before sliding my underwear back into place.

The shadow hovered over me and then slunk across my body. The shape of the man morphed into something larger before it coiled into a dark mass at my side. The image froze. Five, ten, thirteen seconds went by, and it didn't change. It remained that way until I skipped it forward an hour and saw only myself in bed. He didn't return after that.

I refreshed the app but every time I tried to rewatch the video it cut out in the same spot, with him curled next to me. I clamped my shaking hands together and fisted them in my lap. I don't know how long I stared at that image of him frozen beside me.

I trailed my hand between my thighs and carefully slid my fingers beneath my underwear. Wet and tacky. I slipped my fingers inside myself, finding the new wetness that coated me after watching what should have been a living nightmare.

I restarted the video from the moment he entered my bedroom.

I shouldn't be excited by this. This was the monster that had chased me through my home, blindfolded me, and eaten out my pussy. And I was watching him do it again. While I *slept.*

Another memory flashed, of a shadowy figure scooping something up and putting it inside of me. I wasn't brave enough to look for evidence of what that might have been.

"Will you let me give you pleasure?"

I closed my eyes as his voice trickled through the audio.

"You can sleep. Allow me to please you in your dreams."

I slumped back in my chair as I watched him do exactly that, actively fingering myself now, chasing that same dark thrill. Again, I replayed the video and watched as he brought me to climax. On the fourth watch I was coming along with us, my fingers pressing hard into my clit as I circled it and came undone right there in the middle of the kitchen, gripping the arm of the dining room chair.

No sooner did my orgasm start to fade than my anxiety spiked. I shot up from the chair and slammed my laptop closed.

What the fuck was wrong with me?

The buzz of my phone snapped me back into the sane part of reality.

Quint: Can we talk?

Another buzz came seconds later.

Mom: Call me as soon as you get this.

This was too much to deal with. I scooped my phone and laptop up and headed back upstairs. The crawling sensation of roving eyes didn't bother me as much as it had the first couple of days.

I tossed my phone on the counter before running the shower. Once it was hot enough to melt my skin off, I hopped beneath the stream. I let the blistering water droplets paint my skin red. I scrubbed every inch of myself until I was sure I was rid of the stranger's scent and then washed again for good measure.

The footage was useless when I appeared to be a willing accomplice.

I needed to read more of Rosaline's diary and see how she managed to deal with him. But before that, I needed to look for anything Macky might have left behind. If she had left her rules out for me to find, then surely, she had documentation of the creature somewhere.

That's it!

The sketchbook.

I dried off and padded down to the library, hunting through the shelves until I found it again. I didn't remember there being a man in any of the images, but perhaps I would find his face among the monsters.

The first couple of pages were as I remembered, creatures bearing armored scales and curling horns. Headshots of snarling beasts with dagger-long teeth roared to life on the parchment. I flipped through one page at a time, until I came to a sketch of three tall silhouettes. Their limbs and forms were lithe, with long hair that covered what appeared to be naked bodies.

The next page was filled with sketches of eyes. Some were humanoid, while others had pupils in the shape of a diamond. Others had even smaller pupils that reminded me of reptiles, and horned eyebrows.

On a later page, Glamis Manor rose off the paper. I was about to flip past it, but paused when I noticed one of the tall spindly creatures standing in a window.

"Oh, please don't be another creepy creature," I whispered. Whatever this was, it didn't look like a vampire. In fact, it reminded me of a horrible fairytale my mother told me once as a girl, of a tall willowy woman with a blank face, who would take children away and gobble them up if they were bad. I don't think there was a day after that I ever disobeyed her. The story had stuck with me all the way to adulthood.

A twisted and deformed dragon hugged the frame of a mirror on another page. A gaping mouth full of fangs was on the backside of it. Strange plants and flying creatures were pieced together like a muddied collage.

In a swirl of darker charcoal was written: *Things cannot gain power unless you believe in them.*

My phone buzzed again.

Mom: Hello??

"Fuck's sake," I mumbled. I dialed her number and shoved the phone between my cheek and shoulder as I continued flipping through the book.

"Finally!" Mom practically shouted. "I've been trying to reach you all day."

"It's only two, Mom. I slept in a little late."

I could practically hear the roll of her eyes. "Well anyways, I wanted to check in and see how you're doing. How's the place look? Anything worth selling?"

I raised my fingers from the sketchbook, clutching the phone before I dropped it. Vultures come in all forms, but sadly they most often wear the face of family members. "I don't want to sell anything."

Truthfully, it hadn't even crossed my mind to sell any of the antiques that filled the manor. But if Mom wanted to use me to make some quick cash, then I *definitely* wasn't going to sell anything.

"Oh, Sorcha, come on. If the furniture is anything like it was in Manchester then that's a couple of thousand right there."

"I said I don't want to sell any of it. Grandma Macky gave me the house and, well," I paused, looking around at all the books waiting to be read. If I didn't think too much about the stranger, or Glamis's history, it was actually quite charming. I liked the gothic décor and filtered, golden daylight all of the windows offered. Glamis Manor had fallen into my lap by chance. It was a lifeline I didn't know I'd needed until I was finally far away, and out from under my mother's judgment.

"Well, what? You're just going to keep it all to yourself?"

"Yes actually," I snapped. "You and Uncle Ken and Uncle Hank already got your share. Macky left this place to me, and I like it the way it is."

The line was silent for a moment.

"Are you serious? After everything I've done for you, you're just going to take all that money and keep it to yourself? I raised you Sorcha, all by myself. I gave you food, I gave you shelter, I took care of you!"

"That's what you're supposed to do."

"Excuse me?" Mom's voice had gone colder than the Arctic.

I knew I had overstepped, but the grave had been dug so I might as well crawl in. "That's what you're supposed to do when you have a kid. You take care of them. I'm grateful for everything you gave to me, but I don't owe you *my* share of Macky's home when you got your own inheritance. Y'all each got two million."

"You're unbelievable," she growled.

"Why? Why am I not allowed to have this?"

There was a pregnant pause of fuming energy before she finally answered. "Do whatever you want, Sorcha. It's clear I don't mean jack shit to you." There was a loud bang and then the line went silent.

My hand was shaking as I pulled the phone away from my ear. She'd either thrown hers across the room or hard enough on the ground that it'd ended the call.

I shut the sketchbook and held it close to my chest.

I didn't think I would ever be able to escape my mother's judgment. I'd moved out of her place a long time ago, but even living in my own apartment she had managed to force herself into my space, inviting herself over, critiquing the way I decorated, the food I kept in the fridge, the clothes that hung in my closet.

I didn't know what Mom and her brother's childhoods had been like, but it was clear something had rotten them, somehow. Mom definitely had the worst relationship with Macky, and that negativity had trickled down into our relationship. I believed that mothers did the best they could with what life gave them, but I'd spent twenty-six years feeling like I *owed* my Mom something, simply for existing. Like I'd had any say in the fact she'd brought me into this world.

It was toxic.

I'd hoped that putting distance between Mom and I would help heal the wounds that gaped between us. Instead, she was acting as I'd known she would. I was sorry I'd hurt her feelings, but I wasn't upset that I'd stood my ground. At least the call had ended without her screaming at me, until I was the one apologizing for whatever mess she had instigated.

I carried the sketchbook with me into the kitchen and flipped through it as I started the oven for a frozen lasagna. I loved my mom despite her flaws, but she wasn't the most pressing thing I had to deal with right now.

I ran my finger over the charcoal drawing of a male figure with horns curling out from the top of his head. Over the blurred, flaming eyes that glared up at the viewer. Whatever issues my mother and I had could wait. Solving the mystery of my shadowy stalker and the history of Glamis Manor was my top priority.

I swiped the clock app open on my phone and began setting a series of alarms to start after 9 o'clock. One every thirty minutes, in the event I dozed off. I tucked a kitchen knife beneath my pillow, pointing the blade away from my head.

The next time the stranger showed up, I would be ready. If he could only come out when the sun had set, then so would I. I wasn't going to let any*one*, or any*thing* take Glamis Manor away from me.

Chapter 15

SORCHA

The shrill screech of the alarm wrenched me free from the under-tow of sleep that had me in its grip. I groaned, reaching across for the tenth time to shut it up, but the offensive sound cut off before I even touched it.

"Did you set this for me?"

I bolted upright, my eyes wide as they struggled to adjust to the darkness. The moon was high tonight, so everything was generously illuminated. Everything but the stranger who evaded me.

"I'll be honest, I'm a bit flattered by this. But I've never really been a big fan of toys in the bedroom."

I reached under my pillow feeling for the knife that wasn't there.

He had the knife.

Oh God, I was fucked.

I heard it clatter to the floor.

Huh, silver linings.

"Before I allow you to see me, I want us to play another game." He was somewhere behind me, at the edge of the bed, hovering just outside of my peripheral. I wanted badly to see him, but not so badly that I was game to disobey him.

"Which one is it tonight?"

I could practically hear the grin in his voice. "Truth or dare... with a twist."

I swallowed thickly. "Ok." I had a long list of ideas of what the dares could involve, and this time I had the good sense to be worried.

"Good girl," he purred. The words vibrated through my bones, tickling something at the back of my mind when he finished the sound with the soft click of his teeth snapping together. "Get out of bed," he said softly.

I clenched the bedspread before doing as he said. The night air brought chills to my bare legs. I wrapped my arms around myself as I waited for his next command.

"Turn around, Sorcha." His voice circled closer.

I turned slowly and looked upon the most beautiful man I had ever seen. He was the same man that had chased me up the stairs the other night, but gone were the red eyes. Now, they were a pale green, slanted and angular. His face had more color in it than I remembered; some imitation of life blooming beneath the ashen skin.

He was taller than I remembered too, and his muscles more defined. He was big. Everything about him looked big and powerful. Just like in the distorted video.

His dark hair was shorter, and looked as if it had been recently cut. Stray strands feathered at the nape of his neck and across his brow. The lines of his face were somehow as striking as they were fine, as if a sculptor had taken great care in crafting him.

I licked my lips as I struggled to find words. At least the books got it right, vampires were *hot*. Insanely hot. But the stranger wasn't just hot, he was ethereally, unnaturally, beautiful. Everything about him, from the breadth of his shoulders to the slant of his luminous eyes, marked him as a predator. Captivating and deadly.

"What's the twist?" I finally asked.

Those eyes worked their way slowly up my body as he approached, unhurried, until he was standing directly in front of me. Every muscle of his that I could see was taut, like he was going to burst, or pounce. Fear's good sense nudged me to take a step back.

"For every truth you answer you must take off a piece of clothing." An elegant smile fluttered over his face. The curve of his mouth was as dangerous as the rest of him, it only made him more alluring. "If you refuse, your truth defaults to a dare."

My eyes narrowed, earning me another smile that might have been charming if he wasn't so fucking terrifying. This was a lose-lose situation. He would strip me bare and if I refused, I had no doubt his dares would be even worse.

"How do I win?"

He cocked his head. "You don't."

I swallowed. Of course. Because this wasn't about me. This was about him being in control, and me being at his mercy.

"You promise you aren't here to kill me?"

He ran a finger down my arm. No claws... yet. "Would you like to use that as your first question?"

Shit. We were starting now? I guess that was fine, since I had a million questions I wanted to ask. I nodded.

The stranger stepped back and toed off both of his boots. I swallowed again, my blood pounding as I looked down to my clothes. A T-shirt, shorts, socks, and underwear. He had on far more clothing than I did, and it wasn't going to take him very long to strip me down. I'd have to refuse, and take a dare instead.

"I'm not going to kill you," he said smoothly. "That would spoil all of the fun we're having."

I could work with that. The very hot, wicked, man-shaped-creature wasn't going to kill me, he was just a psycho who was going to do goodness knows what else. My toes curled as I remembered the feel of his head between my thighs.

"Have you been thinking about the way my tongue felt inside of you?"

Which time, I wanted to ask. My face burned at the idea of answering him. I clamped my mouth shut.

"Really?" He chuckled. "You'd refuse so soon?" His tongue clicked against the back of his teeth. "I dare you to climb on the bed and touch yourself."

I should have just taken off my pants. But then that would have given him an even better view. I clenched my fists at my side, trying to be defiant but failing when he took a step forward and I moved back.

"Play the game," he whispered.

I didn't take my eyes off him as I shakily moved back. He didn't follow me as I scooted my butt back on the bed, my legs dangling over the edge.

I slid my hand over my chest, my palm grazing my erect nipples. I hated the way my body betrayed me despite how hard I was trying to rationalize with it.

"Not there," he said. "Like you did when you watched your little *film* the other night. Like you did in the kitchen this morning. Oh yes," he chuckled. "I could hear you."

Chills raced down my arms, immediately cooling the flush of embarrassment. "You didn't specify," I said through gritted teeth, but my mind flew to the question of whether he was a vampire or not. If he could be awake, and close enough to *hear* me in the daylight, he must be something else.

His jaw clenched, eyes flashing. They dragged to my other breast as I palmed that one next.

I knew this was wrong but the way he was looking at me… I'd never had anyone look at me that way in my life. Like he wanted to devour me. To worship me. The way his pupils dilated made me just as hungry.

There was a distinct bulge in the front of his pants that told me he was already hard. Was he going to try and fuck me?

I licked my lips, not missing the way his eyes caught the small movement. I had so many questions but if I played my cards right, I would have plenty of time to ask them. "Who are you?"

His long fingers worked down the buttons of his shirt. Popping one after the other until his muscular chest was exposed. I audibly swallowed as he rolled his shoulders back to relieve himself of the material.

He looked like he had been carved from stone. His muscles were defined– too defined – he couldn't possibly be real. With every slight movement, his pale flesh rippled over the ridges and shadows of what lay beneath. Rippled in a very real sense of the word.

Holy shit.

"I'm Corban," he said, drawing my stare back up to his face. His eyes were heated, the pupils bigger than they had been before.

I nodded, trying to gain some control over what was happening. This could be worse. It could have been an ugly psycho that had eaten out my pussy, giving me what I could only describe as a heavenly experience as I came all over his tongue.

Fuck. Is it getting hotter in here?

His eyes dropped down.

My hand had unwittingly moved between my legs. I jerked my hand away, laying it flat on the bed. A tinge of embarrassment warmed the back of my neck.

"What do you like?"

My face twisted. "What do you mean?"

"What do you like, sexually?" The last word came out as a purr.

I bit the inside of my lip. Answer his question or submit to another one of his commands.

"I like.... it a little rough. Not painful but..." Why the fuck was I telling him that? *Lie!* I should have lied. I reached down and fingered off my socks.

His eyes tracked every inch of my movement. "You and I are going to get along just fine."

That answered my earlier question of whether he planned to fuck me or not. That must be game over.

"Why are you here? What do you want?"

Corban didn't move. He arched a thin, perfect brow.

He was giving me the opportunity to demand something of him. I could end this. I could tell him to leave and by rules of the game he would have to... for tonight. I knew he would come back. Or I could keep playing and see what happened next.

I clamped my thighs together. He noticed that too. There wasn't anything that escaped his predatory gaze.

"Fine," I breathed. "I dare you... to let me see your teeth."

Corban's brow furrowed. Was he frowning? He stepped forward slowly and pulled back his lips. I sat forward for a better look. None of them looked sharp.

I grabbed his chin. "Open," I said.

He was practically vibrating beneath my touch as he opened his mouth. Normal, human teeth. Every single one. He wasn't a vampire.

"What are you looking for?"

"Fangs," I whispered. Because while I didn't see any sharp teeth, I did see the shape of his tongue as it moved. It was forked.

And then to my horror, his upper lip peeled back higher to reveal two little slits from which twin fangs slid free, settling perfectly over his normal teeth.

I lurched back on the bed. "I don't want to play anymore."

"You don't have that option," Corban said with a tilt of his head. He thrust his chin out. "Remove your shorts."Before I could bite back, he added slyly, "That was truth."

"That's not– " I started to protest.

He shrugged. "That's the game. Take them off," he said. Commanded.

I made to slide off the bed to do so when he stepped to its edge. "You can stay there." He held out his hand expectantly.

As quickly as I could I ripped them off and crossed my legs, placing my hands over my center. Corban caught my shorts with a grin when I threw them at him.

"Are you a vampire?" I asked. He pulled his belt apart and I felt myself relaxing a little until he undid the button and fly of his trousers. "Belt is fine." But he was already shoving his pants down his hips.

Fuck me.

His thighs were massive, thick and carved just like the rest of him. I only noticed them briefly before I was drawn back to his center. He wore dark grey briefs, through which I could see the outline of the biggest cock I had ever seen. There was a wet spot at the top where precum had started to leak through.

"No," he finally answered.

No? Oh. Then what the hell was he?

I couldn't breathe. Shamefully I couldn't take my eyes off his dick.

I'd only half heard his comment when he asked, "Do you want to taste my cock?"

My eyes snapped to his face. I couldn't do his dare. But neither did I want to remove a piece of clothing. Fuck him.

I swallowed, refusing.

"Good," he said. "I was hoping you'd refuse. Rub your pussy, Sorcha. Show me how wet I've made you."

I was going to combust. The heat that scalded within my blood was either a magic spell he had cast over me or something scientific that would burn me from the inside out at any moment. I could feel my arousal seeping through my panties even before I moved my hand to brush them. I was soaking.

My chest was tight. The sane part of my mind was screaming at me not to continue, to find some way out of this, but the longer he looked at me, the farther away the voice sounded. I stroked my clit through the thin veil of fabric, tracing small circles. I slid my fingers down and back up, smearing my wetness.

Corban inhaled sharply. "Fuck."

Fuck was right. His pupils were completely blown out now, his irises devoid of any color.

"What are you?" I whispered.

"Stone."

I looked past him to where I knew the gargoyles sat coiled on the balcony. My heart slammed to a halt when I looked back at him. The grey skin. The inhuman beauty.

"Close," he said with a crooked smile. "But not quite."

He reached down and removed his socks. I tried to master my expression, to not reveal the disappointment that radiated from me that he hadn't removed his shorts instead.

"Do you want to fuck me?" His question was so crass that I physically balked.

"No," I spat.

Corban's gaze narrowed. "No lies, Sorcha."

"I'm not lying."

His eyes dropped between my legs. "Even if I couldn't see the physical evidence of your lie, I can smell your desire from here. So, I'll ask again. If you refuse, I get to punish you."

I clamped my mouth shut, staring daggers at him. There could be a number of things he would do to punish me, and by how greedy he looked, I didn't think any of them would be good.

He laid his palms on either side of me on the bed. "Do you want to fuck me?"

Yep, there was the fire. Might as well tie me to a stake because I was going up in flames anyway. His cool proximity did nothing to dampen the sweat beading on the back of my neck.

It was wrong of me to want to fuck him, but that wasn't what he wanted to know. Right and wrong didn't matter in this moment. Disregarding that he was a stranger and a stalker; I *did* want to fuck him. I wanted *him* to fuck *me* to be more precise. I let my eyes slip down his powerful form and wondered what it would feel like to be beneath all that muscle.

"Yes," I whispered. Except the word came out choked, barely audible.

Corban's white teeth flashed in the moonlight, his fangs still drawn and vicious.

He was too close. I couldn't relax, much less undress now that he was leering over me. The thrill of danger made my skin ache with need. I twisted my arms and pulled my shirt up over my head.

Cool air made my nipples tighten. A low groan melted from the back of his throat as he took me in. He reached out then stopped himself, his fingers curling into a fist and falling on the bed.

I knew I had been properly blessed in the boob department, but paired with my wider hips and thick stomach they were often overlooked. But the way Corban continued to look at me, his eyes roving every inch of my exposed skin, told me not only that he liked what he saw, but that he desired me.

"Do you want to touch them?"

The corner of his jaw ticked. His nostrils flared as he tore his gaze from my chest to my eyes.

I licked my lips, and the words came out before I could stop myself. "Touch them," I said, taking his silence as refusal.

There was a shift across his face, a shimmer in his appearance I didn't quite catch. It was moments later, when his hand cupped my breast that I registered it to be something feral.

Corban wasn't a man. I couldn't forget that, but when his other hand pressed to my breast, I forgot why that mattered. He took one of my nipples between his fingers and rolled it none too gently, tugging a hiss out of my lips. "I can't wait to suck on these," he said.

I tipped my head back when his grip hardened. It was as if he already knew everything I wanted and exactly how I liked it.

"Can I?" His thick lashes cast darker shadows across his eyes when he looked at me. At this angle, the moon's radiance caught him just right, reflecting an eerie glow in his pupils. The glow all nocturnal hunters had in their eyes. The flashing reflection burned green-white.

I was frozen in his hypnotic stare. Even if I had wanted to speak, I couldn't. Not when his touch turned soft, a gentle gesture that was at odds with the monster gazing back at me.

"I dare you to let me suck these beautiful tits," he said, his thumbs rubbing over both nipples, "and you to watch me do it."

I licked my lips and nodded.

Corban leaned in slowly, his eyes holding mine until his breath cooled the front of my chest, making my skin pebble. He continued to fondle one of my breasts while he held the other in a firm grip, placing his lips over the top of my nipple.

An electric current ran through me the moment his mouth touched my skin. His tongue swirled over the nub. He was gentle at first, moving between one breast then the other. Then he bit down and I swore I was going to come right then and there.

I fisted the sheets. The dark pools of his eyes threatened to drown me. I was tipping over the edge, slipping into the sweet bite of his teeth when he pulled back abruptly.

"Fuck me," I gasped.

A ripple of energy ran through his shoulders. He flexed his fingers, clenching and unclenching his fists.

"Are you going to fuck me?" I panted, giving him the chance to answer but fuck I hoped he went for the dare instead.

A lazy smile touched his beautiful face when he realized it was still part of the game and not an invitation. Corban moved away from the edge of the bed, giving me a full view of his incredible form. I dragged my gaze over every inch of him, from his gorgeous head, down to his thick torso, his strong legs, and back to the cock that was straining to get to me.

He waited until I met his eyes before answering. Eyes that were mercilessly dark, devoid of their usual jade color. A flash of red reflected in his blown-out pupils.

"Yes, I am," he said, and pushed down his shorts.

Chapter 16

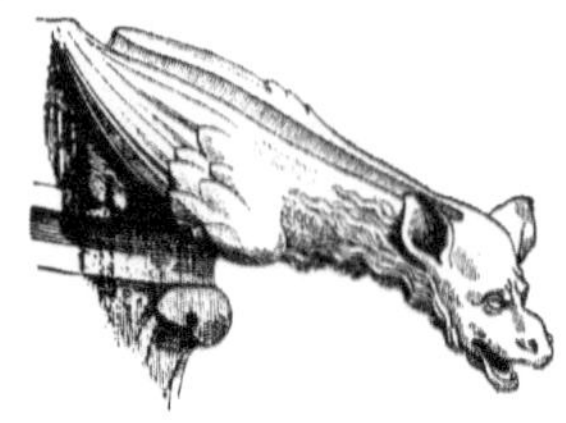

CORBAN

Practically every inch of Sorcha's skin was flushed crimson. She was overflowing with heat, and I loved it. I loved the way her eyes dilated when my cock sprang free. Her lips opened, forming a soft little "O" that I wanted to stretch.

I couldn't restrain myself for another second. Grabbing her chin, I pulled her face up to mine as I swooped down on her. Her kiss was ravenous, teeth scraping against mine as she met me eagerly. Her tongue slipped through my lips first, and I groaned. She thrust it greedily into my mouth, sucking my lip between her teeth.

Fuck.

I'd had every intention of fucking her cunt, but with the way her tongue felt, her teeth sharp and insistent against me, I needed to know what that would feel like around my cock.

I slid a hand around her throat, testing with a little squeeze. She tensed, her tongue stilling only for a moment. I took the opportunity to slide my forked tongue into her mouth and hungrily she sucked it, pulling another involuntary moan from my lungs. I tightened my fingers around her neck and pulled her against me.

"Dare," she said.

My cock jumped at her command.

"I dare you to let me fuck your throat," I growled.

Sorcha's pupils were blown out, her arousal so heady I knew she was acting on pure instinct. Primal energy was radiating off her, begging to be fucked.

She nodded. "Yes. Anything, just let me feel you." I moved away from her touch when she reached for my cock.

Her brows furrowed. Lips, swollen from my kiss, twisting into a pout.

"It's still my turn," I said and leaned down to catch that precious pout in another kiss. "You said you like it rough and so that is exactly how I am going to give it to you. If at any time it is too much, pinch my leg."

She nodded against my lips. "I'll tell you to stop."

I chuckled. "You won't be able to tell me anything with a full mouth."

Her wide eyes dropped back down to my cock. It jerked up, as ready as I was to fill her.

"Lie on your back and hang your head over the edge of the bed."

Her breath trembled between her lips. I loved that she was scared. I loved even more how she pushed through that fear, attempting to regain control that she'd never had in the first place. It was fun to watch her try.

Sorcha lay down as instructed. I couldn't see her eyes as well from her new position, but the rapid rise and fall of her chest told me everything I needed to know. "Open your legs," I said. I stroked my cock slowly, stepping forward.

She parted her strong thighs and licked her lips when the head of my cock was poised over them. I slapped the tip over her lips then rubbed it, coating her with precum. She opened her mouth, her tongue darting out to taste me.

"Good girl," I praised.

I eased my cock into her mouth a little at a time. As much as I wanted to get on with it, I wanted to make sure she was comfortable. I wanted her to enjoy this as much as I was about to. She swallowed, urging me to slide farther inside. Her mouth was so warm and soft. I ran a broad hand over her throat, laying it gently across her smooth skin as it started to bulge.

I've always loved watching a woman's throat stretch around my girth, but with Sorcha, it was even more satisfying. Perhaps it was her deep moans or the way she grabbed hold of my thighs. Or maybe it was how much sweeter she smelled as a new wave of desire flooded her.

"You're doing perfect, my dove." I slid a few more inches in and then drew back, pulling almost all the way out so she could catch her breath before sliding in once more. I did this again and again, feeding her more each time until finally I sank into her completely, my balls pressed against her pretty face.

I shut my eyes and just enjoyed the way her throat flexed around me. She was so fucking tight. Warm, and wet. She raised her hips, and I couldn't help but chuckle at the image. Sweet Sorcha – sprawled before me, my cock deep inside of her and *still* she had more to give. More that she was offering to me.

I slowly pulled back, letting her catch her breath, and then I started thrusting. Slow at first, until her grip on my thighs relaxed, inspiring me to pick up speed.

I slid a talon through the top of her underwear, one side and then the other, shredding them. I didn't care that I was ending the very game I had started early. I needed her taste in my mouth – I'd never had anyone last as long as she did, and it made me ravenous.

I leaned down and pressed my face between her thighs licking, nipping, and tongue-fucking her pussy like my life depended on it. All the while, I kept up my punishing pace. Steadily, *thoroughly* fucking her mouth, though my thrusts were becoming more and more erratic as her flavor overloaded my senses.

I traded my mouth for my fingers when I felt her tightening. "Come, Sorcha. Come for me." The words had barely left my mouth before she was gushing over my hand, her moans deep and guttural around my cock.

"Fuck," I hissed. I eased back, pulling away until the tip of my cock rested in her mouth. She gasped around it, her body writhing, inviting me back inside. I smoothed a hand down her spit-slicked cheek, my other circling around the back of her neck. I let her get a few more breaths in before I slammed back down her throat.

This time I didn't hold back. I cupped the back of her head and fucked her *hard*. The wet gurgling sounds she made as I bottomed out were music to my ears, driving me wild.

My release came sooner than I had intended, and I slammed into her, my thighs tightening around her face as I came. An animalistic roar tore out of me as cum shot down her throat. I could see the outline of my cock pulsing within her, flexing with every rope. I could have stayed like that all night, my hot cum filling her up, when she finally slapped my thigh.

I ground into her face, riding out the end of my orgasm when she slapped me again, harder this time. I pulled back a few inches and then thrust forward, enjoying the feel of her constricting around me as she gagged.

Sharp nails dug into my skin as she pinched me. I withdrew slowly, finally pulling free of her tight throat and swollen lips to let my cock drag across her face.

Sorcha flipped onto her stomach, coughing and heaving for air. Tears, spit and cum covered her face, morphing it into a beautiful glistening mess. I grabbed her by the throat, pulling her to her knees, and kissed her. I forced my tongue into her mouth, savoring the way my cum mingled with her saliva. Her nails were like claws as she tangled them in my hair, pulling me down to her.

She broke our kiss just long enough to breathe against my mouth, "Fuck me. Please."

I kissed her deeply. I couldn't restrain the grin that spread over my face. Especially when a spark of fear entered her scent. She had given permission so easily, and she knew it.

"I will."

"Now. Right now, please," she begged.

I pulled her hair to the side as I crawled on top of her and sank my teeth into her neck. Her blood was as rich and hot as her cum. It was a wine I wanted to get drunk on.

She arched up, crying out. I slipped my fingers inside of her. *So warm,* I thought, *and still dripping. Begging for me to fill her.* From the corner of my eye, I looked toward the sky. It would be sunrise soon enough. I wanted to fuck her, badly, but I also didn't want it to be quick. I would need more than a few hours to leave us both satisfied.

I worked my fingers in her hard while I drank, forcing her to orgasm again, and again. It was beautiful the way she came undone, how messy and vocal she was.

I felt her hand skim across my hips and then grasp my cock, which was still rock hard. She was straining, angling it down towards her center.

When I didn't move, she resorted to stroking it. With her other hand she squeezed my balls.

I ripped my fangs free. I needed to slow down, but it was impossible to think clearly around her. If I wasn't careful, she could easily take control of the situation. I couldn't allow her to think that she had any power over me.

"Please," she said again.

I kissed her, mingling the taste of her blood with the lingering taste of both of our cum. An exquisite combination. "I will. But not tonight, little dove. I want you to think of me as you drift off to sleep. I want you to think of me in the morning when you wake, when lust does not cloud your mind."

"Fuck me," she hissed, but I knew it was a curse this time and not the demand it sounded like. "You're a sick fucking bastard."

I pushed her roughly onto her back and slid down her body, running my hands and tongue down her plush form, squeezing and tasting her as I went. "I am. I am going to do terrible things to you, Sorcha." I kissed the inside of her knee and raised her leg as I slid off the bed, pulling her foot into the air so I could kiss its sole. "And you're going to be begging, like you are now, for me to do them."

I looked down the line of her leg to her pussy, dusted with its dark hair. Then up the curve of her stomach and the swell of her heaving breasts, before I landed on her flushed face. I'd never seen anything so divine.

I wouldn't fuck her tonight, but that didn't mean we couldn't have another release.

"Rub your pussy," I said. I was already rubbing my cock.

Sorcha's eyes never left my cock as I stroked to her. Meanwhile, I was torn between watching her fingers play with her slit and the way her gorgeous face pinched and tightened. Or how her nipples hardened with her arousal.

"Fuck," she panted. "I'm going to come again."

"Do it. Come." Power leeched into my voice. Her eyes widened and then there she was, coming and gushing over the bed once more. I jerked my cock and then I was coming with her, covering her tits and stomach with my seed.

The rush that entered my blood as she gave another part of herself to me made my eyes flutter closed. The feeling was nearly as euphoric as the post-orgasm bliss tingling through my body.

I grabbed her face and pulled her up. "Now go to sleep, Sorcha." I kissed her. "I want you to fall asleep with my scent covering you."

She nodded and kissed me in return. "When will you return?"

I ran a thumb over her lips. "When do you *want* me to return?"

She chewed her lower lip. "Tomorrow?"

I arched a brow. "My, you are a greedy little thing."

"Stop playing games with me," she huffed.

"But you love my games."

"I do." She was practically clay in my palms. So different from the others, to the ones who came before. Them, I had needed to woo with pretty illusions and soft words. To go gently lest I frighten or scandalize them into a bout of pretend guilt. All that time and effort, wasted. And yet here was Sorcha, my wicked, wanting, perfect pet. All here, and all mine.

I didn't believe in soul mates; they didn't exist where I came from, but having this glorious, devilish meal served up to me so easily, had me wondering if there was some truth to the concept. I felt like I had been waiting for her my whole life. Even before the curse, someone had thought to create her just for me.

"Will you let me do whatever I want to you?"

Her brow furrowed. "That depends."

I tsked and drew my thumb over her brows. I was starting to like that look on her too. It was cute. "Have I done anything you don't like?"

The bed creaked as she leaned back to look at me fully. "No, but–"

"Yes or no, Sorcha."

Her teeth worked over her pretty lower lip once more. If she kept doing that, I'd have to fuck it again. A couple of times her teeth had skimmed over my cock, and it had only further fed my desire.

"No," she finally answered.

I tweaked one of her nipples. "Good girl."

She lurched forward to her elbows. "Wait, Corban. How do you know my name?"

I pressed a finger to my lips. "A question for another night."

I stepped back into the shadows that had crept around my feet and had the sweet satisfaction of seeing her eyes widen when I disappeared into their depths.

Chapter 17

SORCHA

Golden light cracked through the gap in the curtains, casting a calming glow over the bedroom. It might have been a relaxing scene had the entire room not reeked of sex, and had my body not been sore and aching with proof of it. I laid there for the longest time, mind spinning over everything that had happened the night before.

I was for sure going to Hell. Because if it wasn't the Devil himself I was sleeping with, it was most certainly *some* kind of demon.

I shoved the sheets and cum-stained clothes into the wash and showered. As messed up as it was, I couldn't help but admire the new bruising on my hips as I scrubbed myself. My throat was raw, and lips still swollen, but otherwise my upper body – aside from the wounds at my neck – was unmarred from Corban's touch. At least he was a considerate monster.

I checked the house to make sure he wasn't lurking somewhere and pulled Rosaline's diary from where I'd hidden it in the library. I set it on the middle of the table and began pulling out the rest of the books lining the shelves, flipping through them in hopes of... what? I wasn't sure. Maybe Macky had stashed something important away somewhere.

Mom had found money behind picture frames in the house she inherited, but since Glamis Manor came with nothing *but* money, I hadn't thought to look for a secret stash. There were at least six hundred books I needed to get through. As I pulled each from its nook, I half hoped one would be a secret lever, leading me to Macky's treasure or Corban's secret lair.

After sorting through at least half of the books, I gave up and flopped onto the couch with Rosaline's diary. If I was lucky, Rosaline would have all the answers I needed.

December 2, 1812

It has been some time since I've written but so much has been happening, that I simply cannot wrap my mind around it all. My angel returned to me some nights ago, which is why I have not had the opportunity to write. Where darkness once left him trapped, he can now walk in the sunlight like any man.

So, he *can* be out in the day? I glanced around, half expecting to find Corban lurking in a shadow, before pulling the diary closer to me. I felt like a guilty child, with my hands on something I wasn't supposed to have, something I'd be punished for should anyone find out. To be safe, I locked the library door and moved to sit on the floor in the corner, where I was pretty sure I'd be out of sight of the windows.

He has been joining me in the mornings and through most of the days. Well, whenever Gerald is not at home, or is busy in his study. His name is Corban, a good strong name for someone as beautiful as he.

Even though I'd suspected the mystery man in Rosaline's diary to be the same one that haunted me, I couldn't help but feel a twinge of jealousy when his name confirmed it. It was a stupid reaction, but one I felt nonetheless. I turned to the next page aggressively.

He is a prince! Can you believe that? And the best part is he wants to take me to his kingdom when he returns. He is from 'Undaland', a place for the divine. He says there are more like him and that is something I can hardly wrap my head around. How can there be more than one creation so divine?

He says there are three things I must do before he can take me to his world. The first is I must give my body to him, the second is that I must give my heart to him, and the third is I must give my will over to him. I was offended by this because does he not already know that he already possesses all of these things? That I would go anywhere with him, should he just ask?

I know you are thinking I am terrible to betray Gerald like this, but I cannot help it. He is dull in comparison. Corban breathes life into me. He makes me feel things I never knew could exist. I thought I knew what love was until I met him. The pleasure he gives me, the devotion he shows, Gerald could never equal it.

I frowned. Corban didn't strike me as the princely type. With that thought came a gut-wrenching realization. Rosaline had killed her husband and then herself. What had triggered her to do it? Or was the story just a story and Corban had killed them both?

I read through a few more pages but Rosaline's line of thought turned repetitive. The next month was nothing but entries where she gushed over Corban and how kindly he treated her. One excerpt even mentioned that he had fed her sweets by hand.

I snorted at the image. There was no way the man that had throat-fucked me stupid last night was the same one playing the gentleman in Rosaline's story.

December 30, 1812

I've upset him. Corban caught me and Gerald the other night. Caught seems like a strange way to term it, he is my husband after all, but when Corban came to call on me and found me in bed with Gerald instead, he was livid. I've never been so terrified of my angel.

I cried out and Gerlad jumped up, but he was gone by the time Gerald lit a lantern.

The crunch of gravel brought me back to reality. I scrambled to my feet and leaned over the back of the couch to see Quint's car rolling to a stop.

"You've got to be fucking kidding me," I seethed.

I marched out to meet him on the front porch, armed with my best "get the hell off my property" face.

Quint was leaning into his car, grabbing, oh for fuck's sake, were those flowers? He jumped when he turned and saw me already waiting for him.

"Sorcha," he started.

I held up my hand. "I don't want to hear it. And honestly, it doesn't even matter. We barely know each other so it's better to not drag this out. Take that—" I motioned to the bouquet gripped in his hand, "—and leave."

Dark circles framed his eyes and as his mouth dropped open, I noted how exhausted he looked. "Can I just say something?"

Annoyance rose like bile in my throat. I ran my tongue between my teeth as I tried to swallow my frustration. On top of it all, was the growing awareness of something *other* dripping into the space between Quint and myself. A prickling sensation crawled over the back of my neck, and I wondered if Corban was somewhere watching everything unfold.

I turned, looking for any sign of him. Rosaline's last entry was far too fresh, and he'd already threatened to kill Quint once.

"I want to ask for a second chance. The flowers won't fix what I said, I know that. I just wanted to apologize. To do something nice, and maybe sit down and talk. I'm not asking you out again or anything. I don't expect that. I'm sorry, Sorcha."

I was only half listening to Quint as I stepped off the porch to look at the balcony. As soon as my foot landed on the gravel the strange dark pressure hit me with twice the intensity. I faltered at the same time Quint did.

"It was all bullshit," he said slowly. He took a hesitant step back toward his car. "What are you looking at?"

The gargoyles on the second floor looked hungrily from their posts, mouths gaping. He said he wasn't, but Corban had to be a gargoyle. No, *close* he'd said. What was similar to a gargoyle?

"I think you should leave," I said quietly.

My gaze moved slowly across roofline, and lingered on the stone dragon-like creature that lay coiled over the porch. Its long neck was twisted and curved, horns rising from its head in vicious points.

"Sorcha?"

I pointed to the creature. "Do you know what that is?"

I felt Quint's presence beside me. "A dragon?"

"But it doesn't look like a regular dragon." It was shaped wrong, its body morphed and hulking. Dread's cool hand pressed into my gut. I flicked my gaze to the rest of the house. Were there more of these things?

"No," he said slowly. Quint stepped in front of me, his back now to the house. If he felt the same presence I did, he was doing a better job of ignoring it than I was. "I just came by to see if you were ok. Those bruises looked really serious."

I tried not to let those words affect me as I walked down the side of the house, Quint trailing behind me.

"Are you ok?" he pressed.

I was getting more agitated by the second, and if this rising feeling was a clue to anything, so was Corban, wherever he was. Chills burst across my skin when I finally turned to face Quint. I looked up into what appeared to be genuine concern reflected in his soft eyes.

That wasn't an easy question to answer. Of course I wasn't fine, but I couldn't tell him the truth and give him more fuel to add to the 'Sorcha's crazy' fire. "I am," I said.

"Has he come back?"

"It's nothing I can't handle."

"Sorcha."

"Quint. It's fine. I'm fine. Let's just forget any of this ever happened." I spread my hands out in front of me. "I've got a couple of things I need to catch up on inside."

"If someone is harassing you, you need to call the cops."

"Because that worked out so well last time." I cut him a sharp look. "And presently the only person harassing me is you."

His brows furrowed and a mean scowl tore across his face. "Note taken," he said, though he didn't sound as bitter as he looked. "I have to be on this side of town again tomorrow. Can I stop by?"

Now it was my turn to be exasperated. I chuckled as I walked past him, making my way back to the front porch. The dark, simmering rage fanning the back of my neck had lessened, but was still very present as its owner and myself tracked Quint to the bottom of the steps.

"You want to get into my pants that bad?"

"I'd settle for another night on your couch." There was a playful lilt in his voice. Men like Quint were hard to stay mad at, and that's what made them dangerous. Or rather, what made my current situation dangerous.

At the end of the day, it didn't matter how Quint really felt about me or that I'd maybe had a little crush on him. It all boiled down to Corban and I, and whatever twisted thing he had in store for me. For us. I thought about the jealousy he'd exhibited with Rosaline.... I doubted his nature had changed, especially given the threats he'd already dished out so easily.

I couldn't put Quint in harm's way, no matter how pissed off at him I was.

I forced myself to give him a closed-lipped smile. "I'll text you if anything changes."

The corner of Quint's mouth quirked. "Sure. If you change your mind, there's another party at the end of the week. It'd be cool if you came."

This time, I did smile. *Persistent this one.* "It'd be cool, huh?"

"Yeah," he said, his smile fluttering wider. "Just think about it. Oh!" He stepped forward and passed me the flowers. "Here, um, yeah." He rubbed his hand on the back of his neck as he made for his car. "I hope to hear from you."

I held the flowers close to my chest and nodded.

It wasn't until I was inside the house with the sound of his car retreating that I lifted them to my face to smell them. I really did love flowers, and it would be a shame to let them go to waste just because I was angry at Quint.

I pulled a vase down from the top shelf in the kitchen, playing with the stems until the arrangement was to my liking. The pinks and reds were a welcome burst of color in the otherwise neutral-colored kitchen. Pleased, I returned to the library and cracked open Rosaline's diary again.

January 3, 1812

Gerald knows. He does not know of Corban exactly, but he suspects something is amiss. Ever since my outburst the other night he has kept a close eye on me and comments repeatedly on how I have withdrawn from him. The nerve! As if he was not locking himself away for months on end with his work.

January 4, 1812

Gerald has become suffocating while Corban becomes ever distant. I cannot take this much longer.

January 9, 1812

Last night I demanded that Corban take me to his kingdom. He said he could not, because I had failed to commit myself to him, body and soul, by still accepting Gerald's affections. I screamed at him that I had! Had I not allowed him to touch me, kiss me in the most intimate ways? Was my unfaithfulness to Gerald not enough? But Corban only grew more angry with each protest that fell from my lips. A fire leapt in his eyes that I had not seen before, and he dragged me to the door that would take us to his kingdom. He told me to try and open it, but it would not budge.

"See?" His voice was like poison, and the way he looked at me, it was as if he were disgusted with me. "My world rejects you because you reject me. You have to give up everything!"

I think I know what I have to do. May God forgive me, but surely this is God's will if the instruction comes from an angel.

January 10, 1812

Tonight will be my last entry. I have prepared a nice meal for Gerald and I. A last supper where I will tell him the truth before leaving him forever. I can't go on like this a moment longer. I have tasted the divine and know now I cannot bear to live without it.

Chapter 18

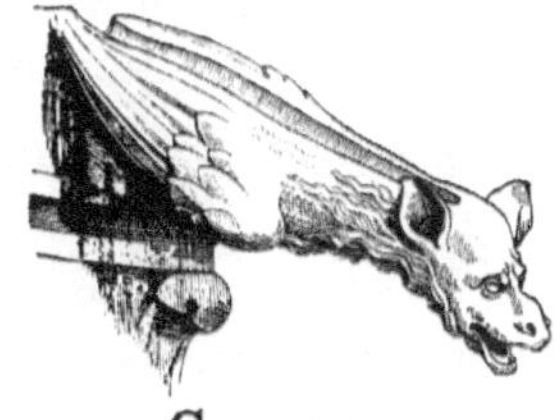

SORCHA

A firm knock echoed down the hallway. I glanced up, the sun was just starting to make its way behind the tree line. Muddied colors washed across the clouded sky.

I opened the front door. "I'm surprised you didn't let yourself in."

Corban touched his fingers to the throat of his black collared shirt and let out a soft hum. "I wanted to give you the opportunity to invite me in."

This was all an illusion. I was not really in control as I stepped back, waving my hand to the side to allow him entry. The flash of darkness in his eyes as he took me in, the slow winding assessment he made of my body, brought heat to my cheeks immediately. The door shut behind him without so much as a flick of his wrist.

He stepped toward me with a predatory smile, but I held up my hand, catching him in the chest. "Wait! We're going to talk first." I looked back at the door, my nerves already shot. What sort of creature could do that? Move objects without touching them, disappear into thin air? My terrible fascination with finding out the answer would be the death of me.

Corban's brows knit together. "Talk? Last night you were begging me to fuck you."

I swallowed as I tried to ground myself. I could feel my body growing hot with want by the simple touch between us. The thrum of his heart was a welcome melody beneath my palm. I jerked my hand away and took a couple of steps back.

Corban followed. "Don't you want to play another game?" He looked absolutely lethal as he prowled after me, matching each step as I backed into the living room. When he drifted into the shadows he seemed to meld into them, disappearing entirely until he moved again, back into the soft glow of the lamplight.

"Yes. But one of my choosing. Twenty questions," I said quickly.

Corban's steps slowed with a cock of his head. He scowled. "Ten."

I kept walking backward until my feet met the cool hardwood exposed at the edge of the living room rug. "That's not enough."

"Twenty is too many. Take it or leave it."

"Fine. Were you watching me earlier? When Quint was here, was that you?"

Corban's head tipped to the side. His eyes caught the lamplight with the movement and that hunter's glow returned, the flash of a cool green reflection. "I've watched you from the very first day you set foot on these grounds."

Fuck, if it was anything like the way he was watching me now, it made it even more concerning. There was something soulless behind the keen, dark hunger staring back at me.

"How do you know who I am? I never met Maxine."

Corban shrugged. "I know all of her children, and her daughter's daughter." He gave me a knowing look. "Maxine spoke of you all, often."

"I'm sure she was complaining when she did."

At that the corner of Corban's mouth tipped up. "It is true she did not speak highly of them. You, though, she only mentioned once, and it was with kindness."

A thousand questions came to mind when it came to Grandma Macky. As much as I wanted to pick his brain about her, I couldn't waste all of my questions on her. Not tonight. "I never met her," I said, more to myself.

A sick feeling overcame me as it dawned on me that she had lived in this house a very long time. Long enough that Corban must have haunted her too. Like he was me, like he had Rosaline.

"Did you ever...." My face heated at the thought. It was clear he'd had *relations* with Rosaline but I hadn't considered he'd also been with my grandmother. "Did you do to her what you're doing to me?"

Corban's eyes glittered like dark jewels. "Did I ever fuck her?" he clarified.

I nodded.

A flicker of darkness flashed across his features. "On rare occasions. Maxine was not much of a team player." Poison dripped from his words as if the bitterness was a physical taste in his mouth.

"Did you hurt her?"

Corban took his time answering. Watching him closely, I could tell that whatever was going through his mind still simmered. Macky was clearly a sensitive topic. "No," he answered thinly.

I crossed my arms, waiting. A low hiss escaped his lips.

"Maxine and I did not get along but I never hurt her."

"Did you force her? I know you crept into my room the other night while I was sleeping."

Corban clucked his tongue. "You're watching me now? I should be flattered, but I'm offended you would think so lowly of me. I have never forced anyone to spread beneath me. And if my memory serves me correctly, you enjoyed yourself the other night while you were *sleeping*." He said the last word as if I had been playing a game with him then too. As if I had been pretending.

"Some would consider that a violation," I said thinly.

He chuckled. "And yet you invited me in. What does that say about you, Sorcha?"

My hands curled into fists, a movement he tracked with a smile. I hated when he smiled like that, like he was one step ahead of me and already laying the trap I was about to fall into.

"Are you done with your silly questions?"

He wasn't getting off that easy. "Why are you here? And I don't mean now but I mean... overall in this house. I know you've been here since it was built."

Red light flickered within the whites of his eyes. "I am part of it," he said simply. "How do you know how long I've been here?"

Well shit. I ignored his question and moved on quickly. I didn't want to have to explain Rosaline's diary, not when I wasn't finished reading it. "What are you?"

Corban ran his thumb over my lip. "Ask another question."

"Why won't you tell me?"

"Because it's so much more fun to keep you guessing." A soft smile spread his plush lips apart. Pointed fangs flashed.

Absentmindedly I touched the marks on my neck. A flutter of nausea hit me when I realized Quint could have seen them earlier had my hair not been down. There'd be no way I could have explained those away.

"What do you want with me?" I asked.

"Isn't it obvious?" He chose that moment to stalk even closer.

I evaded him, slinking my way backward into the kitchen. He was clearly a creature of magic and I didn't want him casting a spell on me. Because that was the only explanation as to why I wanted him so badly. When he touched me, I became a different person. I didn't recognize her, and wasn't in a hurry to meet her again when I barely understood what Corban was. I stepped around the center island, trying to maintain some distance

"Give me a straight answer," I said coolly.

Corban spread his hands on the island and leaned forward. The barrier didn't provide as much space between us as I'd hoped, as he was so tall. He was practically leering in my face at this angle. "I want to give you pleasure, Sorcha. I want nothing more than to fuck every thought you have right out of that pretty little head of yours. I want to consume you."

It sounded more like a threat than a declaration of love, yet I found myself still rooted to the spot before him, despite my instincts screaming at me to run. Because I knew the pleasure he could give me. Something else told me what he had given me so far was just a taste.

I swallowed. "Are you from this world?"

He slid around the edge of the island, his palm making a shushing sound as it caressed the wood. "I'm afraid you've used up all your questions."

"I've let you into my body, the least you can do is let me into your mind."

Something like surprise crossed his features. Corban tipped his head to the side again, hinting at the starving predator lurking beneath his curiosity. "Two more," he said, his words clipped.

"Are you from this world?" I repeated.

"No."

"Why do you only come out at night?" I backed against the counter as he hovered over me. The tall shadow he cast swallowed my entire body, shrouding me in darkness.

He pressed one hand against the cabinet and the other to the neighboring counter. I was trapped. My heart slammed against my chest despite my body warming to the idea of him putting those large hands on me again. Fear and anticipation, they were becoming as close as lovers. Like Corban and I would be if he kept this up.

"Would you like me to haunt you in the sunlight?" My eyes widened as a hand made entirely of shadow stroked down my face, before wrapping a strand of my hair around its finger. I glanced left and right, both of his real hands were still firmly planted on either side of me. *How?!*

His eyes slid past my face to something behind me, and his body seemed to freeze. He became so still I thought he had turned to stone, his skin greying as a tremor suddenly ran through him.

"You're a very bad girl, Sorcha." He plucked one of the stems from the vase that sat on the countertop just past my hip and tossed it to the floor. "Keeping gifts from another man who does not even know you. Foxglove. Hemlock. Nightshade." With each name he tossed one of Quint's stems to the floor and in their stead others grew. Ones I recognized from the garden. "These suit you much better."

I could feel the color leech from my face. "Poison. Those are all—"

Corban sneered. "They're only deadly if they're misused. Oh, don't look at me like that. Did you really think the garden was nothing more than pretty ornamentation when a creature such as I haunts your domain? Macky may have planted the Belladonna Garden, but these days it answers only to me."

For all of the scary stories I had read, I knew nothing about what poisonous plants looked like. Their names rang loud and clear, though and I watched in horror as the sparsely decorated vase bloomed with a deadly bouquet.

Corban's breath stroked chills down my skin. "How does it feel knowing you've invited Death into your bed? That the darkness you seek between pages is blood and flesh before you."

I saw my eyes widen in the dark mirror of his own eyes. Heat fanned the shadows around us. Heat I did not know he could produce, for his hand was ice-cold as it wrapped around my wrist. Within the warring temperatures rose the musk of twin rage and desire.

His thumb moved over my wrist. "It's my turn to choose the game. I am going to count to ten. That is all the time I'll give you," he whispered.

I was already taking a hesitant step to the side. His hold didn't tighten, but neither did he let me go.

"For what?" I could hardly breathe. I tried to rationalize that he was not really Death, that his touch would have killed me if he was. Death could not touch a living thing without consequence, without taking something in return.

"To run. When I catch you," he tsked. He waited until I was trembling beneath him before continuing. "I am going to do all of the terrible things I have promised to you. I am going to punish your cunt again and again....and again." He hissed out the last word, baring his sharp teeth. "Until you are begging for me to stop."

How did something so vile make me so wet? I did not understand how my mind and body worked against each other; how I was a puppet to them both. To him.

"If I win," I started but was abruptly cut off by Corban's sinister laughter.

"You're done winning, Sorcha. Better start running." He flung my wrist away, a movement that jarred me out of my stupor and sent me backpedaling into the island and then the dining table.

"One."

I didn't wait another second before I bolted from the room. I hesitated at the bottom of the stairs, looking up then back to the front door. Corban was fast, I'd seen just how fast when he'd chased me the first night. There wouldn't be a chance in hell I'd outrun him in the open.

I sprinted up the stairs, slamming my bedroom door shut as I passed, then quietly trotted down the hallway to the master bedroom, with its four-poster bed and black duvet. This room screamed *ominous*, but it was the one with the darkest colors, and the only one I thought I might best be able to hide in. I looked around, my eyes landing on the window. A possible escape? Could I hide on the roof?

I could only hope Corban would check my room first to buy me more time.

Closing the door quietly, I moved to the window, then paused.

I am part of it.

Corban's words from the living room moments earlier snaked through my mind. Perhaps he *couldn't* leave the house after all.

Damn it! I should have headed straight for the front door when I'd had the chance, or better yet, grabbed my car keys.

My mind raced. If I could get out the window and somehow down to the ground, I'd be out of his reach. At least for the moment.

"Ten!" His deep voice echoed through the house, and I lurched back into motion.

My heart stuttered when the window didn't budge. "You're fucking kidding me." I dug my nails beneath the edge, trying to pry it up, but for all the upper body strength I had (or lack thereof), the dried paint holding it shut was stronger.

I whirled when I heard his footsteps on the landing.

"Where oh where could Sorcha be?"

"Fuck," I mouthed. I stepped to the next window only to run into the same problem. I was wasting too much time.

The creak of my bedroom door opening down the hall sounded in the same moment that the third window shifted.

My adrenaline skyrocketed as I used every bit of strength I had to shove it open. There was barely enough room for me and yet moments later I was forcing my tits through, pulling and kicking until I was hanging halfway out the window staring at the steep decline of the first-floor roof beneath me.

I kept a firm hold onto the windowsill as I turned carefully to slide my legs free. My feet slid against the worn shingles, and I felt my exposed skin burn as it scraped. I reached up, looking for a way to close the window from the outside, but there wasn't one. Only the person inside could seal it. And that person was staring directly at me, his green eyes full of vicious wrath.

"What the fuck are you doing?" he snarled.

Corban, who had been standing in the middle of the room, was now striding toward me. I scrambled to the left, pressing my palms against the flat wall of the manor as if that would keep me from sliding to my death, or worse. I needed to figure out how to get down without breaking my neck. I rose unsteadily, pressing my chest against the crumbling stone, and looked over my shoulder.

Holy fuck that was a long way down. Maybe jumping down two stories was a piece of cake for some people but for me, who had no clue about parkour or how to absorb the shock of a landing, it looked like a death trap. Still, out here was better than inside with Corban.

"Sorcha, get back inside." Corban had stuck his head out the window and was properly glaring at me.

"Nope," I said, barely glancing at him as I looked for a way down. The part of the roof I was standing on dropped off sharply to my left, but the wall just beyond it that stretched from the ground all the way to the turret was covered with ivy. Ivy that was woven tightly through a wooden lattice. I started shuffling toward it. "You said I couldn't win and I'm going to do exactly that."

"I'm going to strangle you."

"Ha! Going back on your word?" I looked back in hopes of catching a glimpse of humor in his expression.

If I thought Corban had looked angry before, he looked positively livid now. His dark hair was disheveled, his angular face twisted into something downright monstrous. His fangs, already razor sharp, looked absolutely lethal as his forked tongue lashed against them, he was almost out the window himself. "You'll wish you were dead by the time I'm done with you."

Just a little bit farther. I reached for the lattice at the same time he reached for me. I didn't consider that the structure was old and possibly fragile. The moment his talons brushed against my shoulder I jumped. I felt the breath leave my lungs as I landed on the lattice, a few feet lower than the roof, with a loud thwack, my fingers scrabbling for purchase between the slats. My feet slid through the ivy, leaves fluttering around me as the impact shook them loose.

"Sorcha!"

This time when I looked back at Corban I caught the shock – or was that fear? – on his face, before he quickly replaced it with a mask of rage. He sat back on his strong haunches and looked down at me, eyes flashing between red, green, and black. The shift in his countenance might have been comical under any other circumstance. If this had been a cartoon, steam would have been coming out of his ears.

"Looks like I win." Maybe it was the rush in my blood that made me tease him. Or perhaps some sick part of me liked toying with him as he had me these last few nights.

Corban shifted forward onto his hands and crawled toward me. The movement seemed unnatural, his limbs appearing somehow longer, more animalistic from this angle. I swallowed as I managed to get my foot onto one of the slats and slowly lowered myself down, not once taking my eyes off him, even once I reached the ground.

He leered down at me, his eyes impossibly dark. "There is no world in which you beat me."

I took a couple of steps back, throwing my arms wide. "You have to touch me to win and you—" I pointed, "—can't leave the house. Rules are rules."

Poised atop the roof, his claws digging into the gutter, Corban blinked. The reflective glow in his eyes was there, as it had been the night before, as it had been every night, but I was only just starting to acknowledge just how frightening that was. From where I stood, he bore an uncanny resemblance to the monsters guarding the manor, with their fanged snarls and arched backs. All with the same granite grey skin.

"Close," he had said. Gargoyles were symbols of protection and as Corban rose slowly, I knew without a doubt he wasn't a guardian. He did look like Rosaline's angel, though. A vengeful angel perfectly cast in stone.

Corban dropped to the ground in a single quiet movement. The impact of his landing sent me stumbling back so quickly that I tripped, seating myself heavily on the hard earth. He folded his hands in front of him and said, matter-of-factly, "I'll give you twenty seconds this round."

Chapter 19

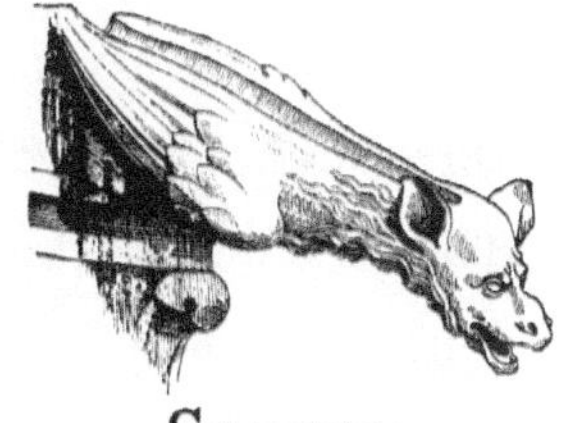

SORCHA

The earth was spongey beneath my feet as I flew across it, into the waiting arms of the crooked trees. My palms were scratched and burning from my fall, stinging all the worse as my nails bit into them, fists clenched as I ran like my life depended on it.

I felt it the moment Corban started to pursue me. A great sweeping shadow of dread shrouded me, threatening to pull me down despite the extra kick of adrenaline. Perhaps he was Death after all, a reaper come to steal my soul.

Branches tugged at my hair, one scraped my arm and then another was slapping me across the face as I hurled myself forward. Of *course* Corban could leave the house. I'd seen him standing in the yard once, after all, hadn't I? But no, like the first idiotic girl to die in a horror movie, I'd taken it literally when he'd said he was a part of the manor.

Fear nipped at my heels, urging me faster. I had no idea where I was going or how large the forest was. I just knew that I couldn't stop. Once I did, once he grabbed hold of me, I was lost. Not just because he would win this game, but because I had a feeling that once he did, I'd never escape his clutches again. Not that I really wanted to – he wouldn't even have to take my soul, if that *was* what he was after. I would give it to him willingly.

The ground shifted beneath me as my foot landed in a soft patch of moss, my ankle twisting as momentum careened me forward and down. I hit the ground with a cry, barely catching myself on my palms, shredding them the rest of the way. I threw my head back, biting my lip to stifle the sob of pain that threatened to tear out of my throat.

Utter stillness enveloped me.

I held my breath to better listen. There was no trace of nighttime birdsong, not a single insect chirped. Even the wind had died. There was absolute silence. I knew creatures went quiet when a predator was close, but surely, I would be able to hear him. Corban was huge, he would be loud. Then again, he *was* magic. I probably wouldn't be able to hear him unless he wanted me to.

I gripped the base of the tree beside me as I tried to right myself. Blistering pain wrapped around my ankle, but I forced weight onto it, testing it gingerly. I let out a shuddering breath and started hobbling forward. There wasn't time to waste when I knew my twenty seconds were already up.

I was alert to every snapping twig, every shifting shadow as I crept forward, but there was no sign of Corban. It didn't matter though, I could *feel* him there with me in the darkness. Every hair on the back of my neck stood on end.

A patch of soft light filtered between the trees up ahead, a beacon leading me out of the maze. A neighboring property? I stepped out from between the final trees and came to a jarring halt.

"No," I said, spinning back around to find the tree line now well behind me.

Ahead of me stood Glamis Manor, in all its glory. Each window glowed with warm light, as if to mock me. I might have been running through the woods blindly but I *knew* I had been running straight. There wasn't any way for me to have completely turned myself around, and stumbled out into the field, only yards away from where I had entered the forest minutes before.

"What the fuck? This isn't possible."

A patch of darkness moved. Out of the shadows cast by my car in the driveway, spilled the tall form of a man. Corban. He looked perfectly composed, his brow free of sweat and clothes finely pressed and tailored. Had he chased me at all, or had he been waiting until I ran straight back into his arms?

"You're only able to leave Glamis when I allow it," he said.

My stomach dropped. "What the fuck are you talking about?"

He tsked. "No need to fear dove," he said prowling forward. "I only intend to keep you here for our games. Which—" he plucked the front of my shirt, "—I've won again."

"You can keep me here?" I breathed.

"Of course I can." His eyes glimmered like rare jewels. He reached for me, one hand wrapping around my throat and the other lacing through the back of my hair. "I can keep you wherever I like. Put you in any position I want."

How did something so violent sound so sexual coming out of his mouth? I knew he could smell the moment my arousal hit by the slow upward curve of his lips.

He slid his thumb over my mouth, the edge of one of his long claws catching my lower lip. "I love the way you play with death. How you invite it in so willingly. Tell me, will you allow me in?" His talons trailed down my throat to the front of my shirt. It sliced apart like silk beneath his touch. "Will you beg for me as you did last night, and the night before?"

His cool skin drew an involuntary shiver from me as he slid his palm over one of my now exposed breasts. His iron grip held me still, not that I tried to get away. I could fight, as my wiser, more rational self instructed, but we both knew I would always give into Corban. Like Rosaline, I'd had a taste of him and needed more.

"Yes," I said hoarsely. "Please, Corban."

"Again." He twisted my nipple between his thumb and forefinger. I rose up on my toes, trying to release the pressure from the sharp pinch of his nails.

"Please."

Swirls of darkness entered his eyes. The bite of his claws found their way into my scalp.

"Please!" I gasped.

"Please what," he hissed.

"Please fuck me."

In a fatal swoop he pulled my face up to his and pressed his cold lips to mine. I laced my arms around his neck as his hands dropped to my ass, and he hoisted me up. I wrapped my legs around him, latching hold to him with equal savagery.

He was like a drug. So powerful that a simple taste was all it took for him to spread throughout my bloodstream. Corban was an addiction I'd always lose the battle against.

One second, we were in the field and the next I heard his boots on the front porch. Warm light spilled around us when the front door opened and he walked us into Glamis' familiar embrace.

He set me down and the moment my feet touched the floor I was tugging at his shirt. He grabbed me by my waistband and yanked me flush against him.

"Take these off, now," he growled, ripping his shirt free from my grasp. It disappeared like smoke. Like it had never been there to begin with.

Fuck he was beautiful. Corban was so unbelievably perfect it ached to look at him. Perhaps Rosaline had been right and he was an angel, one that had fallen from grace.

I wasn't thinking, just following my instincts when I leaned forward and ran my tongue up his smooth chest. A low groan rumbled from beneath my mouth. I toed off my shoes and wrapped my hand around his cock as he pushed his pants down.

Corban's cock was as beautiful as he was. It was long, longer than any I had seen in person or even in porn, and its girth was something to behold. It was a wonder I'd been able to take him in my throat last night. I felt a sense of pride as I stroked down, down, down and then back up, twisting my palm over the glistening head. I took a step back, giving him a gentle tug before letting him go.

I retreated to the bottom of the stairs.

All traces of humanity had fled his slanted eyes. There was nothing but a predator standing naked before me, muscles taut and cock twitching.

He was looking at me just as he had the first time we met and all the times since. Like he wanted to devour me. Slowly, I hooked my thumbs into the waistband of my underwear and pushed them down, along with my shorts, kicking my socks off so I too, was naked.

"Come and get me," I said.

Fire lit behind the pale green of his irises. I turned and sprinted up the stairs.

I'd barely made it to the landing when he grabbed me from behind and pushed me down, his broad chest slamming into my back. We fell to the ground in a heap in front of the giant gilded mirror.

I caught his eyes in the reflection when he sat up, keeping a hand on the middle of my back. He wrapped his other hand around his cock and angled it down. At the first brush against my entrance, he let out an animalist hiss. "Wicked, wicked, Sorcha. You're absolutely soaking."

I shifted my hips up, trying to push him inside. The head of his cock parted me and I let out a shameless moan. I needed him *now*. He leaned over my back once more and took purchase of my hips. With his face pressed against my cheek, his gaze locked with mine in the mirror, he slid inside.

My mouth gaped at the intrusion in a silent plea. More? Stop? Never stop?!

"That's it," he praised. "Look at you." He eased farther in until my silent pleasure finally made a sound, and I groaned, throwing my head back into his shoulder.

"Fuck you're big," I said.

"I know," he said kissing my cheek. "And you take me so well. First your mouth and now your perfect little pussy. You're doing so good. I need you to take a little bit more so I can fuck you properly."

Hysterical laughter bubbled in the back of my throat. There was no way he could slide any more of his cock inside me. I gasped when he thrust forward. "Corban!"

A dissatisfied hiss left him. "That just won't do."

"Won't..." I started. "There's nowhere else for you to go!"

"Shh," he crooned. "It's alright." Corban rolled his hips back and then forward slowly. A deep rumble hummed within his chest.

"You've got to– fuck!" Something between sharp pain and white-hot pleasure ran up my spine when he bottomed out.

He encircled my waist with one strong arm. "That's exactly what we are doing." He shifted his hips and thrust so hard the sound of his flesh smacking against mine echoed down the hallway. "That is what I am going to do to you all night."

I hadn't considered that Corban had been preparing me the last few days. That all of the games had led up to this moment. I had known he was powerful, frighteningly so, but as he started fucking me, I realized how much he had been holding back before. The way he had fucked my mouth was gentle compared to this.

When he *fucked* me, it was the single most soul-sucking glorious thing I'd ever experienced.

He was merciless as he slammed into me over, and over, and over. My eyes rolled so far back into my head I thought I'd never see straight again. There was something primal about being fucked on the hardwood floor, about being practically flat on my stomach, my arms pinned, completely at his mercy. I realized that it was not the house that made the women of Glamis Manor mad, but Corban. Corban and his demented need to possess.

Why did no one tell you going insane felt so fucking good?

He shifted back on his knees. "By the gods," he hissed. Corban rolled his hips forward, his palm coming down on my ass with a loud smack. "You are so warm." He ran the flat of his palm over my reddened skin, his eyes glazing over as he squeezed it roughly.

Sharp talons raked down my back to my hip. I'd had plenty of sex, but there was *nothing* like this. Torn between the pain of his claws and the pleasure of the cold length of him splitting me in two, it was a wonder I didn't die on the spot.

Lust's thick haze shrouded me, enveloping me in a heated embrace as a fresh wave of sweat broke across my skin. "Corban," I begged.

His eyes snapped to mine in the mirror as he increased his pace. A crooked smile flashed across his face. "You are so fucking perfect." He slammed his hips down fast and hard. Once. Twice. Three times, before he crashed over the top of me again and pressed me harder into the floor, lunging forward to lick the sweat off my shoulder.

Corban dug his claws into my hip as he held me to the ground. I didn't know what was more fucked up: that he had me completely at his mercy, or that every twisted part of me wanted it. When I said I liked it rough, I had only ever dreamed of being dominated this way.

My nails scraped across the ground as I tried to free my arms, to find purchase and bear more of his weight. As he pulled back, I thrust my hips up, slapping my ass into a wall of solid muscle. I didn't want him separated from me for even a second. Corban grunted as he slammed forward again.

"I am never going to stop fucking you," he breathed into my ear.

"Please don't," I panted back.

My nails dug into the rug as my pleasure crested. He must have sensed it because he shifted, angling his hips so the head of his cock hit me just right, and then I was coming. I let out mangled cry as I squeezed around him.

"Fuck, yes," he groaned. "Give it to me."

I fell forward once more, my eyes fluttering open as he started to fuck me harder. When had I closed them? Fuck, I wouldn't be able to walk straight after this. The pain and bliss lived inside one another. This is what Heaven had to feel like.

I needed to see the ripple of his muscles when he moved. I needed to see how powerful he looked fucking me. Heavy-lidded I looked into the mirror.

An unbridled scream of terror erupted from the pit of my chest.

Corban clamped a hand over my mouth. "Close your eyes. You weren't supposed to see that."

In the reflection was a woman splayed out on the ground, her tan skin flushed and her long brown hair wet with sweat. Above her, steadily thrusting between her legs, was a grey-skinned monster with large black horns curling from the top of his head. At his back fanned enormous membraned wings that tensed every time he sheathed himself inside her. The monster pressed his face to the side of the woman's and grinned. The clawed hand over her face tightened.

I blinked under the pressure of his talons. I craned my head back, my eyes cutting to Corban as far as I could in the position he had me pinned.

A sultry groan escaped his lips, tickling the air beside my face. "Fuck you smell so good when you're afraid."

Corban looked like Corban but every thrust he made, so too did the reflection. When he tilted his head back, sliding against that spot I loved for him to touch, so did the monster. And as I shamelessly moaned into his hand as he worked to unspool me, I accepted that the woman in the reflection was me.

The monster was bigger than Corban, his skin taut over even larger muscles than the ones straining beneath his human costume.

When his eyes met mine in the mirror, they were blistering red. His lips parted as his speed increased, flashing long canines with sharp teeth in between. He slid his hand from my mouth to my neck, which he encircled with a fierce grip.

I dug my fingers into the ground to steady myself as his speed increased with every second he held my gaze in the mirror. There wasn't a power in the world that could rip me away from whatever trance he had me under.

My chest was close to bursting, my eyes crying tears of pleasure – or fear, I couldn't tell you, and then–

He abruptly shoved my head to the ground, shattering the image of the beast, and pressed his human face to mine. "You're mine now, aren't you, Sorcha?" He groaned as he gave me a deep hard stroke. "Say it."

Fuck that felt good. So fucking good. Too fucking good! I was coming again and fuck it was glorious.

I tried to look back at the mirror but his grip was ironclad. I could only meet his eyes from the corner of mine.

"Say it," he hissed.

"Yes," I breathed. "Yours," I ground out between my teeth as he pounded into me. He was riding me from one orgasm to the next.

Even as I felt myself slipping into the haze of pleasure I reached forward with my free hand. I didn't look away from him as I stretched toward the mirror I knew was directly in front of me.

"I'm yours," I said, my eyes fluttering as he shifted his hips up and hit a spot that had me screaming my pleasure.

Frigid air bit at my fingertips. I curved my nails downwards, something icy-cold giving way instead of hard wood.

I couldn't hold it together any longer and screwed my eyes shut as I rode out the tail end of my orgasm, and felt as Corban started to come inside of me. His sharp teeth clamped over the back of my shoulder as he exploded.

We were a shaking sweaty mess by the time he pulled out of me. His heavy cock slapped the inside of my thigh as wetness spilled between us. The amount of cum leaking out of me should have been physically impossible.

I craned my head up to the mirror. That was no monster running their hands over my breasts. It was not their lips and teeth grazing my shoulder. It was all Corban as he touched me purposefully, possessively. But when I looked down to the hand that I had reached forward with, it was blue with cold, and the last of the snowflakes were melting off my fingertips.

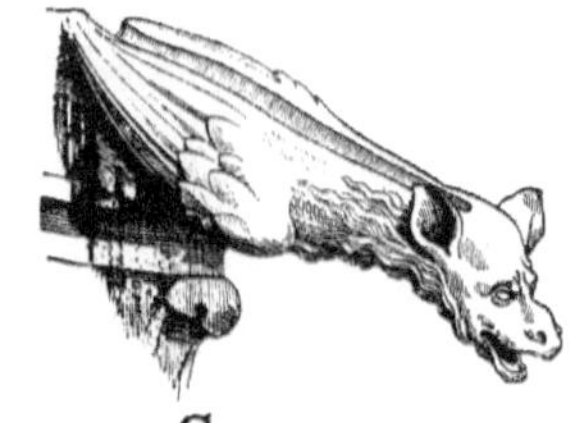

SORCHA

I didn't feel like myself. Would I disappear into the shadows as Corban had done the night before? Like an apparition I followed him into the bedroom, where he climbed into my bed like he owned it. I supposed he did.

"Corban." I couldn't raise my voice louder than a whisper. I knew what I had seen in the mirror was real.

"Hmm?" He pulled me into bed and against his chest. He stroked the swell of my breasts, cupping and squeezing them. It was a welcome break after the intense fucking he had just given me. He'd made a promise to fuck me all night and somehow, I believed Corban was a man – *creature?* – of his word. When it came to sex, at least.

"What are you?"

His finger circled the bud of my nipple. "Sorcha," he growled a warning.

"I saw you." And it fucking terrified me.

"What did you see?" The pluck of his fingers became crueler.

A monster. I couldn't say the word out loud. "You had horns and wings," I answered quietly.

"The mirrors here play tricks," he said.

"It was you."

Corban slid over the top of me, his arms coming down as a cage on either side of my face. "Do I look like a monster?"

Corban was the epitome of dangerous beauty. His body carved like fine marble. His skin was smooth, softer than the stone he claimed to be, and pristine, completely free of marks or blemishes. The panes of his face as sharp as a blade, save for the sumptuous curve of his full mouth. A mouth that housed a forked *fucking* tongue. A tongue I knew was all his and not some creepy body modification.

He was cold until I warmed him.

But did that make him a monster?

"It's ok." I licked my lips. His eyes flicked down to the movement. "It's ok if it was you." I know what I saw. It didn't matter what family I came from; I wasn't mad. The words leaving my mouth didn't make much sense, but I could see with perfect clarity how Rosaline had been so transfixed by him.

I rubbed my fingers together and though the chill was gone, I knew that what I had felt then was real as well. Cold snow blanketed the place beyond the mirror.

Corban's eyes narrowed as he brushed a thumb over my lips. "And if it was? If you knew all this time a monster had been fucking you, then what?"

My heart slammed against the underside of my ribs. The corner of Corban's mouth twitched. "Would you let the monster fuck you again?" He pushed his thumb between my lips.

I sucked on it obediently. I couldn't tell if this was another one of his games or not. Maybe the mirrors had something to do with the final level.

He watched my mouth, moving his thumb in and out as I continued to suck. "Not that your consent matters much now. You already gave yourself to me." He shoved his thumb forward, gripping my chin hard. At the same time, his cock stiffened between my thighs.

I swirled my tongue around his thumb, trying to force it out of my mouth so I could speak. He didn't give me a sliver of opportunity to do any such thing. Not when he angled his hips and pressed his cock back at my entrance.

"Will you let a monster fuck you?" He slid inside of me.

I bit down on the invasive appendage. Corban hissed and removed it only to replace his thumb with his first two fingers. "Keep sucking," he commanded.

He thrusted slowly, his fingers and cock working simultaneously against me. There was none of the brutal claiming he had subjected me to earlier, but there was still power in his touch that gave him total control over me.

The air around his head warped and slowly, like a veil being lifted, dark horns appeared on the top of his head. They were long, larger at the base and tapered to a fine point at the end.

Instinctively I jerked against him but there was nowhere for me to go. I could practically see my wide-eyed reflection in his glittering eyes.

"I didn't tell you to stop," he growled and shoved his fingers farther into my mouth. I coughed and started sucking them again.

Red seeped into his green irises and my heartbeat increased, earning me a wicked grin. "You divine little creature," he purred. The glow of his eyes flickered as he looked back and forth between mine, trying to read me. "You are terrified and yet still, so willing." He rolled his hips for emphasis and I clamped my lips tight to fight off a moan.

He pulled his fingers free. "What do you have to say now?"

I looked at his red eyes and then to the horns spiraling from his dark locks. I reached up at the same time he curled an arm around my waist. He lifted me and shifted back so that I was sitting on his lap. He pulled my hips back and forth, eyes never leaving my face as I touched his horns.

They were as cool as the rest of him, hard and ridged. I trailed them to the base to find they did attach to his skull, then all the way to their tips, which were viciously sharp.

If he was a demon and in the process of dragging me to Hell then I might as well ride down on my own terms. I gripped the curve of each horn, watching his face for any sign that I shouldn't. Corban's lust filled gaze deepened, the red glow invading his eyes becoming molten lava.

I tightened my grip and started to move my hips faster than the steady pulse he had been working into me. Corban's narrow pupils expanded and his grip loosened on my hips as I took control.

I rocked on him, forcing the head of his dick to hit that special spot inside of me. "Does this answer your question?" I breathed. I slammed my hips down and pulled against his horns, forcing a strained grunt from his lips.

His full lips parted, the tip of his fangs making them pucker.

I didn't get to ride him for long before he forced me on my back and captured my mouth in a punishing kiss, ramming his cock hard and fast inside of me.

There was a loud bang and the sound of splintering wood as I wrapped my legs around his waist. I ripped my mouth free of his in shock as the bed lurched on a precarious angle, one of its posts giving way. Corban didn't seem to notice and instead buried his face into my neck, his sharp teeth puncturing my skin as he slid into me again, and again.

Even through the fog of the bite's lust I could tell that it was darker than it had been a few moments ago. It took only a few seconds for my eyes to adjust to realize why.

Giant wings arched over the top of us. Dark, membraned wings that were now hooked into the headboard. An anchor to assist him in fucking me.

There was a demon fucking me. I couldn't hide my fear, the way my body tensed as I saw him like this, but neither could I stop the orgasm that he ripped out of me when he reached between us and pressed his thumb into my clit while his cock drove into me, ever deeper.

"You're perfect," he said. "You're so fucking perfect. I'm going to keep you forever."

My back arched, my eyes nearly rolling to the back of my head as he whispered sweet and filthy things in my ear. I dug my nails into his skin, trying desperately to find purchase on his sweat-slicked back.

"You," I moaned. Corban was horrifyingly perfect. So beautifully terrifying that he left me awestruck. I gripped the hair at the base of his neck, pulling back gently so I could see his face. Carved to perfection. Lethal and commanding.

The orgasm hit me hard, ripping my voice away and I cried out soundlessly.

Corban shifted backward, pulling me into his lap again. His great wings wrapped around us as he stood. I let out a shaking breath as he leaned me back into the cradle of his wings, grabbed hold of my hips, and pushed and pulled me along the length of his cock. He was merciless.

The smooth leather of his wings stroked my body like silk while he pounded into me. This was too much. There were too many sensations that boiled my blood and the way he was looking at me was– Ah!

Corban cocked his head down and to the side as his hips snapped against me. "You are exquisite when you come apart. Just like that, little dove."

I grabbed hold of his forearms, lifting my legs over his shoulders, pressing my upper back hard against his wings and fuck– my eyes really did roll to the back of my head then. The spot the head of his cock stroked was so gloriously delicious I could not hold on to a single rational thought. There was only him. There was only *feeling*. Winding, needy feeling that I chased and chased, angling my hips a little more until the pleasure was blinding.

"Just like that," he purred. Corban's wings tightened around me, hauling me up so I was snug against him. Not a breath of space existed between us.

I stopped caring to count how many times he made me orgasm. They all started to blend together, one after another. Corban fucked me for hours, well into the night, well beyond the threshold of pain and pleasure, and yet I clung to him as if it would kill me to stop. He might have said he didn't plan to kill me, but something told me I was well on my way.

As the dawn sky bled pink around the edges of the heavy curtains, we finally, mercifully, fell down to sleep.

As I slipped into the waiting darkness I knew I was done for. Corban was a monster, a terrifying creature of nightmare, and yet I was undeniably, completely, in his thrall.

Chapter 21

CORBAN

Something about being curled around Sorcha appeased the sickness inside of me, the song in my blood that longed to return to Under. To the winged beasts of the sky and scaled serpents writhing below. To the sounds of endless war and sweeping views of extravagantly built castles. I missed my kingdom. I missed magik, *real* magik. Not the puddle I was left with to dip my fingers into.

It boiled my blood knowing that Phelim had likely dethroned our father and taken the crown for himself. The crown that rightfully belonged to me. If it were true, I'd rip his head from his neck the moment I saw him.

Not much longer now.

It had been decades, centuries, now, since I had been trapped in this absolute hell of a place, surrounded by desperate women and their boring, pretentious husbands. Years bound to the most godsforsaken hovel. Its lack of grandeur only made my need for vengeance burn hotter.

I shut my eyes, mind conjuring the image of the middle-aged man that had stepped into the glowing orange ring like it was yesterday. That snake, with his cursed bargain. Humans aren't usually particularly clever with their deals, but this one had been. "Look into the mirror and speak your greatest desire, to have it granted," he had said.

I had been naive then. I'd thought I was invincible to human treachery, that I was owed everything.

"I wish to be desired above all things."

And that is exactly what he had given me, that nameless man. I never even felt it when the spell struck. One moment I was speaking the words into the gilded mirror, and the next I was encased in stone, frozen in the back of his wagon amongst other stone-carved creatures, helpless in my rage as he carted us from town to town. One by one he sold us off, promising we would protect the homes and churches of those who bought us. Even in slavery gargoyles were loyal to a fault, and so they remained at their posts with their mouths gaping in silent screams. I possessed no such honorable streak. That man had fucked with the wrong monster, and so I would curse every soul that came into contact with me until the day that I broke free.

The salesman had laughed as he'd raised me to my post above the door of the manor that was to become my home. His arms straining at the ropes.

"Desired above all things, old chap? Let's see how you go turning desire into devotion when you're made of stone."

He'd gone on and on, relishing in the trick he'd pulled. My freedom, apparently, would only be gained if another soul willingly traded places with me. If they gave up their body, heart, and soul so that I could regain mine.

I liked to think the stranger could feel my rage when he turned me over to the young couple of Glamis. To sweet unsuspecting Rosaline.

As I watched the sun sink that first night from my perch above the verandah, I felt the stone melt away as life returned to my body. I was chained still by old magik, but free to move and stretch and eat under darkness. I was starved enough that I nearly killed Rosaline on our first night. But I'd had a long while to think of how I would escape my prison, so I stilled my fangs and claws and spoke with her instead. She would be the first of many failures, until–

Sorcha stirred beside me, drawing me away from the nightmare I was forced to relive every time the sun rose.

She stretched, sliding her hand over my bare waist. Her body stiffened and before she could move I had her pinned beneath me.

"Good morning," I purred against her neck. The bruising of my bites that lined it did wonders for her complexion. They were like a choker of violets, blooming in pretty shades of purple and blue.

She looked up at me with wide eyes. "You're here." It wasn't quite a question.

I kissed her. "Thanks to you."

"How?" She kissed me back, hesitantly at first and then more forcefully. I liked that she couldn't help herself. Even while her brain struggled to process what it meant that I had her pinned down in daylight, she gave in to me, flicking her tongue out to meet mine.

Her taste was still sweet beneath the staleness of her breath. She had so many smells and flavors that stirred my hunger.

"You make me whole." Gods, it sounded even more droll when I said it out loud.

She slapped my chest but there was no force in it. "You're so full of it." Her breath was short, laced with amusement and driven by the building lust I could smell between her thighs as I ran my hand up her side.

I didn't know what real love was. I knew that I was infatuated with Sorcha. It felt as if she were made for me. That could very well be the spell at work, as it unraveled itself from me and wound around her. I'd made it this far with only a couple of others in the past, but something felt different with Sorcha. This time, the spell was loosening its hold on me – leaving me free to roam in sunlight and soon, back to Under – but it also seemed to be chaining me tighter to my prey. And I was loving it.

"What if it's true?" I held her green-eyed gaze. Those beautiful eyes that so reminded me of the soft moss that lined my castle walls. Her long lashes fluttered as she fought for an answer.

She opened her perfect mouth to respond, and then her eyes went wide as her gaze shifted past me. I rolled my shoulder back, splaying one of my wings across us as I stretched.

I had considered that my human costume might be more appealing to Sorcha when she awoke, but I'd wanted to know if she'd been honest when she'd fucked me like this the evening before. Whether she could face what I really was, in the cold light of day.

Whatever Sorcha was thinking she hid it well. She took her time in surveying me. The slight tremor in her fingers sharpened my teeth as she reached out tentatively to my wing.

I let out an involuntary sigh when her warm fingers brushed the thin membrane. "Sorry," I murmured when she flinched. I tipped my head back, my eyes half lidded as she touched me again. "I have not been touched in this form in a long while and your heat is a comfort."

That must have emboldened her because she splayed the entirety of her small hand against the leathery surface. Slowly she explored the rest of my wing. She sat up to get a better look at the talon that curved over the top.

"I didn't know anything like you could exist," she said softly.

I chuckled. "That is something I love about you."

She looked up at me, her round cheeks tinged a pretty pink. "What's that?"

"That you take control of your fear. Oh no, it's quite alright. You should be afraid of me. But I absolutely adore seeing you struggle with it – as it goes to war with the desire and curiosity you have for me." I stroked her cheek, which turned a shade darker. "I have waited a long time to find someone like you."

"What about me is different from the others?"

I blinked slowly, savoring her delectable features. The perfect arch of her brows, the soft thrum of her heartbeat. How her lips had a permanent pout to them but puckered whenever she was thinking hard about something. The way her body curved and met my hand with plush softness. "Everything," I said, and meant it.

She hadn't run like the others when they'd finally seen what I really was. *Desired above all things,* I thought bitterly. Desire only got you so far with women who lacked... vision. Looking at Sorcha in the morning light, its honeyed glow leaving feathered shadows on her cheek, I realized I couldn't leave her here. I'd be a fool to leave something so precious behind.

I'd had every intention of switching places with her, of making her the new haunt of Glamis Manor. But as she continued to explore my body and I relished the memory of the way she had grabbed hold of my horns while she fucked me, I knew that I could not abandon her entirely. There had to be some way to gain my freedom and keep her as well.

No one had ever admired me the way she did. Not even a creature of my own realm, when one had been bold enough to touch me, had done so with the hunger and wonder that spooled from her fingertips. While

I relished her fear of me, I thirsted more for the way she battled with it, that she sought to be its master.

"What are you?" she blurted. Heat spread across her cheeks again, like blood dripping into clear water. "Please don't keep me guessing."

I ran my fingers through her long hair. I loved the dark contrast of it against my grey skin. I reveled in darkness. How convenient that all the best parts of her were made of it.

"Are you a demon?" she whispered.

I chuckled. The red stain on her face deepened. Color looked just as beautiful on her as the shadows. "Close," I whispered back, teasing her. I suppose it didn't matter if she knew the truth now. I shifted to the side, lounging my weight on one arm so I could trail down her body with my free hand. "I'm a grotesque."

Her brows furrowed as her heart fluttered quickly. The familiar delectable scent of her fear spiked. "What's a grotesque?" she asked.

"We are similar to gargoyles but our appetites tend to be much more…. Sinful." I traced a claw around her wide areolas, one and then the other. I was keenly aware of how perfectly she fit against me, how warm and soft she was beneath my hardened body. "We hunger for flesh while the gargoyles are meant to protect it. We desire the taste of you to satisfy our stomachs and cocks."

All of that beautiful color leeched from her skin. "You eat people?" she squeaked.

"Oh don't worry, Sorcha. The only feast I'll partake of you is that delicious cunt between your legs." I tweaked one of her hardened nipples. Fresh sweat burst across her skin, glistening like morning dew. She was an absolute treasure.

Her back arched. "Are there more of you?"

"Plenty." Gods I could watch her squirm for hours and not grow bored. I was going to give her body the chance to rest after how long we had fucked last night, but the way she *writhed* beneath me tempted me to do otherwise.

"Are you...from here?" One of her hands slinked its way across my chest.

My head tipped back as I savored the way her fingers trembled. Now was as good of a time as any to tell her about my world. It might make it easier for me to bring her over that final threshold. If she was prepared, she would be less likely to be rejected by the gateway. Hopefully.

I'd hate to have it deny her the way it had Rosaline. When it became apparent Under would not accept her, she had snapped. The gate remained sealed no matter how hard she raged her fists against it. As if the mirror would break through sheer will alone. If she'd only known how many times I had done the same.

I'd had no use for her after that. I'd needed to get rid of her so someone new could take her place and I'd have the opportunity to try again.

Sweet, foolish Rosaline. She hadn't listened. She had given me almost everything, but some corner of her heart still loved her husband. Of course, I couldn't let her lack of faith in the *angel* go unpunished.

At the barest hint of my suggestion, she'd killed him. Poor thing hadn't understood what she was doing until she'd slipped the noose around her own neck afterwards.

As much as I had fumed, I was glad it hadn't been Rosaline that saved me. I wouldn't have Sorcha. Sorcha, with her glorious perfume of fear and desire. Of possibility and opportunity.

"No," I said carefully, looking down at her. "Are you familiar with fae?"

She sat up abruptly, her eyes wide with– not fear. *Oh, silly Sorcha.* A shudder of laughter ran through me as a broad smile touched her lips. It took everything in me not to grab her face and kiss her thoroughly.

"Like High Lords and faeries?"

I shook my head slowly as anticipation wrapped around my heart. Curious Sorcha still had a lot to learn. "Don't believe everything you read in books, my dear." How sweet that the gods had finally shown me favor.

"Oh." Her face dropped slightly, then lit up again. "So you're fae? I've never heard of a grotesque. Are gargoyles fae too?"

As question after question tumbled out of her pretty lips, I couldn't help falling more in love with her. That's what this was, wasn't it? This glorious feeling of being wanted, of having someone adore and fawn over you with such rapture they would overlook the monster and its sins. Her innocence, bubbling up and obscuring the darkness I knew lurked beneath, was going to be her end. I *was* her end. Her inquisitive eyes darted back and forth between mine.

"There are many creatures like and unlike me in the Realm of Underland," I said. "A place few mortals have the privilege of ever laying eyes on."

She slapped a hand over her mouth. "This is going to sound ridiculous, but I've always had a thing for fae. I read about them in books, fantasy books, but those are fiction of course. I didn't think fae were real. And well, they don't mention anything like you. Actually, no they got the wings right." Her eyes darted down to my hips, to what lay hidden beneath the sheets. Did she darken yet another shade? "Yeah, they definitely got the wings right."

"What about my wings?" I flexed them, lifting them high so that they shadowed her.

"Well, um." Her tongue darted between her lips. "They say the bigger the wingspan the bigger, the...." She cleared her throat. She was bright red now, her skin flaming with embarrassment.

"Tell me," I pressed. *Keep squirming for me.*

Her eyes flicked down again. "Corban," she hissed.

I traced my claw over the curve of her stomach to the hair-dusted mound at her center. "Don't get shy on me now. Say it. The bigger the wingspan the bigger the, what, Sorcha?" I forced my hand between her thighs. I slid my middle finger down her slit. Gods she was wet.

"Dick," she choked out.

I threw my head back and laughed. "Well *that,* you can believe." Slowly I eased my finger inside of her and tipped my head down. "Do I surpass your books' expectations? Is my dick big enough for you?"

She grabbed hold of my wrist when I stroked the ridge of her cunt slowly, gently. Her other hand wound its way around my neck as I nudged her to her side so that I could slide in behind her. My hard cock pressed against the swell of her ass.

"Yes," she breathed.

My control was paper-thin as I continued to play with her wetness. I pressed my nose against her hair, breathing her in. "How does it feel knowing this it what you do to me?"

Her breath hitched; her body tightening. "Corban," she hissed. "Please."

I pulled my hand away, smoothing it over her hip as I kissed her shoulder. "Don't worry," I crooned. "I'm not going to fuck you right now. You need to hydrate, and eat." I gave her hip a squeeze. "That way you'll have plenty of energy to play tonight."

What sounded like a groan of complaint came from her throat. "You're going to be the death of me."

I flashed my fangs.

She kept her body pressed to mine as she craned her head back. "If you're not going to torture me, then what do you plan on doing?"

"What do you mean?"

"Well, now that you're free to be in the light," she started tentatively, "is there something you'd like to do?"

I stared at her. Such a simple question and yet I don't think she understood the weight of it. The last time I had been asked what I wanted, I'd been fooled. But I knew there was no trickery in her inquiry. There was nothing but open curiosity and the desire to please. Sorcha wanted to please me.

I leaned forward and kissed her, stroking the edge of her jaw as I did so.

"I want to see what you do during the day when I cannot see you. How do you spend your time beneath my roof?"

Her brows furrowed. "That's it? That's really boring. I mean... I just..."

"Just what?"

"I read. I cook too, but there isn't anything I do around the house that will entertain you."

I sat up, pulling her with me. "Everything you do demands my attention, Sorcha. Allow me to savor you in the sunlight."

I relished the precious minutes we spent lying tangled in the sheets, one creature of many limbs, before I rose, dragging Sorcha into the shower. The water carved pathways across her body, crisscrossing in rivulets that I followed with my tongue. Soft sighs fled her lips as I kneaded her skin with soap and ran my claws across her scalp and through her hair. The simple act of washing together gave me a sense of intimate pleasure not even sex could provide.

As she stepped out into the morning light to dry off, a ray of light cut across her shoulder, obscuring a bite mark I had left there, and I stared. Her soft skin was luminescent, her eyes flashing like cut gems.

I tipped her chin up as I leaned down to kiss her.

Sweet, sweet Sorcha would be coming home with me.

Chapter 22

SORCHA

The sound the page made as I turned it seemed obscenely loud in the comfortable silence of the library. I peeked up at Corban over the top of my book. He looked so out of place against the burnished leather chair. His grey skin had a smooth polish to it beneath his fitted t-shirt and slacks. The black chain he wore around his neck, which I'd only just noticed – had he glamoured it on recently? – glistened the same way his horns did, as if they had both been dipped in oil. He'd glamoured his wings away but he was still much too large for the space he occupied. The library was one of the larger rooms in the manor, but with him inside it felt cramped.

His attention remained downcast, lost in the five books he had been sifting through for the last hour, but I could tell his focus had never left me. Whenever I wasn't looking at him, I'd catch his gaze on me from the corner of my eye. Drinking me in like I'd quench his thirst.

He'd been so gentle this morning that I'd wondered whether the spell had something to do with his cold and ruthless demeanor. If binding him to the house had somehow made him cruel and aggressive. Wishful thinking, considering he'd already told me his kind ate people. As those jade eyes lifted to me, I had the good sense to be scared shitless again. The way he ogled me made me wonder if he was weighing the benefits of eating me, versus not.

It gave the phrase *if he wanted to he would* a whole new meaning.

It was strange seeing him in the daylight. In a way it made him seem less real, like the kind of monster he clearly was should only be able to exist in the deepest hours of the night, or lurking in the shadows. But here he sat, in broad daylight. Reading.

"What is running around in that little head of yours?" he crooned.

I shut my book. Corban leaned forward, setting his own book atop the stack, and rested his elbows over the top of his thighs. The movement was so sudden, so calculated it almost made me flinch.

"You've been trapped here for decades. You've finally told me the incredible thing that you are and all you want to do is watch me... read?" I waved my book at him.

Corban frowned, his brows pinching to the point they touched.

"Don't you want to.... Leave? Go out somewhere? See anything other than these walls?"

He blinked slowly, his frown deepening. Sitting back, he stretched his long arms over the chair. "Leave." The way he said it was like he was testing the weight of the word on his tongue. "Leave," he said again.

"Yeah like... I don't know, we could go for a drive into town. See the water. Why spend another second here if you don't have to?"

His fingers drummed over the top of the armrest. In a single smooth movement he rose to his feet and strode out of the room.

"Corban?"

I hurried after him. Shadows flared down the stairs, whipping my hair around my face. By the time I got to the bottom he was gone. It had taken me only seconds and yet there was no sign of him. I padded through the living room, into the kitchen, and back again. All the doors and windows were shut tight. And all of the rooms were empty.

I felt torn. Something like relief had flooded my system as soon as I'd felt his presence fade away, some kind of relaxation of my fight or flight reflex I guessed. But in the same breath, I was desperate for him to return. Certainly he wouldn't leave me, after finally revealing what he was. Letting me see him in all his glory.

I don't know how I was supposed to go on with my life after experiencing him. He'd ruined all other men for me.

I scoffed. He wasn't even a *man*.

Daylight was fading again by the time he finally returned. I was pacing the front porch, my nails red raw from how much I'd bitten them down. When I turned on my heel for the thousandth time he was striding up the driveway, his long legs eating up the distance between us. My heart lurched.

Fuck. He looked absolutely lethal – and the way he was looking at me! Now *this* was relief. Relief that he had come back. Relief that he looked at me like I meant something. A cruel wicked smile tugged the corner of his mouth, revealing his fangs.

"Miss me?" he purred.

"I thought I finally had the place all to myself." I tried to will confidence into my voice. I hoped he thought my tone was teasing instead of desperate.

"And leave you in peace?" Corban stood in front of me, his face tipped down so the fringe above his brows cast shadows across his reflective eyes. "I had to get something." At the snap of his wrist, a silver chain fell out of his palm. I recognized the locket from the first night we met.

"You tried to give it to me before. What is it?"

Corban twirled his finger, motioning for me to move. I did, lifting my hair off my neck.

"A good luck charm." He looped his arms around me and grazed his cool fingers against my collarbone as he fastened the clasp.

"For what? It certainly hasn't warded you away. Ah!" I jerked away from him as a sharp stinging pain slid up the back of my neck. I whirled, one hand holding the locket in place against my chest and the other diving for my neck.

Corban turned out his palms. At the end of one of his long claws was a smear of blood. "Oops," he said and stuck his finger into his mouth.

"What the fuck." I rubbed my smarting skin. "Be careful with those things." I thumbed the door of the locket.

"The locket holds a piece of the manor, one of the mirrors, if you recall. With you at my side and the charm in your possession, I think Glamis will let me go."

I frowned, turning the locket over. "Have you tried this before?" Is that why he tried giving it to me the first night?

"No, but it is a theory I would like to test now. You've anchored me into the light. Now I need you to anchor me to the manor. I've never gotten this far with anyone before."

His voice wavered ever so slightly. It sounded ominous, like what we were about to do was forbidden.

"Besides," he ran a thumb over the hollow of my throat, catching the chain on the end of his nail, "I like how pretty my token looks around your neck." He slid two of his fingers over my shoulder and took a step back. Raising his hand, he twisted his wrist and made a graceful downward motion. A warm tingling sensation started at the top of my head. It trickled down my shoulders, arms, and the rest of my body. Down, down, down. "It will take the place of my other marks on you for tonight," he said with a smirk.

I looked down at my legs. The bruising, bites– they were all gone, save for the "C" carved above my knee. I touched my throat tentatively. Smooth skin replaced the bite marks that had graced it moments before.

It was then I realized he had changed my clothes as well. Gone were the shorts and horror film t-shirt I had been wearing. In its stead was a little black dress that hugged my chest and cut off at the middle of my thighs. The entire thing was somehow sophisticated, yet sexy at the same time. It accentuated my curves perfectly. Especially the neckline, which highlighted my full chest and the locket that rested above my breasts.

Something about this felt incredibly wrong. I couldn't put a finger on it, other than that Corban seemed too eager. But the feeling ebbed when I looked up into his wicked green eyes. Whatever spell he had cast over me, I would happily be a slave to it.

Did I have the power to break his curse? This felt like a real-life fantasy. Dark, like one of Grimm's fairy tales, but magical all the same.

He wrapped an arm around my waist, pulling me against his muscular chest.

"How generous," I breathed. I gripped the front of his shirt to steady my shaking hands.

He hunched down and brushed his nose against mine. "This is just the beginning, Sorcha. Now, let us see if this works and get me the fuck out of here."

Corban was stiff as a board as we made our way down the driveway. He'd hesitated before getting into the car and I'd wondered if he'd been worried whether he could really leave or not. But as Glamis disappeared in the rearview mirror, I wondered if he wasn't having second thoughts about me instead.

"Everything ok?"

He turned his head. That was another thing he either couldn't or refused to change, the gleam in his large ever-changing eyes. Every time light from a passing car or streetlight hit them, they lit up like reflective mirrors. "Everything is fine," he said silkily. He looked back out to the road. I could feel the tension leave his body as he settled back into his seat. "Everything is just fine."

We went into the first nice place we stumbled across.

I just couldn't wrap my mind around the fact that I was sitting across from him, at a place called White Porch, and that he looked completely human. This was the first time I had seen him without any trace of the monster lurking beneath his skin.

In fact, there was *color* to his skin. Gone was the ashen grey. Blood heated the top of his sharp cheekbones; it warmed his full lips. Even his eyes, as they swung to me, were not as hungry as they had been earlier that day.

Despite his 'human' costume, his very inhuman presence radiated lethal power that commanded the room. From the second we had walked in people couldn't stop staring. Corban's chin remained lifted as if he were preening from all the attention he was getting. If only they knew what kind of creature he really was.

I leaned forward. "What are you doing?"

"What am I doing?" he asked, his voice dropping as low as mine.

I motioned to him with my glass of wine. "You look different, and I don't just mean the lack of wings and horns."

A slow smile spread across his face. "You brought me back to life, Sorcha. I merely want to thank you for doing so."

Pressure expanded beneath my ribs. It was twisted, wasn't it? That those silly little words were enough to make me feel special? As much as I tried to fight it, I couldn't suppress a smile of my own.

He took my hand and pressed it against his lips.

We ordered nearly everything on the menu. I hadn't questioned how we were going to pay for it all – I certainly didn't have room in my budget, but Corban seemed unfazed. I went to the bathroom and by the time I returned he was shutting the black leather booklet that held our check.

I sipped my wine, fighting the urge to open it up to see if he had actually left any money. Did fae have credit cards?

Corban leaned back in his seat, his eyes on my mouth as I took a drink. When I swallowed his gaze trailed down, following the liquid in the movement of my throat, and gradually halted at my chest over the locket.

"People are staring," I hissed.

Corban cocked his head. "As if they haven't been the entire time we've been here."

"I think they were curious about you before, but now it looks like you want to fuck me on this table, and people are taking notice. Cut it out."

A flash of red entered Corban's eyes. "But I do want to fuck you on this table." He leaned forward. "What do you say we give them a show?"

I choked on my wine. Sputtering turned to coughing and our server who had been reaching to collect the check placed his hand on my shoulder instead. "Are you alright?" he asked.

A bolt of nauseating energy zinged across the table. Corban looked absolutely murderous as he stretched his arm toward me, blatantly flashing his claws.

Fuck's sake, he's going to rip the guy's arm off.

I waved him off. "I'm fine." I pointed to my throat. "I just swallowed the wrong way."

Our server jerked his hand away and stared dumbly at Corban. His eyes went wide at the sight of his taloned hand.

"You had no trouble swallowing me," Corban said playfully, a stark contrast to the venom of his gaze.

I lurched up from the table when the red glow pooled in Corban's eyes again. "We were just leaving." I risked a glance at the bewildered server. "Thank you." I shot Corban a warning glare, but he wasn't looking at me.

He rose smoothly, towering over the young man, who took a couple of steps back instinctively. The tension was so thick I swear I could hear it crackle through the air. He leaned forward, pressing his lips close to the poor guy's ear. I couldn't hear what he was saying, but by the color draining from the waiter's face, I could guess.

The server nodded, his eyes blinking rapidly.

Corban eased back and gave him a playful slap on the shoulder. "Have a good evening," he said coolly. He turned to me, slid his arm through mine, and led us quietly out of the restaurant, completely unperturbed that the entire place had gone silent, and that every eye remained on us as we made our departure.

"You're a menace," I said the moment we were outside. "What did you say to that poor kid?"

Corban's possessive hold slid around my waist. "I told him he was lucky I didn't cut off his hand to enjoy for a midnight snack. That he was fortunate I'd already eaten."

I came to an abrupt halt. "You did not."

"I did," he said matter-of-factly. "I also told him that if I caught him so much as looking at you again, I would take his eyes."

"You can't just threaten people like that. They'll think you're serious."

He stepped in front of me, his touch moving like oil over the fabric of my dress. The chill of his skin cut right through the barrier and made me flinch. "But I am serious. You belong to me. Just as I," he hesitated, only a moment but still he hesitated, "belong to you." His thumb stroked my collarbone, soothing the tension that had wound its way through my body. "That's what we are to one another now."

Corban let his eyes roam over my body. I don't think I would ever get over the appreciation I saw there. He was undeniable. I slid my hand over his, twisting it until our fingers were intertwined. Despite the cold of his skin, warm tingles raced up my arm and slowly, so very slowly, like the gradual spread of a drug through my veins, seeped everywhere else.

The sun was making its final show of the day, casting splashes of gold and pastel orange across the waterfront. The colors painted Corban in dreamy warmth.

"Who said I belong to you?" I said, as I fought for some semblance of control.

A feral glaze swept over his eyes, the grip on my hand took charge. "Why don't I just remind you?" Corban swooped in and pressed his mouth to mine.

His taste was an elixir I would willingly drown in. I didn't recoil when his forked tongue brushed against mine. I welcomed it, sucking him deeper into my mouth.

The trickling sound of laughter broke the spell between us. Corban drew back, his pupils completely blown out, eyes now devoid of all color. His cool breath pulled my gaze down to his parted lips. His fangs had lengthened. The predatory essence had returned to his being. Gone was the gentleman he had been playing the part of earlier.

He looked like he was fighting to say something. He opened his mouth once, twice, but nothing could have prepared me for the words that fell from his lips.

"Sweet Sorcha, will you come with me to Underland?"

Chapter 23

SORCHA

I ran my fingers over the still throbbing cut on the back of my neck as I watched Corban order us a round of drinks. He had asked me *that* question, and I hadn't been able to give him an answer. Instead, I had dragged him into the closest bar I could find and ordered two shots. Both of which I took for myself.

The idea of Underland – not *Undaland* as Rosaline had thought – of fae, sounded absolutely insane. Not that I knew much about it with how secretive Corban was. But if the realm was anything like him then it had to be incredible. Beautiful. Ethereal. Dripping in magic.

Yet I knew some things were too good to be true. That was the other side of the coin. Beauty was often a disguise to hide the ugliness and evil that lurked beneath. And I knew Corban wasn't good, not even a little bit. I told myself that I'd only warmed to him in the first place because of how *physically* good he made me feel. How worshipped. It wasn't until today that I'd felt the tug of other emotions, when he'd fawned over me. And why wouldn't he fawn? I had given him something no one ever had.

I needed to learn why he had been cursed and the truth of what had happened to Rosaline. To Grandma Macky and everyone in between. I'd be an idiot to trust him blindly after all the games he had forced me into.

A woman's shrill laugh from across the room jarred me from my thoughts. She was standing in front of Corban, nervous energy radiating off her ridiculously quaffed blonde waves as she prattled on about something. Hunger filled Corban's gaze when he tipped his head down toward her, eyes narrowed. My heart lurched, but this wasn't anything to be jealous over. The hunger reflecting in his eyes was pure animal, there was nothing lustful in his gaze. Corban wanted to eat her.

"Sorcha!"

Oh fuck me. I turned just as Corban's head snapped in my direction.

Quint threw out his arms, his navy t-shirt stretching across his chest. "Hey." He grinned. "It's good to see you."

Panic alarms blared inside my head. They were so loud I couldn't hear anything he was saying. This was bad. This was really bad, and about to get a thousand times worse the moment Corban came over.

As if in answer to my rising alarm, a wall of jealous fury slammed into me.

"I see you got my text."

I turned, scanning for the grotesque over my shoulder, but he was gone. The woman he had been speaking to twirled the straw in her drink. She swiped her free hand over a glistening droplet on her cheek, took a deep breath and looked up, blinking quickly like she was fighting back tears.

If Corban was the reason for her tears, she was lucky all he did was hurt her feelings.

"What text?" I licked my lips. Corban should have been impossible to miss. He was taller than everyone else here with a face that could have been slapped on the cover of every romance book ever published.

"I asked if you wanted to meet here tonight. Wait, you didn't get it?"

I tugged my phone from my purse. Six unread messages stared back at me. One was from Quint, another from my friend Lauren back home, and the remainder were from my mother. I hadn't heard my phone go off, hadn't even felt it vibrate.

"I see it now," I said, tucking the device away. "Sorry, it's been a long day." I looked past Quint, half expecting Corban to be looming behind him. Where the fuck did he go? I scratched at the back of my neck as I turned the other way.

"Oh, ok." Quint clapped his hands together softly. "Look, I get you're still probably mad. But since we're both here, will you let me make it up to you? Drinks are on me tonight."

The stale breath he blew across my face is what finally drew my attention back to him. Glassy eyes, flushed cheeks. Quint was drunk or on his way quickly to it.

"I have to go." If I left, then Corban would be forced to follow me. If the locket really was an anchor, he would have no choice but to chase after me. I gave Quint a half-assed smile.

Someone yelled for Quint across the room. His brow furrowed and he waved them off, his attention fixated on me. "Are you really going to be like that?"

"Let it go," I hissed.

Quint ran a hand over his face, a forced smile plastered underneath it as I made to move past him. I made it a single step, one that brought me to his side, when Quint's smile faltered, his eyes darting behind me. His pupils expanded and whatever he was about to say never passed through his parted lips.

A cool possessive touch slid around my waist, fingers digging into my flesh, as Corban pulled me back against his hard chest. "Who's your friend?" He didn't purr so much as he growled.

Quint stumbled back.

I'd known Corban would be angry seeing Quint, but the nausea that kicked me full in the gut was heinous. Vile and deadly. I was too afraid to look at him because by his tone, by his intoxicating power, it was clear he wanted to rip Quint's throat out. No wonder he had let the girl be. Why bother with her when there was better prey to be had?

"Ah, t-this is Quint," I offered. The words were dry in my throat.

What had I done? I'd unleashed a monster into Bristol, and here was Quint practically on a silver platter.

I knew that Corban's threat from the other night – about slitting Quint's throat – was no bluff. If I'd not played his game, he would have killed him. He would do it now if I didn't get us out of here.

"Quint," he said, letting the name drip like acid from his tongue.

Somehow Quint had managed to grow balls of steel. That's the only explanation I could come up with for why he stuck out his hand. "And you are?"

"Corban," the grotesque answered, sliding his palm into Quint's.

"Quint's a friend," I offered. *Idiot, Corban knows exactly who Quint is.* "We were catching up, but I told him we had to get going."

"And how do you know Sorcha?" Quint pressed. "I know just about everyone in Bristol and I've never seen you before." He tried to pull his hand back, but Corban wouldn't let go.

Fuck.

Fuckfuckfuck.

Corban's grip tightened. "Yes, you have."

Quint's brow furrowed. "What?"

"You've seen me before. Don't you remember?" Corban cocked his head to the side so that the dim light of the bar hit his reflective eyes.

I pressed my hand against Corban's where it wrapped around my hip. "We really should get going."

He let Quint's hand go abruptly. Quint jerked it against his chest, flexing his fist as blood rushed back to his fingers.

"What's the rush, love?" Corban drew his finger up my throat and pressed into my throbbing pulse. "Don't you want to finish your drink first?" His eyes flicked down to my hand, where a lavender colored cocktail had appeared. I flinched, both of my hands flying up to my chest. Corban snatched the glass out of the air before it could hit the ground.

"Love? Are you her boyfriend?" Quint had the audacity to sound incredulous despite how pale he still looked in Corban's company.

"No." "Yes." We answered at the same time. I curled my hands around the locket to hide their trembling.

"Quint, can you give us a minute?" I snapped. My nerves were shot and being caught between them, one jealous and one murderous, was making it difficult to think clearly. I didn't give him the opportunity to answer before I spun around, grabbing hold of Corban's shirt and forcing him backward through the crowd.

He turned fluidly so he was now the one to herd me, forcing me back into a low-lit corner beside the bar. He hunched forward, his hand sliding to the wall beside my head. "Careful," he growled.

"I think we should go home," I said.

"Now? When we're having so much fun?" He leaned farther forward and swiped his tongue over my cheek. "I quite like this defiant side of you, but I'll warn you, get in between me and that boy again and you'll not like the way I punish you after."

"Leave Quint out of this. He doesn't mean anything, he is no one–"

Corban sucked the back of his teeth. "If he is no one then you'll not miss him."

"That's not the point. I don't want him to die!"

Corban ran two fingers down my neck, following the line of the chain, past the locket, and pressed them hard where the pulse of my heart was the strongest. "You are mine, Sorcha and there is not anything or anyone that will take you away from me."

Heat pooled in my stomach. It spread downwards, flooding between my thighs with an intensity only he knew how to drive.

"I have waited far too long for this moment. I will not be bound to Glamis a second longer than I must. I will kill anyone that stands in the way of that by thinking they have access to you. Do you understand me?"

I shouldn't be enjoying this. My heart should not have sped up the way it did. My breath caught at the pressure of Corban's fingers when they pushed harder. He wasn't just threatening Quint, but me. He would destroy everyone around me just to keep me. To win his freedom.

There was a sick part of me that basked in how possessive he was. The danger of it sent heat straight to my core. This was all incredibly fucked up, him threatening another man over me, his deadly interest, the ravenous way he looked at me. Even with his claws hidden they were hooked inside of me, tearing me apart as he liked.

Everything about him was wrong and yet I whispered, "I'm not going anywhere."

Our faces were so close together our noses touched. He inhaled every time I exhaled. The sound of my pulse overpowered the music and voices in the background. I could smell the fear and excitement within my own sweat.

A wicked smile carved Corban's face apart. "Good girl." I hadn't realized he was still holding onto the cocktail until he slid it into my hand. "Now, finish your drink."

I wondered if Corban had slipped something into my drink. Or if perhaps he had glamoured it and the liquid had been replaced with faerie wine. Because the moment I finished the glass, giddy warmth filled my body, overflowing until I was a bubbling laughing mess. I twirled in front of him, showing off the dress he'd tailored.

The grin plastered on Corban's face made me even giddier. I hadn't seen him smile like that yet, with no inhibitions, or trace of malice.

"Aren't you a pretty thing." He looked up at me from the red leather booth he sat in. He grasped my hips and pulled me between his legs. "I agreed to leave your friend alone but what am I to do with everyone else staring at you?"

I looked over my shoulder. Men and women were throwing glances our way. Others *were* outright staring.

"They're staring at you!" I gazed down at him. "Look at you!" I motioned up and down his body with my glass, which was magically full again.

"Look at *you*," he said. "Look at them watching you."

A dim lamp hung over our table, framing half of his face in orange and the other in gray. Shadows of nearby patrons cut through the green glow of his eyes periodically as they passed across the bar. I leaned forward the moment he tipped his face up, my forehead knocking against his before my lips found his mouth. It wasn't my best kiss, sloppy and clumsy. Corban grinned, opening his mouth when my tongue snaked through his lips.

I swayed my hips to the music as I pulled away. I turned to face the crowd, lifting my arms high above my head and moving in time with the beat. I tipped my head back so that my hair spilled into Corban's lap. Felt him tug at the end of the strands, pulling my head back farther, exposing my throat and chest to anyone brave enough to look.

I shouldn't have let Corban tempt anyone that way knowing it would move them up on his shit list, but I couldn't help it. He made me feel alive. I wanted them to see how powerful he made me feel.

Through heavy lids I scanned across the room until I found Quint. He was standing amongst a group of men and two women. His brother-in-law was yelling something in his ear that had Quint shoving him backward. He snapped something back and then turned a cold-hard stare my way.

Something should worry me about the way Quint was looking at me. About the way his friends hissed in his ear. Whatever thought was trying to form in my head disappeared when Corban's hand palmed my ass.

I whirled to face him. "Be careful where you put your hands."

A perfect brow arched. In response his hand slid to my front, to the hem of my dress, and he tugged me forward. My legs buckled and I slid a knee between his thighs as I all but fell into the booth with him.

"Corban!"

"Mmm, yes love?"

That was the second time he had called me that tonight. It gave me a warm rush and sent a pleasant tingling sensation zinging across my skin.

I held his glimmering stare over the rim of my glass as I took a sip. "We're in public." I placed a hand on his shoulder and leaned back, placing my foot back on the ground with the other.

His fingers remained pinned to the hem of my dress. "We are. Stay facing me, but keep dancing," he said, petting my thigh with his fingers. "No one can see you from this angle."

"What are you– Corban!" The slide of his hand moving under the front of my dress sobered me up in moments.

"No one will be any the wiser." Wicked delight blazed in his eyes as he moved his sinful touch to the heat between my legs. One finger, then another stroked the length of my slit. I could feel my wetness slick between us, already soaking the thin fabric of my underwear. I don't know how my body was able to keep up with him as sore and torn as it was. I swayed my hips after a moment's pause when I realized I was being too still. Corban pressed his thumb against my clit as I moved, his other two fingers still stroking me, drawing more heat and wetness from my aching body.

"You are glorious, little dove. How I love watching you sin." With the turn of his hand he slid his fingers inside my panties. I lurched against him, my hips rolling forward to meet him and far too suddenly to be in sync with the music.

I flicked my gaze to the right to see if it was true that no one could see anything.

"Eyes on me," Corban growled.

I met Quint's gaze and then Corban pushed his fingers inside of me.

Shame hit me like a tidal wave but was forced down at the curl of his wicked fingers. I looked down on Corban, at his beautiful, upturned face, laced with rapture.

This was wrong on so many levels and yet I didn't try to stop him as he pushed farther inside, pressed harder on that little bundle of nerves. If anyone caught us we would be tossed out, or worse, arrested. I'd never be able to show my face in town again.

His throat bobbed. "Would you ride me here?"

Oh fuck me. "Absolutely not," I breathed.

Corban leaned forward, his free hand sliding up the back side of my thigh. "What if it pleased me?" He worked his fingers in and out of me, slowly gaining speed with each stroke.

I knew Corban liked to move quickly, but this was lightspeed. I could brave him in private but there was no way in Hell I was going to let him take advantage of me in front of a crowd. "I'll please you at home."

A guttural groan left his throat. "Please, Sorcha." He rolled his thumb harder against my clit.

The way he said my name in time with his touch nearly undid me there and then. If I didn't stop him now there would be no telling him to quit. "We have to stop." I took a half step back that was cut off by the iron press of his grip on my thigh. I glared down at him, trying desperately not to roll against his touch again. "Corban."

His tongue slid between his lips. "I love the way you say my name when you're panting."

And I was panting. He was driving me closer to the edge. My nerves were on fire. From his touch, from the thrill that someone might see us. It felt like I would fall out of my skin any second. His fingers worked between the sore sensitive flesh to the point I could hear my own wetness between one song dying and another starting.

His eyes narrowed as mine widened.

"Keep dancing," he commanded. I shook my head even though I moved my hips to this side and that. I didn't want to obey and yet I was afraid of what would happen if I didn't. "Dance until you come. I want my hand glistening, Sorcha."

"Fuck," I gasped.

"That's it." His fingers worked furiously, stroking hard and fast against the upper ridge of my pussy.

I rolled my hips and moved my arms to the side. I knew the song playing but the only tune I focused on was the bass of our breaths as they deepened and the slick slapping his palm made against my flesh, against my clit, sending in shockwaves through my entire body.

I stiffened and fell forward, my hand slapping down on his shoulder. I dug my nails into his shirt, trying to find purchase on his skin beneath as I came. My hair fell around my face, mercifully concealing it as I let out a silent sound, my mouth gaping in sheer ecstasy.

Corban's grin was corrupt. He pulled his fingers free and slid them into my mouth. "Taste how ready you are for me."

I was thankful for the curtain of my hair because I don't think I could have stopped myself from sucking his fingers clean. I ran my tongue between them until he pulled back and pushed them against the middle of my chest, easing me back. He gave my body an appraising look, starting with my heeled feet all the way to the mess of my hair.

"Let me clean up and let's go home," I said before anything else that might damn us both could pass between those beautiful lips, which were parted, no doubt ready to issue another filthy command. "I'll do whatever you want, let's just get home first."

Corban's brow arched. "Whatever I want?"

I'd probably regret saying that, but I nodded. "Yes. Anything."

At the lift of his chin I turned and made a beeline for the bathroom. With every step, I could feel the eyes of the bar following me.

Chapter 24

SORCHA

The cool touch of the mirror against my forehead grounded me as I leaned over the sink in the single stall bathroom. It stank of piss and cheap perfume. Of spilt beer and fried cheeseballs. None of those things sobered me up enough to dampen the heat that still coursed through my body.

Corban had made me come in a bar full of people. And I had let him.

I took a deep breath as I leaned back to look at myself. My skin was flushed, sweat dotted my hairline and my lips were red and full from where I must have been biting them.

"I'm going to Hell," I muttered. Or Underland rather, if Corban had his way.

I ran a hand through my hair. I needed to get a hold of myself. Corban had far too much power over me and had set us both on a collision course. We needed to get out of here, I needed to get him to Under, and then Glamis would be all mine.

The final thought sent a nervous tingle through my chest. Did I want Glamis without him?

Two raps on the door broke me out of my thoughts. "Just a minute!" I called. I brushed my hands through my hair again and down my dress as if I could wipe away the freshly fucked look that still glazed my eyes.

I opened the door and stopped dead. Quint threw a quick look over his shoulder before pushing me inside, forcing me back.

"What the fuck are you doing?" I tried to dart around him but he was faster and slammed the door shut, throwing his back against it.

"Sorcha, I need you to listen to me." He grabbed hold of my shoulders.

"Ow! Quint, that hurts. Let go of me." I tried to raise my arms to push him away but couldn't from this angle.

He gave me another hard squeeze that made me wince before letting me go. He threw up his palm. "Just. Listen. Ok?"

I crossed my arms over my chest. "Yeah, outside. Now!"

His eyes snapped to mine. They had a wild look to them that reminded me of an animal caught in a snare. An animal that would bite just to save itself. "I don't think you're crazy. I never thought you were. That story I told you about seeing a monster with your grandmother was real."

"Oh my gosh, Quint. Are you fucking serious right now?" I pinched the bridge of my nose and tried to move past him, only for him to block me again. I pointed my finger sharply in his face. "*Stop* trying to win me over. You think I'm crazy. You don't think I'm crazy. I don't really care anymore. What I do care about is that you have me trapped in a bathroom right now."

"It's him!" He reached for me again then curled his hand into a fist, drawing it back to his side. "That dude you're with," he pointed over his shoulder, "that's who I saw."

Shit, I'd actually forgotten the story he'd told me. About the man with long horns who had kissed the top of Grandma Macky's head. Ok, well,

I knew Corban was real – obviously. I should have put two and two together earlier.

My heart hammered as I reassessed the crazed look of Quint's eyes again. He wasn't just an animal that would bite, he was one that would chew off its own leg, hurt everyone around it, just to get away. I could smell it on him. Beneath all the alcohol was the sweet scent of fear and desperation.

Dread filled the space between us. Corban was going to come looking for me if I didn't get out of here soon and there was no way he was going to let Quint off a third time.

"Quint," I said slowly. "I need you to listen to me very carefully, ok? True or not, I need you to let me out of this bathroom right now."

He flung his head back in exasperation. "Are you even hearing what I'm telling you?" He gestured wildly back at the door. "That is not a man out there. That is a monster. This isn't a game I'm trying to play with you. Rob recognized him too; he's one of the guys that was there with me that day. We don't talk about it because how could that have been real, right? But it's him."

The dread wound tighter, stalked toward us. I looked around the small space. Were the shadows getting darker?

"Quint," I warned. I pursed my lips and moved to the side as I slowly inched my way to the door he was still pressed against. If I could get him to turn his attention with me, turn his body with mine, then maybe I could duck out.

His eyes narrowed, stopping me in my tracks, and he looked at me. Really looked at me. His gaze dropped down to my legs that were now bare and blemish free. But they hadn't been. I'd shown him the bruises. "Holy fuck. You know. Is he what hurt you– holy fuck you saw him! It was *him* you saw that night. That broke in."

I would have to try a different angle. "We can talk about this later when you don't have me trapped. Corban is going to come looking for me and I'd very much like to leave before that happens."

"What has he been doing? Is he holding you hostage?" He took hold of my arm again and looked over his shoulder, then to the vent and to the mirror. His eyes darting around like he could find another exit. "I can get you out of here. Get you away from him."

"Let go, Quint." I jerked my arm against his grip, but it just tightened.

"No, it's okay. I'll get you away." Those fingers curled tighter, tighter until I could feel the bruises expanding across my skin. "I'll get you away and it'll be fine. We'll get rid of him."

"Quint!"

The door crashed open, sending Quint flying past me into the wire rack of bathroom supplies. I caught hold of the railing beside the toilet the moment Corban rushed in, the door banging shut behind him.

The shadows that had been gathering at the corners of the stall exploded. Black tendrils writhed like snakes, striking and snapping like they could jump free, and latch hold to something for real. I pressed myself against the railing, my nails chipping away the cheap paint on the wall behind it as I cast about for something, anything that would help me get us all out of this situation.

Corban twisted his fingers around Quint's neck and in a single graceful movement lofted him into the air. "Remember me now?" he snarled. "You were just a boy, sticking your nose in places it didn't belong. Clearly, not much has changed since then."

Quint gurgled as he kicked. His feet made solid impact against Corban, but the grotesque didn't so much as flinch.

"So many times I could have killed you. So many times I've spared you."

"Corban," I whispered because it was all I could manage, terror closing my own throat. Quint's face was turning purple, his eyes bloodshot where they should have been white.

"I meant to let you live tonight, but then you went and touched her." Corban gave Quint a good shake for emphasis. Quint clawed at the hand around his throat, his kicks becoming twitches.

The smell of piss was stronger now and, oh– Quint had pissed himself. The denim of his pants darkened between his thighs.

Corban's eyes blazed bloodthirsty red, with all consuming hate. He was going to kill him.

I reached out a shaking hand, my eyes locked on the vicious set of his face as the glamour he held over his appearance flickered. "Corban," I said, louder this time. "Corban, look at me please."

His nostrils flared before he flicked his glowing gaze down to me. I could only see one of his eyes, as his focus still almost entirely on Quint, a deadly attention fierce enough to burn a hole through his head. I would have stumbled back were I not already pressed against the wall. His *eyes*– their pupils were slitted, vertical like a vipers'.

"I'm fine. He didn't hurt me. Corban, please let him go." I rested my hand on his muscled arm.

"Give me one good reason why I shouldn't snap his neck." At the widening of Quint's eyes Corban's sneer deepened.

He truly was a sight to behold. There was such unbridled fury roiling from him that I should have been running in the other direction. Instead, all I could do was stand there in awe. I had the good sense to still be terrified of him, but something was clearly cracked inside my brain that held me there completely captivated.

"It would make me happy if you did." I conceded, tilting my chin down when his nostrils flared again and he turned in my direction. "It would make me happy if you didn't kill anyone tonight. If you came home with me instead." I had no real feelings for Quint, but I didn't need Corban thinking I might.

Bang! Bang! Bang!

"Hey! You can't be doing that in there!"

I jumped as another series of bangs shook the door. I looked from it to Corban. Quint's eyes were rolling back in his head, his tongue slightly poking out between his swollen lips.

I slid my hand up over Corban's where it gripped Quint's neck and pushed down, slowly lowering it until Quint's feet touched the ground.

"I'm going to need you all to step out or we are going to drag you out. This is a place of business, and we can't have you in there doing... whatever it is you're doing."

I might have laughed at the situation if Quint hadn't fallen like a sack of potatoes out of Corban's grip. He hit the ground with a solid thud. They thought we were in here screwing. My gosh, they had no idea someone was almost murdered.

I kept a firm grip on Corban's hand as he came back to himself, his eyes flitting over Quint. He ran his tongue over his teeth, the split ends curling over his upper lip.

"I'm not going anywhere. I was never going to," I said.

"Dammit! Open this door right fucking now!"

"We'll be right out!" I called.

"Now!" The man shouted back.

How were we going to just walk out when Quint was unconscious between us? I looked down at him sharply and stared until I saw the shallow rise and fall of his chest. Oh thank God, he *was* breathing.

"Do you trust me?" Corban asked.

I looked back at him, at those eyes that remained blood-thirsty red. Not even a little bit, and yet I nodded that I did.

Corban yanked me to his side without warning. The darkness that had been writhing in the corner erupted into pungent black smoke. Cold suffocating shadows enveloped us. I gasped as the chill forced its way into my nostrils, down my throat. I clawed at Corban's chest as the world froze around us, encasing me to him like a vice.

As quickly as the shadows attacked, they disappeared. I heaved, sucking in air and stumbled back, my hand still firmly grasped to Corban to anchor myself. He kept his hands on my elbows, his fingers flexing.

I blinked and nearly stumbled again.

We were outside. We were beside my car, to be more precise.

"What?" I looked around. There were no stars out, no moon. The sky was lightless, heavy with gray clouds.

"We should leave before they think to come looking," he said, rounding to the passenger side.

I could still feel his shadows crawling on my skin, prodding. "What did you do?"

"You've seen me meld into the shadows before. I brought you with me this time." He tapped the roof of the car with a long claw. "Hurry up, Sorcha, before I change my mind. My will is strained, and I would love nothing more than to march back into that bar and finish what I started." He slid my keys over the roof of the car. I touched my purse absentmindedly. When had he stolen my keys? Did he think I would have left him?

A car passed by, and his eyes flashed bright as the headlights caught them. I grabbed the keys before they fell to the ground. With shaking hands, I shoved them into the lock and then into the ignition. I was so numb to everything, to Corban teleporting us, to him nearly killing

Quint, that I couldn't feel anything. I couldn't feel the smooth curve of the steering wheel beneath my clenched palms or the stick of leather to the back of my legs. I felt nothing until Corban reached over and slid his hand over the top of my thigh.

And then it all came crashing down like wild lightning, shocking my senses to life.

Corban's magic was like fire in my blood. The heady thrum of it pounded the entire drive to Glamis. As his hand slid higher, my stomach coiled and my breath caught.

I looked over at him. His lashes brushed the top of his cheeks before he looked up at me, pulling his gaze from my lips, or heaving chest, I couldn't tell which. He slid that wicked forked tongue between his lips slowly, as if he was tasting me. As if he could taste that despite the fear warring in me, that I was growing warm and wanting beneath his icy, yet burning touch.

I focused back on the road, but try as I might I couldn't focus on it.

Corban had nearly killed someone for me, killed them *because* of me, and a twisted part of me liked it. I liked how he had rushed in to save me. I liked even more the way he was currently sprawled out in my passenger seat, his eyes locked on me like I was prey. I didn't want him to kill Quint, not then and not now, but fuck if it wasn't hot knowing he could do it. Would do it if someone threatened me.

A bolt of magic shot out of his fingertips to my center, making my thighs clench.

I'd barely put the car in park before Corban unbuckled my seatbelt and was dragging me into his lap. I grunted when my head hit the ceiling. Our mouths locked together while I fumbled for the lever on the seat and it tilted back with a jolt, giving me better access. I ran my hands under his shirt, his broad muscles coiling and flexing beneath my shaking fingers.

One of his hands grasped the curve of my ass and the other wrapped around the side of my neck. "I can't help myself," he breathed. "I don't want to hurt you, Sorcha, but I have to be inside of you."

I kissed him so hard our teeth knocked together. My hands worked his belt apart. It should have been physically impossible to want him as badly as I did. Corban was a curse I could not break.

He slid his claws between my thighs, careful not to slice my skin, and cut through the fabric separating me from his vicious touch. I pulled his belt apart and then the button and fly of his trousers.

"What have you done to me?" I moaned as I struggled to pull him out of his pants.

Corban's sharp teeth flashed in the darkness. He pushed my hands out of the way and lifted his hips. In another motion he pulled me down, sinking me onto the length of his cock in a single, agonizing motion. "Claimed you," he groaned. "You were always going to be mine and I will never let you go. Never let anyone else have you. Not even for a moment."

He cupped the back of my neck as my head lolled back and I started rocking my hips against him. Glorious aching pleasure shot through me.

Fucking in a car isn't the most elegant way to have sex, which worked perfectly for a pair like us, who fucked like animals. He let me set the pace until I sat forward to catch my breath. Then he grabbed hold of my ass, lifting me up slightly and then pumped his hips up to meet me. Over and over again until I was gushing all over his nice black slacks.

"You're so fucking beautiful coming undone. So. Fucking. Beautiful." He rammed hard into me, accentuating each word.

I leaned forward, pressing my breasts into his face as I found purchase on the headrest and held on for dear life. He pulled down the front of my dress so that my breasts popped free and then sank those delicious fangs into their soft flesh. He bit me again, and again, until he found my nipple and sucked.

The windows were fogged. Our bodies were slick with sweat. The entire car smelled of sex. It was suffocating. Intoxicating.

He lifted his head at the same moment he pulled me down. He held me over his blood slicked face, his eyes glowing a terrifying red. "I'll not let him or anyone else live that comes near you again."

I clenched around his length – that I swear got even harder – as he said those words. How did such evil words unspool me?

The corner of his mouth tugged upward, flashing his fangs again. "Does that turn you on, little dove? I can feel your pussy gripping me, begging me to cum inside of you." He rubbed his face against mine, smearing the blood from my chest over my mouth and cheeks. His breath fanned against my ear when he said, "I'll kill for you, Sorcha. Tell me how that makes you feel."

I shook my head. I couldn't answer him, not when my body was so desperately trying to lie. Because I couldn't want that. I didn't want anyone to die. But every threatening word he said while inside of me wound me tighter, made my pussy grip his cock harder.

"Tell me that doesn't get you sopping wet," he hissed. "I can feel you dripping down my balls."

Corban wrapped an arm around my waist and fucked me. Hard. Fast. He pounded into me viciously, all the while looking up at me with his mouth agape and his eyes alight. The glamour shifted and his skin greyed, his black horns spiraled out of his dark hair, jutting past the headrest.

I let out a guttural moan that brought a lethal smile to his mouth. I ran my hand over his sweat-slicked forehead and into his mess of black hair. I slammed my hips down as he brought his up. Heat flared inside my core, expanding to every cell of my body.

"You'll never get me to admit that." I ground my ass into his pelvis.

Challenge flashed in his eyes, and he snaked a hand around my throat. I don't know what got into me, but I wasn't going to let Corban win. Not this time.

I grabbed his chin with my other hand and pulled his mouth farther open. "Tongue out," I said.

His eyes sparkled before he slid it out. I leaned over him as I gathered the spit on the middle of my tongue and slowly, so slowly let it drop out of my mouth into his. It had barely touched his tongue before he slammed our mouths together, forcing his forked appendage against the flat of mine.

"You'll never win against me. Not tonight, not ever," he growled. "But for spitting in my mouth I'll give you something extra special. Are you ready, Sorcha? I'm going to make you cum so hard you'll see stars."

Corban grabbed me by the ass again and fucked me harder. My grip slipped in his hair, and I latched onto one of his horns as he slammed into me at a rate that should have killed me. My mouth opened and what started as wordless cry turned into a mangled scream of pleasure as all sense left me and there was only Corban.

His thick length forced me apart again, and again. Wet squelching filled the silence between our breaths and moans. The heat inside of me exploded, white hot and debilitating as he pushed farther than he should have been able. And just like he promised, I saw stars, burning bright white lights that flooded my vision.

Corban chased me over the edge, slamming into me once more before a torrent of heat poured into me from his cock. I clutched at him, both of my hands now held fast to his horns as he jerked and spurted inside of me.

I knew he had corrupted me then. Because in that moment, as I looked down on him, with galaxies still in my eyes, I think I loved him.

Chapter 25

SORCHA

Grease popped and sputtered, raining tiny burning droplets on my bare hands. I'd thought the smell of bacon would have woken Corban when I could not, but I heard nothing as I pushed the crispy strips around the pan.

At least for me the smell of food always got me up quickly.

He'd stayed with me all night and was still next to me when the sun rose, but had barely moved when I tried to wake him. Just pulled me closer when I'd tried to get out of bed. Not once did his deep, sleep-heavy breaths falter.

I fiddled with the locket I still wore around my neck. Perhaps it had something to do with the curse, and he had expended too much energy too quickly? We had been away from Glamis the majority of the evening, plus he'd teleported us out to the car. I sighed. I didn't know how we were going to separate him from the manor entirely if this deep sleep was a side effect.

I rolled the shred of bacon around in my mouth, chewed and swallowed. My feelings were a mess. Help Corban, don't help him. Be afraid of him, possibly be falling in love with him.

I stacked more bacon onto a piece of toast and took a massive bite. I needed more information. I'd been blindly letting Corban lead me into his schemes. I needed to know for certain that what I was doing was the right thing, I needed more than his word to go on, basically.

I made my way back to the bedroom quietly. He hadn't moved an inch, his large body sprawled over the bed, both wings now draped over either side of the mattress. His glamour must have unspooled while I was cooking.

I ran my fingers through his hair, scratching my nails over his scalp. Corban let out a heavy, contented sigh. I waited another few minutes to ensure he was still in a deep sleep before padding downstairs to the library.

I pulled Rosaline's diary and the sketchbook from their hiding spots. If there were other accounts tucked away there wasn't time to search for them. I reread Rosaline's last entry and flipped through the remainder of the book to make sure I hadn't missed anything.

January 10, 1812

Tonight will be my last entry. I have prepared a nice meal for Gerald and I. A last supper where I will tell him the truth before leaving him forever. I can't go on like this a moment longer. I have tasted the divine and know now I cannot bear to live without it.

Chills raced down my spine. That's the night she would have killed Gerald. To prove herself to Corban. My fingers froze between the pages. Corban said he needed three things to be free. What if he was lying?

What if he needed a sacrifice to shatter the curse entirely? No, he would have gone ahead and killed Quint if that theory was correct. He was too desperate for his freedom. Right?

Unless that sacrifice is you, a little voice taunted.

I looked up, my ears straining for any sign that he might have woken. I didn't hear anything but that didn't release the tension from my muscles. He could spill from a dark corner and I'd have no idea how long he had been lurking there.

I swallowed, tucking Rosaline's journal beneath a couch cushion before turning to the sketchbook.

Monsters of various forms were outlined in charcoal. I flipped past the pages I had already seen. Flipping, flipping until I slowed. Slowed as the images morphed into the shape of a man I recognized.

Corban's face was gaunt, narrower, like the apparitions sketched earlier in the book. But it was him. The eyes were unmistakable, their cruelty palpable.

On the next page *"fear the night that would consume the light"* was written. Next to it was a stunted looking dragon with long tapered horns and curved membraned wings. I'd seen that dragon before. I flipped back to the beginning of the book until I found what I was looking for. The first image of the dragon with its diamond-shaped pupils.

Vertical... slitted pupils... like the ones I'd glimpsed last night, when Corban had been lost in his rage.

My stomach dropped. That wasn't the only place I'd seen the dragon. I jumped from the couch and ran outside. It couldn't be.

All doubt vanished the moment I stepped off the front porch and looked up.

The arch above the doorway was empty.

Where the twisted dragon had coiled over the entrance, there was nothing but a vacant space.

My heart thundered. I looked down at the book, to the likeness I should have seen carved in stone. Corban had never come to me in this form, but it was him. There was no other explanation as to why the space was free, while he slept in my bed.

Another memory came to me, of a long dark shadow slinking into the manor and morphing into a man. The shadow on the video.

My tongue felt dry when I tried to swallow.

I pulled my phone out of my pocket and snapped a photo of the doorway. Even if I never showed anyone– at least I would have the proof for my own peace of mind. I flipped to the next page, scurrying back to the library. Only this time I shut the door and turned the lock.

I hope to God that no one has been put in a position where they must find my account of the monster. I made certain he could not get to my children, or their children. If he has, then his magic is stronger than I feared. His will more hungry than I could have imagined.

There is no light in the darkness. Only things made of it can slink out in the night. Evil things that want to devour.

His silver promises are empty. Do not let him out.

The creak of the floorboard above my head forced me off the couch. I scrambled, snatching the sketchbook from the floor as it went flying from my lap, and sprinted across the room to hide it.

A soft clink sounded when I dropped the volume a second time. "Oh fuck me," I whispered. I forced the book between two others, snatched the object from the floor and hurried to the door. I threw the lock aside before taking a deep breath, fighting to regain my composure as I pulled it open.

Corban stood in the doorway, his brow arched when I stumbled back, my hand flying to my chest. "Fuck's sake!"

A slow turn of his mouth that couldn't quite be called a smile touched his face. "Did I scare you?"

I scowled at him. "Obviously." Could he hear how loud my heart was beating?

He looked over my shoulder. "What are you reading?"

I took a step back to let him enter. He tucked his wings close to his body and hunched forward to cross over the threshold. "Not sure yet. I was just browsing. There are so many to choose from." I watched him carefully as he crossed the room and dragged a long finger down the spines. "Have any recommendations?"

Corban snorted. "Half of these are useless; they carry no truth in them."

"All fairy tales?"

Corban looked over his shoulder, a cruel smile on his face. "Oh, the fairy tales are all real." He cocked his head.

Don't see it. Don't look at it, I silently begged as his gaze cut to the shelf where the sketchbook wasn't fully tucked away. I don't know why I didn't want him to find it, only that I knew it was urgent that he not.

"How are you feeling?"

Corban hummed quietly. "Tired, but well." He threw a grin over his shoulder, his lips parted to continue when his gaze snagged on something.

Please no.

He reached for the sketchbook that was so obviously out of place between the traditional hardbacks. His fingers grazed the bowed spine, stiffened over it and then tugged it free. Shadows flickered–no those were the clouds moving across the sun. Everything was fine.

"What's that?" I piped up.

His jaw noticeably rippled as it clenched. "This was Maxine's." He hesitated before opening the book.

My heart raced faster. The warning I'd read repeated through my head so loudly I feared Corban would hear it. *Do not let him out. My children, or their children...me!* Realization smacked me full in the face. Macky hadn't had a relationship with me, with mom, because she'd been trying to protect us.

From Corban.

Something akin to sadness washed over his face. The proud arch of his wings drooped with the drop of his shoulders. "I told you before we did not get along well, but I liked your grandmother. I hated that we could not see eye to eye."

I swallowed, willing the dryness coating my throat to go away. "What happened to her? With the two of you?"

The shuck of paper sliding against itself sliced through the air as he turned another page. His gaze lingered on the image of the three tall figures. Their lithe forms seemed to sway on the page. Slowly, he brushed his thumb over them, almost affectionately, before he turned to the next image. A portrait of himself, thin and gaunt.

"I never told Maxine what I was. I didn't have to. She was well versed in things of my world, though to this day I have no idea how she could have known about Under. She feared me."

The thing I'd grabbed from the floor felt cool and hard in my palm. I slid my hands into my back pockets, shoving it there for safe keeping. "I thought you enjoyed being feared. You like mine."

"Oh, yes. But Maxine never played any of my games." He held out a hand and curled his fingers, beckoning me toward him. When I stopped at his side he rested that large hand over the back of my neck. "I can smell you on the pages, Sorcha. Tell me, how far did you get before you thought to hide this from me?"

His eyes remained planted on the sketchbook, on the gnarled and twisted dragon. The weight of his hand was light, and that scared me. I was used to him being vicious and lethal, this calm coolness somehow frightened me even more.

"Not far," I lied. The corner of his jaw ticked like he could sense it.

"But you did try to hide it," he pressed.

Was his hand getting heavier? No, he hadn't so much as moved. Fuck he was so eerily still. While the wings and horns fascinated me, they also made it impossible to forget that he was a predator. At least when he wore his human costume it was easier to pretend.

"Yes," I said.

"Where are the others?"

"Others?"

His eyes snapped to me then. "The other accounts. Diaries. Where are they?"

I shook my head. "That's all I've found. I thought those were just drawings."

Corban frowned the longer he held my gaze. When I didn't back down, he gave a curt nod and let his hand drop so he could flip through the sketchbook more quickly.

What was there that he didn't want me to find? *Others* meant there was more than just Rosaline's to be found. How many women had Corban tormented and failed with?

How many women had he killed?

I dismissed the thought in case he was able to track my attention to where her diary lay hidden beneath the cushions of the couch. Instead, I asked a question I already knew the answer to. "Are you the dragon over the door? That's you in the book, isn't it?"

"The grotesque," he said. "Yes."

"Why haven't you come to me in that form?"

Corban shut the book and slid it under his arm before turning to me. "You're already fucking a monster, Sorcha. Would you fuck a beast too?" He grabbed hold of my chin when I flinched. "While I do enjoy feasting on your fear, it is not my desire to scare you to death. I much prefer your heart beating."

"How kind," I choked.

The smile he gave me looked strained, forced. He held up the sketchbook. "I do not know how far you truly got but you cannot believe everything that you read and saw. Your grandmother was not in her right mind at the end."

Mad Maxine.

Ridiculous Rosaline.

What were all the others called?

Stupid Sorcha. Because of Corban, because of the spell he cast over us.

Even teetering on the edges of terror, I found myself wanting to tip forward into his arms. Fall into his chasm and never see the light of day again. It was toxic, this sway he had over me.

"Why do you say that?" I asked softly. "Is there something bad in there?"

His silver promises are empty. Do not let him out.

What was so terrible about returning him to his realm?

"A mind gone lost is always tragic," he said. He cocked his head one way and then the other, assessing me. "The only harm I mean to bring to you is what I have already brought. I will not hurt you more than I already have."

"I believe you."

Corban's lips pouted. "You're a terrible liar, Sorcha. Do you know how I know? Because I can see the damned diary sticking out from under the cushions." He clucked his tongue. "Now get down on your knees. I want to feel your lying tongue around my cock."

Chapter 26

CORBAN

The slam of her heart against her ribs was like music to my ears. Its steady pump was the only thing that kept me grounded. I don't know whether I was more angry, or afraid that she had read those bitches' diaries. They had too much of the truth in them. Truths that Sorcha could not find out lest she try to pry herself from my hold.

I was so close, so incredibly close to sealing her fate to mine. I would not fail this time. I refused.

I stroked her throat with my thumb, pressing harder into the vein at her neck with each swipe.

"Two truths and a lie," she blurted.

"I've already sniffed out your lie, sweetheart," I growled. "Down on your knees and if you do a good job, we can play a different game after."

She had the good sense to look afraid. Her fear wafted up into my nose. But so did her heat. The two had become close as lovers, perfuming the air each time I loomed over her.

"It's only those two, I swear. I didn't know there were others."

Truth? Her heart hadn't kicked an extra beat like it had before when she was fibbing.

"I want Glamis," she said. "Macky left it to me, and I want it. I'll do whatever I can to free you and get you back to Under. I was looking to see if there was a way to free you that you hadn't already tried before. A clue they may have written but didn't understand for themselves."

Lie.

One lie. Her heart stuttered violently at the end. She had read something in Maxine's sketchbook that scared her. But the other part? Why the hell would she want Glamis when she had me?

I squinted down at her. "Why do you want Glamis?"

She rubbed her fingers together, a sign of just how nervous she was. "I've never had anything of my own. It feels like magic here and I want to keep it."

I scoffed and twisted my hand so that it collared her throat. "I am the magik, Sorcha. Who do you think feeds you by keeping the cupboards stocked? Where do you think your entertainment comes from when I am not buried between your legs? These books," I nodded to the shelves, "are one of the few things I have allowed to stay that are not of my own making."

Her eyes widened. They darted to the shelves and back at me. "None of it's real?"

"It is real because I make it so." I ground my molars together.

"So without you...."

"There is no Glamis," I finished for her. "That is why I asked you to come with me to Under. I do not want to be parted from you, but also..." I flicked my eyes to the ceiling, to the windows. "All of this is nothing compared to what I can give you. What is one old house compared to an entire realm? Once I am restored to my homeland there will be endless possibilities. All wholly and completely yours."

Sorcha worked her teeth over her lower lip. Gods I almost had her. She was right there, teetering on the edge. I could feel the bond between us vibrating. She just needed a little push and she'd tumble right over into the right decision.

"I find it hard to believe. You've been playing with me this entire time–"

"So, let's keeping playing. You love my games, but allow me to play one of yours."

Sorcha shifted against my hand, trying to widen the distance between us. I let Maxine's sketchbook fall to the ground in exchange for grabbing hold of her waist. Not yet. I couldn't let her go before pulling her into the deep end of my want. I needed her to drown in my desire. Drown in me.

"Two truths and one lie. Places far grander than Glamis will be yours. You will be happier apart from me. I am so madly, deeply in love with you."

Air blew out of Sorcha's lungs in a fatal exhale. My own breath became trapped in my throat as the confession left me. I hadn't meant to say it, not yet, but the truth was out there now. Or was it? Is that what this electric wave flowing between us was? Love?

Her heavy breasts heaved. "What are you doing to me? Why do you insist on playing these vicious games with me? You've just told me you can give me everything. You know that I'll never be happy without you. And I know you don't love me." She placed her shaking hands against my stomach. "A creature like you cannot love."

I hunched over her. "You think that is the lie?"

"You've given me two lies and a truth."

I pressed my forehead against hers, angling my face until the tips of our noses touched. "Little dove, that is not how the game works."

A tremor ran through her body as if it had erupted from her core. My sweet Sorcha, so incredibly brave, so determined, was pushing her way through that fear. Ignoring whatever warnings Maxine had left to her.

A little farther.

"Which is the lie?"

She shook her head. "I can't."

"Say it." I pushed her chin up so I could brush my lips to hers.

"Corban," she pleaded. Begged.

I slid my fingers beneath her shirt and groped her warm skin. "Then let me to show you the truth."

There wasn't a single part of me that was made to be gentle. I enjoyed pain. Both inflicting it and being on the receiving end. I *reveled* in it. I knew Sorcha enjoyed how I touched her, but she needed to know I could be tender. That I was capable of love, of holding her delicate heart in my hands without crushing it.

She stifled a moan behind her lips when I kissed her neck. "Don't do this to me," she begged.

I ran my tongue over the divots of my fang marks. I slid my tongue along her jaw and planted a soft kiss to her lips. "What am I doing?" I trailed my hand from her hip down the swell of her ass and squeezed. I'd never get over how full she was against me.

"You're going to destroy me." She pulled her face away while simultaneously pushing her hips into my hand.

I pressed my mouth to the top of her head, breathing her in while I moved my hand to her waistband and worked her underwear and pants down her hips. "That's not so terrible, is it? Don't you want to see the stars again?" I pushed her firmly against the bookcase, earning another startled exhale.

She grabbed hold of my shoulders as I slid to the ground to relieve her of her clothes. I lifted one of her bare legs to kiss the sole of her foot. She took her bottom lip between her teeth. Her straight white teeth worked it furiously. She'd make herself bleed before I could if she kept at it.

"Careful, love. I haven't quite gotten past not wanting to fuck that devious little mouth of yours." I traced the line of her smooth leg, opting for kisses instead of sinking my teeth into her flesh like I craved.

Her back arched, shoulders pressing into the books as I climbed higher up her leg until I was at her sweet, hot center. I couldn't stop my devilish grin even if I'd tried. She was soaking wet. Gods I could already taste her.

"Eyes on me," I instructed as hers threatened to close. I made a slow show of gliding my tongue over her slit, swirling it over the bundle of nerves that always made her breath catch, before dipping it inside her.

"Oh fuck," she groaned. Her hips snapped forward involuntarily, forcing my nose against her. I breathed in, pushed my tongue farther, and ate. I devoured her like she was my last meal, like she was the first thing I'd tasted after starving for a thousand years. Like my very life depended on it, and maybe it did.

I pushed and pulled my tongue, twisting it inside her. I worked her right to the edge then pulled back to suck her clit. Sorcha's hands dove for my head, one in my hair, the other at the base of one of my horns. She rocked with the motion of my tongue.

I sucked harder. As she thrust against my face, I took the opportunity to slide my fingers inside of her. Her cheeks flushed bright pink. Beads of sweat dotted her forehead like crystals, collecting and dripping down her face.

I twisted my fingers and curled them over the upper ridge of her pussy, back and forth until she tightened around them, trying to push me out. I pressed the flat of my tongue against her clit, worked my fingers faster, and then sucked.

Sorcha's head slammed against the books, her back arched. She gripped my fingers like a vice as she came hard and sudden. Was there anything more beautiful than watching a woman come? Than watching Sorcha come?

"Do you see the stars, love?"

Sorcha's fingers flexed in my hair. "There's so many."

I kissed the inside of her leg. "Shall I show you the universe?" I licked where she had dripped down on her thigh then looked up at her, arching a brow.

"Yes, please." She flashed me a lopsided grin.

I gave her cunt another quick lick before standing up. I took a step back and took my time in glamouring my pants and shirt away. Her eyes dropped down to where I stroked my cock. Slowly they worked their way up my frame, to my face, and back down again.

"I'll never get over you. You're so fucking beautiful," she breathed.

I moved forward and scooped her up. I held her by her ass while I worked my cock across her slit and up her stomach. "That's all you. You're perfect."

She laughed. It was a sound I rarely heard her make, and I loved it. Breathless and uncertain. She wrapped her legs around my waist as I poised at her entrance, her arms around my neck.

"You are. So, ah!" She tensed when I pushed into her. "So, so perfect."

It was painful not to fuck her thoroughly. I was grateful for the distraction of her heady moans and sweet kisses. I kissed her gently, told her how divine she was. How beautiful she would look covered in jewels and with a crown atop her head. It didn't matter if she heard my words or if only my tone registered. She was becoming undone beneath me, melting, dripping, coming into bloom.

Sorcha's pussy tightened around my cock. Her legs pulled me in when I started to withdraw. "Show me that universe you mentioned."

By the gods. Yes. Sorcha was mine. In that moment I knew she had been made for me just as certainly as I had been created for her. I fit inside her perfectly, her body molded precisely to mine.

I kissed her. "Hold tight," I growled.

I rocked into her, shoving her back into the bookcase until books tumbled all around us. She anchored one hand on the shelf behind her and fisted her other to the ridge of my wing. I lowered my face until my forehead was pressed to hers, so that the only thing I could see were those beautiful emerald jewels she had for eyes.

Soft gasps turned to high-pitched pants.

"Louder," I said. "Let me hear you scream."

I fucked her harder, obliterating any act I had left that I was playing the gentleman. Sorcha's scream crested as she orgasmed. I fucked her right through it, on into the next.

"Fuck. *Fuck!* It's too much. You're too much, Corban," she choked.

"Give me one more." Sweat dripped from my brow to her flushed chest. Her tits bounced with every thrust. I wondered if I was trading one curse for another, if she had not somehow ensnared me the same way her cunt gripped my cock. "One more, little dove."

I was close to breaking but she needed this. She needed to know I would put her first if only she gave me everything I desired.

And just like that Sorcha was screaming unintelligible words as she came once more. So hard that she was dangerously close to forcing my own cum out of my balls.

I groaned, and leaned my head back, simply enjoying the way she gripped my cock as I worked into her. Gods above and below, she was everything.

When I opened my eyes again, she was still looking up at me, her eyes large and glassy. Wanting.

I licked her lips and kissed her.

"I want your mouth," I said.

"Take it," she breathed. "I don't think I can give you anything else. You've wrung me dry."

I grinned and rubbed my face against hers before dropping down to her throat, then running my tongue up to her ear. I took her lobe between my teeth and sucked. "Will you let me finish there? Will you swallow every drop?"

She nodded, her fingers digging harder into my flesh. "All of it."

I eased out of her, dropping her legs carefully to the ground before moving behind her so that my back was pressed against the shelves. As she turned to face me, I made a show of stretching out my wings, their span taking up almost the entire wall. My cock bobbed and glistened in front of her face as she dropped down.

She looked up at me like I was a king. A god. Oh, she had no idea what I was truly capable of. She took hold of my cock and fuck– the wicked little thing ran her tongue from the bottom of my balls all the way to the top before she sucked the head into her mouth. She did it again, this time wrapping her tongue around my length, licking up her juices.

I leaned my head against the stacks as good fortune finally graced me in the form of this unbelievable, filthy, perfect woman and her greedy mouth. The weight of the curse fell loose about my shoulders and pooled around her knees. Lust was one of humanity's greatest sins, which was why it was the easiest weapon for me to wield when winning my freedom.

Desired above all things, I thought hazily, as I enjoyed the feel of my balls smacking against her face. If Sorcha would give me that, would give me everything, no matter which form I wore, I would give her *worlds* in return.

Once the others had realized they were losing themselves to me, binding their souls to mine, they had stopped letting me in. Had stopped letting me taste their flesh. A parasite, Maxine had called me.

Sorcha was either oblivious or too far gone to care about the consequences. To notice the invisible binds anchoring her to Glamis.

Or maybe, she was as in love with me as I was with her.

I felt it the moment the spell broke, like the snap of a thousand chains shattering all at once. My hips lurched forward, forcing my cock down the length of her throat as the sensation ripped a guttural sound out of mine.

"Gods," I gasped. Holy *gods.* White light burst behind my eyelids. I grabbed hold of her head on instinct and rocked into her, staring blindly into nothing, feeling every single thing. Every sense felt gloriously sweeter. How dulled everything had been, trapped beneath the weight of the curse.

Sorcha's mouth had driven me wild before, but now the flex of her muscles around my cock set my nerves on fire. The smell of her brought me to the shining lights I had introduced her to. Euphoria. That's what I was on the brink of.

A wet choking sound snapped me to attention. She was staring up at me, drool running down her chin. Her teary eyes as wide as her gaping mouth around my cock. I brushed a thumb down the side of her cheek.

"You perfect little creature." I was so close to coming. I needed to come. I needed to know what it felt like now that I was free. Finally, truly free.

A muffled moan vibrated up my cock in response. I eased my cock slowly back until the head was out of her throat resting on the top of her tongue. Her cheeks hollowed out as she started sucking.

"Good girl," I purred and sank my fingers back into her luscious hair. I let her set the pace, taking over as she bobbed her head up and down. I wasn't going to last much longer.

She flattened her tongue to the underside of my shaft and pressed up as she sucked. It was a direct line to my balls that had them tightening even further. She must have felt me tense because she did it again, harder this time, and pressed her teeth into the top of my cock.

 She was too good. This was too fucking delicious. I didn't have time to warn her before I started coming. Thick hot jets of cum shot into her still sucking mouth. I held her eyes, watching her take every last drop, sucking like *her* life depended on it. Like she was sucking my soul right out of my body. Sucking whatever venom of the curse remained straight into hers.

Sorcha fell back gasping once the last drop hit her tongue. Tears and drool covered her face. I was on her in an instant, kissing and licking every drop from her. Her mouth met mine eagerly.

"You're perfect. I love you. You're so fucking perfect, Sorcha. Thank you. Thank you."

Thank you. Thank you. Thank you.

I ran my finger along the faint mark on the back of her neck. I was going to keep her forever, and she had just given me everything I needed to do so.

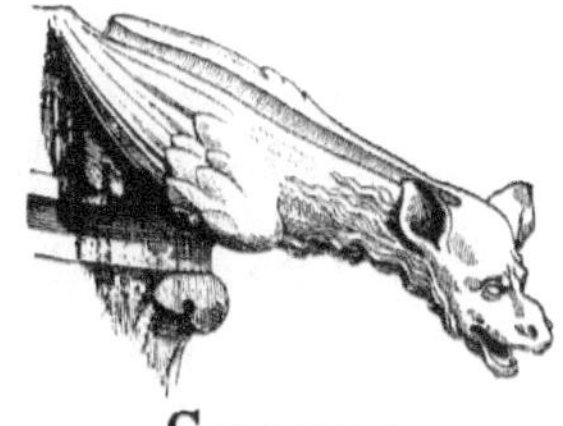

SORCHA

Corban stayed on me like an addict chasing a high. There wasn't a day over the next week that he wasn't filling me with his cock or tongue, sliding under my skin like a needle. As toxic as it was, I loved it. It felt like worship when he caressed me, his fingers carefully kneading my worn muscles and rich curves. Reverence filled his eyes with radiant light. Color graced the tops of his cheeks, and his body, which had always been ice cold, had begun to warm to mine.

Something had changed after that day in the library. Something that revived and softened him, yet his hunger for me was no less ravenous.

We hadn't spoken about him leaving Glamis, and I was too afraid to ask. Every day had been so perfect, and I did not want to break the spell by bringing up the inevitable.

Selfishly, I hoped he'd changed his mind, and that this adoration was his way of showing me that he would stay.

"I love you," he had said. I hadn't been able to shake those three little words. Over and over they played inside my head. He'd been so wild and desperate when he said them. His eyes as raw and open as I had ever seen them.

My heart and head worked actively against each other. Part of me wanted to return the words, say them right back to him, but the other was afraid that him saying what he did was just another play in one of his twisted games.

I don't know what happened to the sketchbook and diary. When I finally worked up the courage to ask about them Corban had looked through me with cold, flat eyes. "What books?" As if they had never existed.

Whether he kept them hidden or destroyed them, I never saw them again. It made the matter of his affections more unnerving. Within the week he had become softer, kinder, gentle in the moments when he was not buried between my legs. It was so out of the ordinary that I daresay I missed his darker nature. At least I knew what to expect of him that way.

It made it all the stranger that he no longer hid himself from me. The wings, horns, red eyes and stone-grey skin were there to stay. Even the shadows had started to move with him. Every time he entered the room they would gather at his back, his feet, as writhing tendrils between his fingers. Any time he left me alone, they too would retreat.

Corban was up to something, and it was only a matter of time before I found myself trapped in another one of his games. I could feel it like an electric crackle in the air. Something powerful and dangerous was building.

I reclined in the rocking chair I'd moved from the front porch to the upper balcony. My feet were perched on the railing between two of the gargoyles. They both looked over the front drive. One's ear was broken off and the other had a great gash carved down its back. I had tried speaking to them but if they heard me, if they were even alive, they never answered.

The sun was making its slow descent behind the trees. Dark orange painted the sky with luminescent strokes of color. It really was beautiful here. Magical even.

I scratched the back of my neck, ran my hand into my hair and sighed. Corban had created quite the haven within his prison.

If this is what he could do with magic while bound, what could he do in Under? I'd been toying with the idea all week, what it would be like to leave everything behind and run away with him to the fae realm.

I thought to my books. To the one I'd read where the mortal girl was turned fae and married a High Lord. Or the other who was given a crown and a throne. Would I be granted immortality? Power? Did I want that?

I'd be an idiot to refuse Corban. Right?

Corban *was* Glamis. Without him, what would the manor even look like? Could I let a being as otherworldly as him slip through my fingers, and go on with my life alone, in order to hold onto something materialistic?

Something caught the corner of my eye. I looked over my shoulder to the parlor behind me. It had appeared so barren and dusty a moment ago, hadn't it? Another one of his tricks probably.

My phone buzzed.

Mom: *Are you going to stay angry at me forever or are you going to grow up?*

I rolled my eyes. Of course *I* was still the problem.

Me: *I'm not selling anything. Drop it.*

I hated matching her energy, but I was tired of being walked over. Being with Corban had given me a little bit more of a backbone. A little.

My phone buzzed.

Incoming call: *Mom*

"Who are you texting?" Corban's silent presence never failed to startle me.

"My mom," I said, bumping her call. I tipped my head back to look at him.

Corban leaned against the doorframe, taking up the entirety of the entryway. He was dressed in charcoal linen pants, belted, and a fitted short-sleeved sweater top. He spun a ring on his finger, one he had recently acquired that matched the chain around his neck. It looked like a signet ring, with a moth stamped into its face in sterling silver. Though I couldn't see the skull in its wings, I assumed it was a death's-head.

The scar above my tattoo itched. I ran my hand over it absentmindedly as he watched me with a tilted head.

"Do you miss her?" The aloofness didn't match the glint in his eyes.

"I told you I'm not going anywhere if that's what you're worried about."

The corner of his mouth twitched into an almost-smile before it jerked away. "You couldn't if you wanted to."

I sucked the back of my teeth. He swept around me and leaned against the railing, where he casually placed his hand atop the broken head of the gargoyle. He stroked his claws through the granite, chipping off flakes with each strike.

"Sometimes," I finally answered. "I love her, but she can be...difficult. She's been pressing me to sell off pieces of Glamis." I watched him carefully for any sort of reaction. A jump in the corner of his jaw was there, then gone. "I told her she can never have any part of Glamis, but she's greedy."

"Most humans are," he said. "Tell me, did you want Glamis before or after me?"

I met the challenge in his gaze. "I uprooted my entire life to come here. What do you think?"

He gave me a long look before turning his head to look out over the property. His eyes slid over the woods and then to the long drive that ended at the iron gate. "Perhaps you should give her a piece of it. Something that will satisfy her appetite."

I scoffed. "The will states–"

"I wrote the will, Sorcha." His eyes snapped to me momentarily before darting off again. "The part about the money at least. I was desperate, and I needed you."

I shut my mouth, which had dropped open. "Was any of it real?"

He held out his hand. I looked from his closed fist to his face before extending mine in turn. Gold coins spilled out of his palm, landing in mine. They bounced off each other and dropped to the ground. The moment he shut his hand the coins stopped flowing. I clutched what was left in my fist, looking about the ground which was now littered in gold.

A thistle topped with a pointed crown was carved into each piece. Script in a language I didn't recognize framed the image. The edges of the coin had a dull red coating.

"All of it was real. I had to make sure that whoever came to me would be willing to stay."

I didn't know whether to be offended by Corban's original treachery or grateful that he was finally opening up to me.

"You've been bribing me." I said thinly.

Corban purred, the sound sending a thrill through me. "I've been see-ing to your comfort and needs." The clack of his claws came to a stop as he made a sharp swipe against the granite, knocking one of the horns off the gargoyle. It hit the top of the banister before disappearing somewhere into the gathering darkness below. "Enjoy the spoils, Sorcha." He kissed the top of my head.

I caught his hand as he eased back. The faint light of the sun dipping behind the trees highlighted his sharp features. The shadows of night's arrival slithered over the banister all the way to his feet. He turned out his hand, palming one like you would a snake.

"Where are you going?" I asked.

He flicked his wrist, sending the shadow scurrying up his arm before tucking a piece of hair behind my ear. "I have a surprise for you. I need to finish preparing it."

I scrutinized him. Corban had been softer, but he wasn't exactly sweet. On instinct my hackles rose.

"Don't look at me like that," he chuckled. "You'll like it."

"Another game," I tested.

At that he grinned. It was broad and feline. "Would you rather have dinner with me in my home or take a walk through moonlight?"

"Care to elaborate?"

Corban shook his head.

I chewed on the inside of my lower lip. There wouldn't be a full moon for almost a month, which meant this option had something to do with magic. I was hungry, but I was far hungrier to understand just how powerful Corban was.

"A walk in the moonlight sounds nice." I said carefully.

I wasn't ready to go to Underland. I was only just starting to accept what Corban was, and then there was the bomb he had dropped on me about the will being crafted by his own hand. I needed time to process everything. And to figure out exactly what he was up to.

A dark glint sparkled in his beautiful eyes. "And so we shall." He ducked his head, brushing a kiss across my temple, before turning on his heel to leave me with the turmoil of my thoughts. "I'll return for you later this evening," he said over his shoulder.

I leaned back in the rocking chair, thinking. Whatever Corban was up to, I needed answers first. I grabbed hold of the balustrade as I lurched forward, to keep the curved legs from knocking into the ground. *Later this evening* could mean anything, I had to move *now*.

In the post-coital bliss that had followed Corban and my escapades in the library last week, I'd almost forgotten about the small object that had fallen from Macky's sketchbook. I'd only found it again the following afternoon, when finally trying to create a little order in the chaos of my bedroom by putting some clothes away.

A key.

A key that had been burning a hole in my pocket ever since. I'd been too afraid to pull it out lest it be one more thing Corban didn't want me to have. With the way he had reacted to the diary and the sketchbook, I suspected the key would be the same – or worse. And with him being stuck to me like glue, I hadn't been able to test my theory.

The only locked door in Glamis. I'd never thought much of it, but I should have. Obviously, I should have. I had tried to open it once on my first day and then forgotten about it completely. Until I found the key.

Locked doors hid secrets, and in a place like Glamis, ruled by a fae creature, it had to be something good.

Or terrible.

Tiptoeing down the stairs to the ground floor, I held my breath as I slid the key into the lock. I waited a few moments, heart thundering in my ears, but Corban didn't appear. Even without his looming presence, something about the key sliding home made my skin crawl.

I took a deep breath and turned my wrist. The door held, then gave way with a hiss of air. I pushed it all the way open.

The smell of something sweet filtered through the air. A sweetness that reminded me of overripe, rotten fruit. That smell, while vaguely pleasant... wasn't right. I knew it wasn't right and yet still I looked inside.

Steep, narrow stairs angled into darkness. I cast my eyes about and spied a switch on the inside wall. Flipping it did little, the weak light illuminating only the first ten steps, leaving the rest to be swallowed by the gloom.

Perhaps this door had been locked for a reason. I took a hesitant step down, my ears straining for any sound from Corban or from below me. The steps were so narrow I had to turn sideways to fit my foot on them comfortably. There was no railing to grab hold to, just dull red brick. No way this was a regular basement.

"Don't let me break my neck," I whispered.

BANG!

The sound was loud enough to make me jump straight out of my skin. My foot skidded and I dug my nails into the wall to keep from tripping to my death.

Bang! Bang! Bang! I whirled to face the still open door.

"Sorcha!" My name was followed by a series of garbled voices. "Do it, hurry up."

I couldn't tell if it was the same voice as the first but they sounded riled. I'd only made it down five steps, but I scrambled back to the top and darted for the front door where the angry voices were rising.

There was another bang against the door, splintering the frame. And just like that my fear was replaced with anger.

"Hey!" I yelled. Whoever thought they could come into my home and destroy it was in for a rude awakening.

The voices muffled. Someone peeked through one of the windows framing the door. Quint.

This fucker.

"Sorcha, let us in."

Us. Fuck, had he called the cops? Quint alone would have been bad enough but bringing back-up? For what? Fuck, he really did have balls of steel to show up here after Corban had nearly killed him.

Or he was just a straight-up fool.

I jerked open the door. Mottled, dark green bruising crept out from beneath Quint's collar. The red imprints of Corban's claws looked fresh, as if he were still bleeding from the strangulation attempt. Petechia spotted along his face, matching the red coloring in his corneas. If anything, time had only made Quint's battle wounds look worse.

Jeremy and three other men stood just behind him. One pulled his sun-faded baseball cap down to hide his face; his companion, a blonde, looked at the ground with him. The other wore a 90's band tee. In his white-knuckled grip was a wooden bat.

Before my mind could register the weapon Quint grabbed hold of me as the men pushed inside.

"What the fuck are you doing? Hey! Get out of my house!"

"Where is he?" Quint asked. He jerked me roughly against his body, his head swiveling left and right, his bloodshot eyes darting furiously.

"Come out, come out," one of the men called.

"I live alone, dickheads," I snarled.

Quint pulled me so hard that my feet skidded against the ground, the toes of my shoes clipping the uneven, broken floorboards as he dragged me over the threshold to the front porch. No– the floorboard were fine, perfect as always. I blinked away the wonky image of the house and whirled on him. "Let go. What the fuck is wrong with you?"

He stopped abruptly and looked down at me. "What the fuck is wrong with *me*? That fucking monster has been torturing you and when I tried to save you, he nearly killed me."

I turned into his body, trying to find leverage to break free. "He isn't torturing me."

"He's a monster, Sorcha. I saw him."

"He attacked you because you cornered me in a fucking bathroom. What did you think was going to happen?"

"I'm trying to save you," he shot back. He opened his mouth and closed it, gaping like a fish. "He has you under a spell, doesn't he? That's what this is."

"This isn't beauty and the fucking beast, Quint." How ironic that that is *exactly* what this was. The mortal woman had fallen for the grotesque beast, and an angry mob of men had shown up to do something about it. As far as fairy tales went, it was a classic.

Glass shattered from somewhere inside the house. I froze, allowing Quint to pull me farther away. Another sound of something breaking came from somewhere upstairs. They were destroying the house. They were going to destroy the house– my house!

I'd never felt rage before, but I supposed this was as good a time as any to experience it for myself. It swirled inside my belly and clawed its way around my heart, up my throat, into my face until my vision flooded red. Piercing talons sunk into the muscle within my chest, pumping my blood faster. And then everything went white hot.

The next second I was looking at Quint's shocked face. Maybe it was something I had said in the period of disassociation, or perhaps I had hit him. In any case I took the opening of the stunned, stupid look he wore and slammed my elbow as hard as I could into his nose. His head jerked back. A half second later, blood burst from his nose in an almost comically delayed reaction.

"Fuck!" He threw his hands up to his face as I slipped out of his hold and backed away.

"I will kill you before he does if you don't get your friends the *fuck* out of my house," I snarled.

"You fucking bitch. My fucking nose!" His words came out thick and wet. Quint winced as he spit out a glob of blood. Not that it helped, the torrent kept coming.

"Corban!" I screamed. I knew Corban would kill them, but they had to have known that when they walked in.

One of the men I didn't recognize, the blonde, appeared in the doorway, blocking it. His eyes were wide, as if the commotion outside had summoned him. He looked from me to Quint and back again. I span on my heel and ran.

After a garbled shout from Quint, the man followed. His heavy steps pounded on the front porch, keeping pace with mine as I cornered the house, heading for the garden. It was a gamble, but if I could lose him in the hedges, I'd be able to double back through the kitchen doors.

What had Corban said in the kitchen that day? That the garden answered only to him?

Let's hope it knew whose side I was on.

I was no athlete, but a burst of adrenaline sang through my blood when I heard his steps leave the hardwood of the porch as the man chased me onto the lawn. No, that was two people chasing me. Quint was right behind him. I didn't look to confirm, I just pushed harder.

I'd traced the patterns of the hedges from the parlor balcony plenty of times, but I hadn't actually fully explored the garden on foot, and as I broke through the entrance archway, under its fragrant wisteria, I tried not to let the sudden rush of dread slow me down. Pausing for only a heartbeat to get my bearings, I took off in the direction I instinctively knew would lead me to the archway closest to the kitchen.

"Sorcha!" Quint panted– spat. I could feel his anger, his humiliation, burning the back of my neck as they both chased me. Fuck he was fast, he'd overtaken the other guy and was right on my heels. Every time I turned a corner – I didn't remember the garden being so large when I'd looked down on it from the balcony – I thought I'd lose him, only to feel him closer than ever, and gaining.

The deadly flowers Corban had replaced Quint's bouquet with flashed past, blurring together as I sprinted on. Somewhere behind me and to my left, on the other side of the hedge, I heard a muffled sound and then a loud thump. Like someone had tripped and fallen.

The garden seemed to be urging me onward, an invisible thread connecting me to my goal despite the impossible turns I had made, the impossible distance I had covered. There was nothing natural about this silent, rustling space, but I was hoping I could use that to my advantage.

I made another right and there – the archway – a mirror to the one I'd entered from, rose in front of me. A burning stitch clawed up my side as I tried to force myself to find another gear. I was almost there. It was so close.

But Quint was still right behind me. And he was reaching for me.

Something snagged my ankle and I stumbled, my legs buckling a little as I almost wiped out.

Quint's momentum sent him sailing over the top of me, straight into the hedge. "Sorcha!" he shouted, trying to untangle himself from the weed-like fronds. "I'm trying to *help* you. What the fuck are you doing? Stop running away from me!"

A second stitch crawled up my other side. I couldn't fucking breathe but neither could I stop. I glanced back, just in time to see a gnarled root slipping back into the earth at the base of the hedge to my left. Had a fucking *hedge* just helped me evade Quint?

I supposed it wouldn't even be close the most insane thing to have happened to me at Glamis Manor.

Issuing a silent thanks to the garden I was back on my feet and running again before Quint could right himself, crossing the lawn that separated the house from the looming hedges and the secrets they clearly held.

My legs burned as I took the back steps two at a time and wrenched the French doors open, before whirling to slam and lock them behind me. Without waiting to see where Quint had gotten to, I blew through the dining area, into the living room, where I slid to an abrupt halt. The guy with the bat was mid-swing, and as he looked up, it slammed into the TV. On the screen, a man was laying on a pile of glass, choking on his own blood. Some horror rerun I had left on after breakfast.

Ironic.

I didn't think as I grabbed an ornate vase from the nearest shelf – one of Macky's priceless knickknacks I guessed – and charged straight at him. I wish I could have relished the look of surprise in his eyes. Too bad my body was moving faster than my brain, and swinging the vase at the center of his face before he could so much as raise an arm. *Crack!* I reaffirmed my grip and hit him again. On my third swing he caught my wrist and hurled me to the side.

I cried out as I landed, hard. The vase bounced on the rug. Perfectly intact, as that wasn't what had cracked. The man's face was covered in blood, and beneath that, it was a mask of fury.

"We're here to *help* you," he said. He twisted his grip on the bat.

Somewhere else in the house, I heard the sound of glass shattering.

I backed away, rising to my feet as I did. "I don't need your help. Besides, destroying my property is going to earn your ass a first-class ticket to jail."

"Quint said you were crazy." The man swiped a smear of blood from his cracked brow. "But he really downplayed how insane you are."

"Haven't you heard? Everyone that comes into Glamis goes nuts."

Hands grabbed me from behind the same moment the man swung at me. I let whoever it was take the brunt of my weight and dropped to the ground. I looked up just in time to see the smooth edge of the bat miss me and slam into Quint's chest.

He released me, winded, and I rolled away. As I stood for a second time, the temperature suddenly plummeted. Goosebumps sprouted over my arms as my hair began to stand on end.

Corban!

I bolted. I didn't need to see what he was going to do to these assholes. I made a desperate push for the closest door I knew could be securely locked.

Someone yelled from upstairs, a high-pitched scream that sounded anything but human, and definitely not like anything you'd expect from a grown man. It was followed by a loud bang and a storm of footsteps. I slid through the still open door of the basement, my vision laser focused as I whirled to close it behind me.

Quint's bloody face blurred as he charged through after me, but he didn't know about the narrow steps I was standing on. He made a grab for my arm but instead pushed me back, his momentum tipping us both into free fall.

I stared up in horror as the doorway grew smaller, and the first jarring impact of the steps drove into my back, whipping my head backwards. Completely out of control, I flipped head over heels. Down, down, crashing, and rolling, I made the horrible tumble down into darkness.

Chapter 28

CORBAN

The mirror rippled, distorting my reflection into an elongated face atop a long, coiled neck and scaled body. Quiet thrumming rattled the frame. There was a sudden burst of darkness across the glass, like frost climbing over steel, that revealed a pathway blanketed in snow and shadowed by twisted white trees.

"Underland," I breathed.

I reached a shaking hand toward the moonlight, my body bracing for the violent pain that had attacked me all the times before. My fingers passed through. Cold. Frigid cold met my fingertips. I pushed my hand farther.

My vision blurred as I twisted my hand one way and then the other. I knew it had worked – well, had *hoped* it had worked – but here was the proof. After so many years, so many lives, I was finally and truly free.

I pressed my chilled hand to my chest, letting the cold seep into my fast-beating heart. After all this time, the mirror that had gotten me into this mess was finally letting me go. I stepped forward, letting the cold seep into more of my body as old magik sank into my bones. It gripped my hand, pulling me forward like a lost love.

Something snapped me out of my daze. I don't know if it was a sound or a scent, but I was aware something had shifted. I turned my head, my fingers curling, still holding onto the other side. I opened my eyes slowly, not realizing that I had closed them.

A loud crash echoed from somewhere in the manor.

I looked down the white-lit path once more before taking a step back into the mortal world. My scaled reflection rippled in the mirror. "Don't go," it seemed to say. "Come back. Come home."

It was a scent, I realized. The house reeked of sweat, rage, and fear. Fear that did not belong to my Sorcha.

There was a loud crack from downstairs, but another, much closer crash came from Sorcha's bedroom. I stepped into the shadows, materializing beside a man. Oddly, he was hammering a small table into the mirror that hung across the room from her bed.

It was one of the five boys that had come to Glamis all those years ago. He was older now, as Quint was, as they all were. They thought I hadn't seen them hiding in the bushes, the scraggly things. One would expect that aging would have made them wiser. Would have kept them away from the horned monster and its lair.

Apparently not.

"What are you doing in my home?" A hiss trickled down my long throat as I shifted, letting my gnarled, taloned forelegs drop to the ground.

The man whirled, his eyes going wide. They flicked from my snarling face to the wings curving over my back. Shadows spilled beneath all four of my clawed feet. They wrapped around his legs, holding him in place as the color seeped from his thin face.

"You're real," he gasped.

"As real as the day you first saw me. Scarier now, aren't I?" I grinned, letting him see the sharp teeth behind my scaled maw.

"I'm sorry. I'm sorry. I didn't know you were real."

Sorcha's pained cry echoed up from somewhere below.

I had not felt such fury since the day the mortal man tricked me into stone – when he had bound me to this godsforsaken manor – but in this moment, when a pained sound not of my own making came from the woman I loved, I grew white hot with rage.

The man tried to move. His body lurched, but my shadows held him firm. He wailed. There is something particularly delicious about the moment when a man loses all his inhibitions and really *screams*.

He tried to shield himself with the table, but I cracked my horns through it like it was an eggshell. Somewhere behind me was the sound of someone running. They weren't going to be fast enough. Nothing was faster than my strike. I opened my fanged jaws and snapped the man's head from his neck, ripping it free and swallowing it down as I turned to face whoever was stupid enough to come to his rescue.

The second man was already retreating by the time I turned around. I shot after him.

Magik coursed through my blood, my veins. It sang through every part of me that had been denied its beauty for so long. I let it devour all mortal flesh and let my true form expand. My claws crushed the floorboards as I shifted and slipped into the walls of the house, while he ran further into its depths, trying to escape me. No matter, I relished a panicked chase.

I flowed through the bones of the manor in pursuit, not giving much thought to who he was or why he was there. He was in the way of me getting to Sorcha. He had something to do with her getting hurt, and someone who hurt Sorcha would *not* be allowed to live.

I sent a ripple of my power forward, and the door of the bedroom he had been running for slammed in his face. He darted to the right, but I slammed that door shut too.

"Run, run as fast as you can," I cajoled.

I emerged from the shadows behind him and dropped my head down, letting my wings spread wide so that they blocked his exit. Foolish as he was, he tried to dart past me. I twisted my head around slowly to follow him, letting him think he could wriggle away. The moment he cleared the underside of my wing I lunged, sinking my teeth into his shoulder.

He let out a broken curse that was cut off entirely when I shook him violently, spraying blood across the walls.

"Who are *you* to come into my home?" I asked, dropping him. Gorgeous, pink fleshy tissue bloomed from the tear in his shoulder. I snaked forward and bit down again, snapping the tendon and earning myself a shuddering scream. "To make my woman bleed?"

"I didn't. I didn't touch her. Holy fuck, don't kill me. He talked us into coming." A dark stain spread across the front of his pants.

I curled my lips. "I can smell her on you," I seethed.

"Please don't." His breath was coming in ragged pants. For as much blood as he was losing, he was surprisingly coherent. He rolled onto his belly, and using his good arm as leverage, tried to crawl away. I followed him, clacking my claws together intentionally to enjoy the way he flinched at the sound.

"It has been months since I tasted flesh." I stepped on his back, forcing him to the ground with a sharp talon that I slowly embedded in his spinal cord. The man's scream sent shivers down to the tip of my tail. "So allow me to thank you for sating my hunger."

The crunch of his skull beneath my teeth was delicious. I licked his flesh from my lips, wishing there was more time to savor him, before tossing the body to the side. Blood spattered over the hallway in a gory arch, painting the walls crimson.

I twisted my way down the stairs and through the foyer, slithering across the short hallway that opened into the living room. Oil-slick trails of magik seeped in my wake. It thrummed within my blood. I flicked my tongue, tasting the air. The overpowering, metallic tang of blood was a living thing. Not hers, and yet it sharpened my fangs into vicious points.

A third man was striding out of the kitchen, a bat in one hand and a cloth in the other, which was pressed to his forehead. He stopped dead at the sight of me. Unlike the other two, he didn't try to run. The spike in his scent revealed how desperately he wanted to, but he remained still, his grip on the bat tightening.

I pulled back the scales, forcing them beneath my skin. My wings twisted backwards and down, finding their way beneath flesh too, where they wrapped lovingly around my bones. I allowed the horns and hellfire in my eyes to remain.

"We should have killed you," the man said. "We should have come back and killed you."

I flicked a piece of debris from my shoulder as I stalked toward him. "You could have tried."

The man threw the towel at me and with speed faster than I anticipated, gripped the bat with both hands and swung it toward my face. I had just enough time to dodge it. The wood collided with one of my horns instead of what would have been my jaw. I grabbed the bat and pulled him toward me with a vicious yank.

"I do love it when they fight," I taunted.

It drove the man into a frenzy. When he couldn't jerk the bat free from my grip he threw a punch into my throat. The sound of his knuckles fracturing was a sweet symphony.

I grabbed the collar of his shirt as a wave of pain blossomed over his face.

"W-what the f-fuck are you?" he sputtered.

I hunched forward, lowering my face to his so that our lips nearly brushed. "I am the foundation of this house. I am the stone heart that beats within these walls. I am the grotesque that steals your loved ones. I—" I ran my forked tongue over his face, "—am the monster of Glamis Manor."

My shadows, which had been waiting patiently, struck. They pulled the man's arms and legs apart, suspending him in midair. I slid my hand down his chest, letting my claws rest over the galloping heart beneath.

"And you, my sorry friend," I said, looking up at him as I lifted him higher into the air. The red light of my eyes cast his face in an eerie glow. "Are a dead man."

I thrust my hand into his chest, through the breastbone until my fingers wrapped around the pumping muscle. He was still screaming when I pulled his heart from his chest.

The defiant light dimmed from his eyes with the final exhale from his lungs. I released him and watched with satisfaction as he crumpled to the floor. I took in the blood drenched organ in my hand. "Pathetic," I muttered, crushing it with a flex of my claws before I dropped that too.

I cocked my head, listening for any indication of where Sorcha might be. I cursed silently that I had not sensed the commotion sooner. I'd been consumed by the mirror, by my plan to bring her with me. Too intoxicated by Under's pull that I hadn't felt a damn thing. Gods, what would have happened had I let it take me completely? There was no guarantee I would be allowed back into the mortal world once I crossed over.

I stepped into the kitchen, retracing the steps of the dead man. Glass littered the floor, and the French doors, their windowpanes completely shattered, were thrown wide open.

I tasted the air. Sorcha's scent was everywhere, laden with fear and anger. I could tell she'd been through here only minutes before.

"Guys! Where the fuck are you? Get me *the fuck* out of here!" A voice trickled in from outside. I loped down the back steps, pausing at the latticed western entrance to the Belladonna Garden, from where the panicked voice rose again from behind the hedges.

"Guys! Jeremy! I'm not fucking around!" Even through the tightly woven hedges I could taste his terror.

A slow smile spread across my face, ripping the seams of my human mask as my scales revealed themselves once more. I could hear my prey pacing, hear the frantic beating of his heart. Beneath his sweat I could smell Sorcha's desperation. She was, or had been, in there with him.

I ran my tongue over my sharpened teeth as I strode into the garden. The hedges shifted, poisonous plants bowing as they parted, opening a direct path to the sweat-slicked man. He had his back to me as he stared helplessly at the impenetrable vegetation before him, his torn t-shirt damp and muddied. I could see the rashes blooming on his pale, bloody skin from the thorns and barbs that had already started their vicious work. I was tempted to pounce immediately, to drive my talons through his skull, but the predator's sensibility pulsing through my veins urged patience. I had not hunted like this in a long while, and the game of it thrilled me.

"Lost, are we?" I did not bother to contain the lethal rage and hunger that laced my voice.

The man whirled, his hands clenching into fists. I heard the air leave his lungs as he looked me over, the assessment made all the more delicious by just how quickly the blood drained from his cheeks as his gaze locked onto my face. A face that I knew was crooked and wrong, the costume of my human flesh tearing ever further as my true form pressed outward. I allowed my eyes to shift, the blood-red light of my irises casting my prey in an unholy glow. I let the length of my spine uncoil as my tail swept behind me. Part man, part monster, a patchwork of beauty and horror.

Pure, delectable fear flooded the space between us. My mouth started watering.

"Where is she?" I let power drip into my voice, its echo filling the space between the hedges, which seemed to lean in in anticipation.

The man stumbled back against the hedge, his arms spreading wide in an attempt to hold himself upright. His mouth gaped, opening and closing dumbly. I advanced until I was right in front of him, until I could see the tears gathering in the corners of his blue eyes.

I took his chin between my claws. "Where is Sorcha?"

"H-house," he gasped. "S-she'sss in the house. –got out," he stammered. "I-i can't get out. She d-did."

Annoyance flickered through me. "How many of you are here?"

"F-five. P-please." One tear, and then another fell down his dirt-scuffed cheeks. I followed them down, making an assessment of my own. He was filthy, it was clear he'd fallen and been lost to the maze, whereas I knew Sorcha would have been welcomed through without hesitation.

Five. So, there was only one left...one I suspected was with Sorcha unless she had evaded him too.

The bastard would beg for death when I got my talons on him.

But first...

"Shh," I crooned, cupping my hand over the man's mouth. I pulled at the magik in my blood, at the traces of it that lay buried deep within the mortal realm's soil. The hedge shivered behind the man, parting and then wrapping around him like a lover's embrace. His eyes were impossibly wide. It sounded like he screamed the word "please" into my palm.

"You should never have come here."

Roots snaked out of the earth to trap his wrists and ankles. They threaded around his thighs, his chest, tightening in a lethal embrace. He lurched, his back arching violently. Another muffled scream graced the underside of my palm.

I smiled, flashing my fangs. "Hurts, doesn't it? People don't give plants nearly enough credit these days, but they can be quite vicious. Quite effective in the ways they usher in death."

I lifted my hand from his face as he started to shudder, in order to best hear the cough that rattled his lungs as he fought for breath. I leaned forward and pressed my mouth against his, slipping my forked tongue down his throat to taste the terror, the poison that now burned through his veins. The man's body convulsed. The hedges crushed him further, and I heard the sweet sound of ribs cracking. I withdrew slowly, savoring death's flavor as blood bubbled over his lips and down his chin. His lips parted as if to make some final, useless plea.

In place of words, elegant stems dotted with white flowers sprouted from the bloody hole of his mouth, reaching for my kiss. I brushed my thumb over them, grazing the fresh blooms of foxglove.

The man stopped shaking. His empty eyes looked almost as red as my own, such were the veins that had burst around their irises. The flowers danced in the last shuddered exhale of his breath.

Smiling to myself, I turned back to the house as the hedge continued to pull him back. In, in, in it dragged him, until all was once more still and silent, and no trace of the blue-eyed man remained.

I slid my bloodied hand through my hair as I entered Glamis once more, senses expanding in every direction in search of Sorcha. Stepping back into the foyer, my eyes traveled over the destroyed and gaping front door, its wood warped and splintered. I kept turning. There, in the middle of the hallway, another door stood open.

A fucking door that was supposed to be locked.

My blood simmered as I stalked forward. Where had she found the spare key? Oh, that little liar was in big fucking trouble.

I stopped at the top of the steps as the smell hit me. *His* smell.

"You stupid little boy," I hissed. Of course it had been Quint to lead the posse. He'd fancied himself the hero, Sorcha's white knight in her twisted fairy tale. How unfortunate that he was too slow. How foolish of him to be born human. I couldn't wait to see his face when I showed him that in the real world, the monster eats the hero every time. That these so called 'happily ever afters' were nothing more than fiction.

Chapter 29

SORCHA

Everything hurt. Pain radiated from my back, my ribs, my forehead. The drop down the stairwell had been so long I was pretty sure I'd hit every part of my body multiple times. I vaguely remembered Quint careening over me mid summersault.

I blinked, letting my eyes adjust to the darkness. I wiggled my fingers and toes and slowly, very slowly, tried to move the rest of my body. As far as I could tell, nothing was broken, just banged to Hell and back.

I gripped something cool and smooth to my right as I forced myself to sit up. Something rigid was digging into my back. It felt like I had landed in a pile of wood, rocks maybe? Whatever it was, was sharp and jagged.

The sickly smell was more intense down here. So putrid I had to cover my mouth with the back of my hand to keep from gagging.

Shapes slowly bled from the darkness. I could see mounds of something at the bottom of the steps, to the side— that might be a table. I pressed the heels of my hands against my eyes and blinked again.

"Oh fuck," I hissed as I shifted to my aching knees.

Somewhere to my left Quint answered with a groan.

I had to get up. The light at the top of the stairs was my only goal. Once I got up there, I could lock Quint in and deal with him later.

I braced myself as I eased onto my hands and knees. One of my hands slipped into something wet, and mushy. I jerked back on instinct as I fought off the urge to imagine what exactly would feel like that. Something round with two small, evenly spaced depressions met the underside of my other hand. A bowling ball?

Macky had been an odd lady. Perhaps whatever was down here was a part of weird hobby. Yes, that's what it was. Something weird. But not too weird. Weird enough, though, that I didn't want to think about it.

I stood just as a weak light popped on.

Quint was standing off to the side with his phone held out in front of him. He swiped his thumb across the screen until a brighter, smaller light illuminated on the back of his phone. He panned it in front of him. I took a step to the side, hoping to somehow slip past him before he saw me, when my shoe scraped one of the hard things against the ground. That light swiveled toward me, momentarily blinding me.

"Get that out of my face." I held my hand up.

Quint inhaled sharply but he didn't move the light. "We have to go," he said.

"You have to go. Do you have any idea what you've done? I was just going to call the cops on you before, but you have *no idea* what Corban is going to do to you."

"Do you? Do you know what he's capable of?"

I reached for the phone, trying to shove it out of my face. "I've been living with him for the last month. I know exactly what he'll do when he finds you. He would have killed you if I hadn't stopped him the other night."

Quint grabbed hold of my wrist and pulled me to him. I snagged the front of his shirt as I stumbled into him. "You know about this?"

"If you don't stop grabbing onto me!" I slammed my fist into his chest while simultaneously trying to free my arm. "I'm going to *break* your nose this time." I wound my fist back to do just that.

"Sorcha."

Something in the way he said my name made me halt. So hushed and gentle, like he didn't want to startle me. There was no aggression, no bite to his words.

I turned, following the dusty path of the light through the blackness. Stacks of greyish white objects littered the floor. At first it looked like rubble. Weird, elongated rubble. Some were more rounded, with uneven holes in the middle.

My stomach dropped.

Not sticks and stones. Skulls and bones. These were bodies.

I looked down where I imagined I had been sprawled out moments before. A man, or what used to be a man lay propped against God knows what else. Chunks of his rotten flesh were missing, like they had been bitten out. Distinct holes marred his torso, torn clean through the blood-encrusted overalls and flannel shirt. His arms were stripped clean of flesh and tendons. His *head* was missing.

A pair of yellow leather gloves jutted out of his pocket.

The groundskeeper. The man that had been sent to ready the house for me. The one the librarian had mentioned.

Bile rose from my gut and I hunched forward as I hurled. What I had compared to the scent of off fruit earlier had been the sweet decay of bodies. Quint grabbed the top of my shoulder as another wave of nausea kicked me in the stomach, and I hurled again.

"Come on," Quint hissed. He pulled me back, but I couldn't move. Not when I was still taking in just how many bones were scattered around us. How many bodies were there?

Quint tugged me harder and I slapped his hand away.

"Sorcha, what the fuck? We have to go." Quint rounded in front of me and tried pushing me instead.

My breath was shallow, too shallow. Every time I blinked, I saw a new face, or what was left of one. Another burst of air from my lungs turned white in front of my lips. It was cold. So cold down here in the dark.

I turned.

Where was she?

Quint cursed under his breath. He followed me across the room as I flailed amongst the bodies. Death burrowed its scent up my nostrils. Where was she?

Quint grabbed me and started to pull me back to the light waiting for us at the top of the stairs.

"Let go," I whispered even as I let him drag me to the steps. Where was she? Where was Macky?

"You're going into shock, Sorcha. Let me help you. Will you stop fucking fighting me," he ground out when I twisted in his grip and kicked him in the shin.

"Let her go."

The voice poured down the stone steps, radiating power. Corban's tall silhouette dominated the doorway to the ground floor, blocking all but a glimmer of light. He took each step slowly, deliberately. His feral red gaze slid from Quint to me. He looked my body up, down, and up again as he made his assessment. What must I look like amongst the horror? He had a strange look in his eye I'd never seen before.

Quint's grip tightened on my arm again, drawing Corban's attention back to him.

"You're a fucking monster," he said.

Corban cocked his head. "You've always known that. It's why you ran away the first time." Blood was splashed across his face and hands. In the twinkling light of Quint's phone, I could see it glistening on the black fabric of his clothes.

Quint must have noticed it the same moment I did. "Where are they? Where are my friends?"

"Don't worry, you'll be joining them soon." That look simmering in the crimson light of his eyes, it was cold rage. Icy and lethal, so much more terrifying than the fury that had ruled him the last time he tried to kill Quint. And we all knew it.

Quint audibly swallowed. "Let us go, and I'll never come back. Let me take her with me. We'll never speak a word of this."

"A little late for that, isn't it? If it wasn't for your *words*, your little friends wouldn't have joined you on your, what shall we call this, *quest?* That's what this is, isn't it? You thought you were saving a damsel in distress?" Corban's teeth flashed. They seemed larger, sharper than I remembered them being. "I hate to break it to you, but the princess likes the monster."

Quint let go of my arm and dug into his waistband. He pulled a dark wooden hilt from the holster hidden beneath his jeans and held it out. Didn't he know a knife wasn't going to do anything? The blade would shatter before Corban did.

"He's stone," I said quietly, almost to myself.

Quint turned to look at me, his brows furrowed. His eyes flickered between the two of us before they narrowed in on me. His lip curled, as if he had just realized something, something that disgusted him.

He was shockingly fast for a human. The movement snapped me out of my daze, but I was still too slow to block him. Before I could lift a hand to defend myself Quint had grabbed me by the shoulder and hauled me against him. The blade of his knife pressed against my throat.

He was using me as a literal shield against Corban's rage.

Somehow that was still less frightening than the creature that stood before us. Corban cocked his head unnaturally, the points of his horns glinting in the dimness. Red light brushed the top of his cheeks where his eyes quite literally glowed. It made the blood splatters on his face shine like rubies.

"You want her, you can have her, but you're going to let me go first," Quint said.

"Quint, you fucking–" I made to grab hold of his fist, but it only served to push the blade closer. I felt the sharp sting as it split my skin. "You *fool.*"

"Shut up, *shut up,*" Quint hissed. "You know what this *thing* is, and you don't seem to mind him or whatever fucked up shit he gets up to in this *creepy* fucking house." His voice was shaking now. "He's a demon. He's possessed you or something. So," he directed his words to Corban now. "You let me go, or I kill her."

Corban's head tilted downward as he let out a menacing hiss. He seemed to be looming larger, filling the cellar, sucking all the air from the room. "No more saving the damsel?"

I opened my mouth to spit some choice words of my own, but the blade pressed harder, and I swallowed them down. Surely Quint wasn't stupid enough to try and bargain for his life. Not when the evidence of Corban's lack of mercy was piled all around us. *There had to be the remains of one hundred bodies in this cellar, or more.*

"Fuck no," he spat. "She's clearly as crazy as every other bitch that's lived in this house if she would choose you."

Oh no he didn't...

Consequences be damned. I threw my elbow back into his gut with as much force as I could muster. The impact jolted the blade across my throat, a warning bite, but Quint only tightened his grip. I could feel him steeling himself.

He was serious. The notion chilled me.

The corners of Corban's mouth pulled back, cutting farther into his cheeks. "Over you? Of courssse sssshe would." He hissed long and loud, his breath steaming in the air as the temperature dropped violently.

Corban struck faster than I could blink. His face turned scaly and ghastly. Long fangs flashed a breath from my own face as he lunged.

I felt Quint's arms tense for the impact, the one that held the knife jerking violently as I instinctively turned inward, trying to create some space where there was none–

Too slow. I was too slow as Corban ripped Quint away from me. As Quint's clenched hand ripped a white-hot line across my throat.

Something hot and wet sprayed over the left side of my face as Quint let loose a mangled scream.

I slapped my palm against my neck, but the wetness burst between my fingers. *Blood.* It was my *blood.*

Fog floated from my lips as I exhaled sharply, then gasped for air. Air that tasted like metal.

Sounds seemed somehow muffled. Somewhere, it sounded so far away, was the song of metal striking stone. *The knife...*

There was the briefest sound of a struggle, then an awful, wet tearing sound. Wetness splashed the other side of my face.

My eyes drifted to my right, fixed on the figure hunched over Quint's body. The figure who had just relieved him of his throat. The figure–

"Corban." Except I couldn't get the word out. It felt choked. Why did his name taste so funny?

All fire evaporated from his slitted eyes when Corban lifted his head. He let Quint's body fall and grabbed hold of me before I could follow suit. He enveloped me, pressing a cold hand to the side of my neck.

"He won't take you from me," he said. "Sorcha. Love, look at me."

Corban's other hand gripped my chin, dragging my gaze away from Quint's jerking body. His touch was so very cold and sticky. The rush of an ocean filled my ears. For a brief moment, I felt like I was back in Miami, surrounded by the waves and the noise of the city. That this was all a sick nightmare.

I shut my eyes. They say manifestation can make anything happen if you believe in it strongly enough. I manifested, wished, that I was in the white linen sheets of my bed, in my room overlooking the harbor. That when I opened my eyes, I would see tall glistening skyscrapers. Any moment now I would hear my mother's condescending tone from somewhere down the hall.

"Sorcha."

I blinked. I was floating toward a light at the end of a tunnel somewhere high above.

The glow of Corban's eyes drew me in as he looked down on me. "Let me take you away from this place of darkness. From this nightmare. Will you let me?"

The darkness never left. The rich metallic bubble of blood was still in my nose. Yes. I needed to leave. I needed to get out of there. Get away to some place better. Get away from the violence and evil that was gripping my soul so hard it would permanently bruise once it released me.

If it ever released me.

I nodded into the hand still pressed against my throat.

"Good girl," Corban said.

The room slanted as we fled the darkness and turned the corner that led upstairs. I swear I could see a body lying in the hallway. I grabbed the front of Corban's soaked shirt. Trying desperately to hold onto something. What? I didn't know.

The house seemed to waver with each step he took. I looked on, dazed, as the walls splintered; the fine wallpaper seeming to tear off in strips as mold bloomed across it. The marble of the columns dulling, cracking. Tilted, empty frames decorated what had just minutes before been the glowing, lush entryway. The whole wretched scene flickered beneath dusty lights.

Another step. The manor snapped into pristine focus, all order restored, before the illusion faltered again, shuddering into an image of ruin.

Bright crimson splashed the crumbling ceiling and walls of the top floor. The scene seemed to pulse: perfect, broken, gilded, decrepit. In both versions, the red stains remained.

Red footprints leading in the opposite direction we had come stained the rug and floor. Corban reaffirmed the pressure on my neck, forcing my head tighter against his chest. He must have come through here before. But that couldn't be right. Those footprints weren't from a pair of boots, they were clawed, and there were *so many*.

"Gods," Corban whispered. "I'll forgive the centuries you have forsaken me if you *do not fail me now*."

How strange, Corban was *praying*.

I'd never seen him like this. Fierce determination and desperation were carved into the striking grey lines of his face. I was the one that was supposed to be frightened, not him.

Shadows flickered in my peripheral and there at the top of the stairs stood the grand gilded mirror. Or it had once been a mirror. There was only a subtle reflection of me and the winged grotesque against a snow-covered landscape, white-blanketed trees, and darkness.

Corban's grip on me tightened as he lengthened his stride. I braced for impact with the glass but was met instead with an all-consuming, soul-fraying cold.

And then there was nothing at all.

Chapter 30

SORCHA

The steady drum of rain pulled me from oblivion. The sound of it grounded me, slowly reeling me back to the waking world. I inhaled crisp, cool air. The sudden blast of it in my lungs made me realize how very cold it was.

I burrowed farther into the covers that were tucked around my body, cocooning me in a warm embrace. Somewhere down the hall I heard dishes clinking.

I didn't remember Mom popping over, but I wasn't surprised that she had let herself in. It would explain the drop in the thermostat.

I took a deep breath and stretched, finding the courage to open my eyes and face the day.

There were no pristine white walls of my old bedroom in Miami. Nor was there the terracotta sheets and old antique furniture of Glamis. I lurched upright, the movement bringing such a sharp, stabbing pain to my throat that immediately my hand went flying to it.

The room was a soft dove grey, save for the black vaulted ceiling, which glistened like starlight. From it hung the most magnificent chandeliers

I had ever seen, their strands woven together like spiderwebs. Little diamonds of light dotted each thread like droplets of glowing dew. Fur rugs covered the midnight stone of the floor, which shone with the same luster as the ceiling.

Three arched cathedral windows graced one of the walls. Their iron framing was set with countless red jewels, simmering like coals.

I pulled my knees up to my chest in the center of the bed. A bed that was larger than any I'd ever seen. With black sheets, black furs, black throws. Black everything. Everything glowed with subtle magic. It was perfect. Ominously perfect. A gorgeous, harmonious haven all cast in pale, gentle light.

Moonlight.

That's when it all came rushing back.

I ran my fingers over my neck, blindly feeling for the tear in my throat Quint had made.

A dread weight settled over my shoulders. I clutched the sheets against my chest and followed that thread of fear to the far corner of the room where a stone-colored beast hunched in shadow.

Glowing red eyes gazed back at me.

I held my breath as the hulking shadow moved. Its body and legs were long, with bulging muscles. Giant leathered wings flexed, and the grey scales covering its flesh rippled and sparkled in the chandelier's light. It unwound a great deal, revealing just how massive the monster really was. It wasn't a dragon, but it favored one. If dragons had ghastly faces and crooked, stalking movements. It was grotesque. With each step forward, something about it changed.

I pressed my back against the headboard as all sense fled me. I was frozen. My heart slammed against my ribcage, threatening to burst free the closer the thing prowled.

The beast shifted again and this time it looked a bit more like a man. Not quite human, with its grey skin and spiraling horns, but enough like one that I recognized him.

I let out a startled gasp when he stopped at the edge of the bed. He looked more beautiful than I had ever believed he could be, a stark contrast from the horror he had been seconds before. His hollow cheeks were fuller, his hair sleek and shining. He was larger, his torso thicker and shoulders prouder. Even the red of his eyes shone a little brighter. He was magnificent.

I already knew but still I asked, "What have you done?"

"I brought you home," he breathed. He smiled softly, something like relief flashing in his eyes when he sat at the end of the bed and I didn't move away. "I brought you to Underland."

I looked at his very normal hand resting on top of the covers. How easy it was for him to change faces. How incredibly foolish I had been to trust anything about him.

Heart in my throat, I shook my head. "I didn't want to come here. I told you I wanted Glamis."

"You played my game," he said with a tilt of his head.

"What game? Murdering those men? All those." Oh my gosh, the bodies. There were so many bodies. "Those people," I choked.

Corban sucked the back of his teeth. He cocked one brow high. "Would you rather have dinner in my home or walk in moonlight? Don't you recall?"

"You tricked me." Tears filled my words with moisture, making them thick and heavy.

"Oh love." I recoiled when he reached for my face. A look of disapproval pinched his lips, distorting his perfect features. "Either answer would have brought you here. Underland is my home and moonlight graces my land. I saved you."

"He was trying to protect me from you!"

"That boy almost killed you, or have you already forgotten the way he sliced your throat open? Weak men will destroy anything that scares them. They have no care who gets hurt in the process, so long as they save their own asses. You should be thanking me."

"What you did was monstrous. *You* are a *monster*." As if I didn't know that already; hadn't known it since he knocked on my front door and chased me through the house.

Corban slunk up the bed until he was straddling me. His palms pressed into the wood on either side of my head. "Yesss," he hissed, long and low so the word dragged out. "A monster you willingly let in to your body, your mind, your heart, and out into the world. I never tried to hide what I was from you." He gripped my chin when I looked away from him, forcing me to stare into those pulsing red orbs. "You gave yourself to me of your own free will. You knew you were fucking a monster the entire time, well before you grabbed hold of my wings and horns when I was deep inside you."

He swiped a tear from my cheek that had escaped one of my eyes.

"What are you going to do with me? Will you finally kill me? Like you did everyone else?"

Corban took a deep breath. "Love, I never planned on killing you. Do you want the truth?"

What truth could be worse than the horror I had already experienced? Than all the murders I had seen evidence of?

"The truth is I planned to leave you in Glamis, transfer the curse from me to you." He ran his fingers along the side of my head, pulling at my hair carefully as he parted the strands. "You see, Glamis is nothing without me. It wasn't just the food and treasures I made real; it was the house itself. I was the living beating heart that pumped blood into that cursed place. Without me, without a soul, Glamis does not exist. There was nothing for you to keep, without me there."

His eyes flickered back and forth between mine as he continued to stroke my hair. "Your grandmother was a keen woman. She knew about me. Well, not *me* exactly but she knew about fae. About real fae, not the silly little princes in your story books with pretend powers and soft romances. Fae that come from Underland, from the Seelie and Unseelie courts.

"'Mad Macky' they called her." The corner of his mouth cocked at that. "Maxine was perhaps the smartest woman I ever met. She was a challenge I'll admit I was sore to lose to."

All the times my mother had complained about Grandma Macky, had she known? Had she even entertained for a moment that there might have been truth to her rants about monsters and ghouls? Was the woman in the window my mother told me of as a child real? Was the cruel nickname, given in spite, based on nothing at all?

"Did you kill her?" I asked.

The stroke of Corban's hand slowed, his touch gentled. "As much as I would have liked to, she stole that opportunity from me. If she'd been more thorough with the hiding spot of her will, perhaps you would have escaped me too."

"I don't understand. If you needed me to break the curse, to take your place in Glamis, then how am I—" I looked around the room, "—here?"

A low hum purred inside Corban's chest. It sounded like stones grating against each other. "Because I left a piece of Glamis inside of you." His fingers crept to the back of my scalp, down to the slope of my neck, caressing gently.

I dropped my hand to my stomach in horror.

Corban chuckled. "No. No Silly Sorcha." He stroked the back of my neck affectingly. "It is rare for fae to have children and much harder to do so with a human. No, I left it somewhere safe. It was the only way I could pass my curse onto you and bring you with me. Don't worry, it can't be removed. I made sure of that. Our night out solidified my theory."

Rain splattered against the windows. The storm had picked up rather quickly. A flash of lightning brightened the room as if to emphasize a point.

"And now?"

"Now I am going to make you a queen." He grinned, flashing long pointed fangs, so long they touched his lower lip. "Queen of the Unseelie. While you were resting, I was getting everything ready. I had some unfinished business to take care of, but with that now out of the way the throne is ready for my ascension. For our ascension."

"You're a prince?" I choked out. So he hadn't been lying to Rosaline all those years ago.

He grinned again. "A king, now, my love." His fingers wrapped around the back of my neck. He settled himself closer to me. The cool breath exhaling from his lips fanned against mine.

"I'm scared," I said. "Of this place, of you." Corban had always scared me, but this had finally driven the knife home. I had died, or almost died. I assumed all five men had died, not to mention the numerous bodies piled in the basement.

The entire time those bodies had been there I had been fucking him. I had been letting Corban inside of me while his curse infected and condemned me. I played each of his games willingly, tying my soul to his. His to mine.

"Don't be scared, Sorcha. I love you. I'm going to love you forever. For all of time." He nudged my nose with his. Instinct had me tipping my face up so that it was our lips that touched next.

"How long is that? Can I go back? My mother." *My mother.* Guilt slammed into me like a ton of bricks. We had always had a strained relationship but the idea of never seeing her again gutted me. Worse was that she would never know what had happened to me if I didn't go back. I didn't want that to haunt her. What horrible things she would come up with? Would the town spin something as tragic as Rosaline's story?

"A long time," he said with a kiss. "Your home is here, Sweet Sorcha. My changeling giving her life up for mine. To save me."

Corban pulled the covers down, pulling me with them. He kissed me and this time I kissed him back. "Saint Sorcha," he said, dropping his lips to my throat and collarbone. With each kiss he called me a new name, erasing all the crazy names that were given to the mad women of Glamis Manor. "Savior Sorcha."

I opened my legs when his tongue slid over the sensitive line of my neck. His cool body pressed to mine. He must have glamoured his clothes away. Or had he been bare this whole time?

"Successor Sorcha. You will make a fine queen."

Queen.

The title had a pretty ring to it. As scared as I was, I could not deny the thrill I felt. How my heartbeat changed from its gallop of terror to a steady thud of morbid fascination.

All I had wanted was a place to call my own. I only had to last one year, and I would have inherited Grandma Macky's wealth. A wealth I imagined was as real as the manor itself. A work of fiction, a fairy tale too good to be true.

I slid my hand along Corban's face and pushed him back gently so that I could see him. Beneath the red was the faint jade green of his eyes, a reflective glow that heated as he looked back at me. He kissed my wrist before I let my touch travel up to the horns on his head.

The broad span of his hand slid over my knee, pausing briefly so that his thumb could brush the scar of his ownership, before sliding up my thigh as he pushed my legs farther open.

Maybe I had been a little mad even before Corban, what with my obsession with the dark and macabre. Was this not just the start of my own, twisted, happily ever after?

I arched into his mouth as it grazed my chest.

The final thing I knew about Grandma Macky was that she loved her family. I could feel it in the cold yet hot press of Corban's body to mine. That the only reason she had shut out her children was to keep them safe from the monster that haunted her halls. Her cruelty is what drove my mother down south to Miami, so that Macky might never meet her one and only grandchild. Just as Grandma Macky had wanted. Not because she didn't love me, but to keep me safe from the monster that now coiled around me.

"What's going on inside that pretty head of yours?" Corban crooned. He hovered over my stomach, poised to travel even lower.

Grandma Macky wasn't batshit crazy. *She* had been the saint. She had given up her life to save everyone else. She would have succeeded if Corban had not been equally desperate. Corban would have been forgotten had I not been such a fool.

"What happens now?" I asked.

Corban slid his tongue across my naval. "We live," he answered. "Free. You and me, for all eternity."

I had let Corban lead me this far, what other choice did I have left but to accept my fate?

"Tell me you love me," he murmured against my center. His wicked forked tongue flicked between my thighs, tugging a sigh from deep within my soul. Was it even my soul anymore?

I had never been touched by anyone with such cruel affection. Had never had a man worship me the way Corban did. I had watched every horror movie ever made and had been working my way through every book, but none of them could have prepared me for this. Even the dark romances with their twisted happily ever afters had lied.

Free? Hardly.

They don't tell you when the villain gets the girl, the crown and jewels he offers her are just pretty silver shackles in disguise.

And yet, the weight of them wasn't as heavy as I imagined it would be. Corban was a horrible, wicked creature that I gladly welcomed with the arch of my hips against his mouth. His mouth that had been covered in blood the last time I saw him. He caressed me with those possessive hands that had killed. For me.

"Tell me," he said. One split of his forked tongue slid inside of me while the other lapped at my clit. It was something he hadn't done before and as I looked down I realized why. He had let a little more of his costume slip to reveal a much wider; much longer tongue. He took hold of my hip with a clawed hand as I involuntarily ground against him.

"I do," I said. There was no coming back from this. No salvation awaited me at the end of my life, however long that might now be. Corban had damned me and with every prayer he lapped against my center, the farther I fell. I grabbed hold of his horns as he pushed me back by my thighs, angling me so that he could better feast.

A broken sob cracked from my lungs. "I love you," I choked, as if it were forced from me. I hadn't meant to say it but there it was. The truth. I loved Corban. Every manipulative, evil part of him.

Corban twisted the entirety of his tongue inside of me before he pulled back, unfolding my body. In one luxurious motion, he slicked it up my stomach across my breasts, and to my open, waiting mouth. In the next motion, he was inside me, filling me so completely that I saw stars. Stars that made up galaxies I had never seen before.

"What a magnificent queen you will be. What a beautiful wife," he purred.

There was nothing in that moment except for Corban. Beautiful, terrible Corban. The pleasure he had given me before dulled in comparison. This– This! was bliss. This was *real* magic. Unbridled and wild. Decadent and sinful. My skin felt like it was on fire, my soul begging to be consumed.

Corban slid his hand around the back of my neck, his fingers nestling just beneath my hairline as he tugged my head back. "Look at how lovely you are."

I looked up as the veil fell from his face, into the slitted eyes of a monster, and smiled.

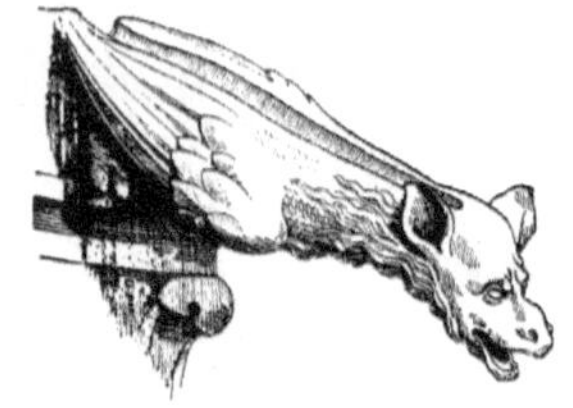

Gravel crunched under the wheels of the dark blue Chevy as it came to a halt at the top of the drive.

Next to the sedan squad car. Why was there a police car at Glamis?

Brenda Grendel stepped out of the truck, her high heels sinking between the tiny black stones. She cursed under her breath, resting her hand on the door as she straightened.

Yellow tape blocked the front door, barring entry. Not that anyone would ever set foot inside Glamis Manor. The whole town knew that anyone who went in never came out. That whatever evil lived within drove you mad or drove you to death. At least, those were the stories Macky always told them as kids.

Brenda had been to Glamis once, but that was so long ago she could hardly remember what it had been like. Vaguely, she recalled the gargoyles, but she could have sworn the house had been made of wood, not stone.

It was supposed to be a vacation home but after a single weekend that resulted in one of her brothers needing stiches from an animal scratch on his back, and the other being thrown down the stairs, Macky packed the family up and never brought them back. Once the kids were grown and moved out, Macky had gone away too. Brenda still didn't know if she had been at Glamis Manor the entire time, or if she had bounced between the other broken-down shacks she owned. What she did know, was that Macky's last days had been spent in this hell hole.

"Sorcha!"

It had been weeks since Brenda had heard from her daughter. She knew she'd been hard on her, but that's how it went between them. They would butt heads more often than not, but at the end of the day they would be right as rain. Except Sorcha hadn't called her back. Hadn't answered any of her texts after their last argument.

Brenda flipped through her phone, double-checking the address to make sure she was at the right place. The selfie Sorcha had sent all those weeks ago showed a beautiful manor in frame behind her. This couldn't have been the same building. It was decrepit, crumbling, quite literally falling apart at the seams.

Sorcha had described the house as being in pristine condition, elegant, and on one occasion, as magnificent. What stood before Brenda was a rotten structure that *could* have been all those things. Once.

Voices flitted past the fluttering yellow tape strung across the gaping front door. "I don't know how we're going to explain this to the community. How do five missing men turn into one hundred and twelve? There was no space at the morgue, they had to take the rest over to Providence County."

Brenda's heart faltered at their words as she stormed up the steps. "Hello?" She ducked under the yellow tape, her eyes skimming the dusty, dilapidated foyer until her gaze snagged on the black stains along the stairs leading to the upper levels.

The sound of footsteps came from her right, dragging her attention away from the dark spatter. An older gentleman, followed by a clean-shaven man strode through the long hallway. The older of the two was in a tan suit, pressed with sharp lines, while his companion donned the typical uniform of an officer.

"This area is blocked off, ma'am. I'm going to have to ask you to leave," the older man said.

Brenda shook her head. "My daughter lives here. She hasn't been answering her phone and—" her eyes snapped back to the stains, "—what's happened?" It was all over the walls.

A flash of a memory darted through her mind. A spiral staircase, distinctly different from the straight, sweeping stairs before her.

The men looked at each other in blatant confusion. The younger one ran a hand over his face.

"You look a little young to be Maxine's mother," the first said. The officer beside him gave him a funny look.

Brenda scowled. "My daughter, Sorcha, inherited my mother's place. Maxine's place. She moved here about two months ago." She stepped farther into the foyer, peering over their shoulders into the living room. There were more stains behind them, except these still held their color. The stains weren't black, they were dark red.

"Ma'am, I need you to step outside. Come on now."

Brenda planted her heels. As steep as they were, she didn't waver an inch. "Where the fuck is my daughter?"

"Lady, your daughter isn't here. There's nothing but bod–" The younger officer snapped his mouth shut when the older man shot him a glare.

Brenda's chest clenched. Her eyes flashed back to living room, to the second floor. "The... what?" Bod...bodies. The stains– it was blood.

Blood dried black like that. "Oh my god, is my daughter...?" She couldn't finish. She couldn't breathe!

"I saw the house. She only sent me one picture of it, but it didn't look like this," Brenda insisted. "Where is she? Did something happen to her?" No, that couldn't be the reason Sorcha hadn't returned her calls.

The older man took her by the elbow and eased her outside as her knees buckled. "What's your name?" he asked gently, settling her on the front porch

"Brenda. Brenda Grendel. My daughter, Sorcha." Her eyes brimmed with tears. Her shaking hand dove into her pocket for her phone. Her thumb skidded across the screen several times as she let out a broken curse. "Here. This is her. This is Sorcha." Brenda looked up at the young officer. "What happened? Has anyone reported her missing?"

The officer took the phone, his face paling slightly. Did he see the same thing she did? That the house was whole in the background?

"You! You know her. What happened?" Why weren't they saying anything?

The officer grimaced. "I don't know her. It's just—" he gave a look to the older gentleman, "—there's stories about this place." He turned the screen to the man and dropped his voice. "I think those boys killed it, August. People in town said there was a haunt in Glamis. And look, it's the same house, but this one is..." He trailed off.

August, the older man, squinted at the picture on the phone. "You're telling me you believe in ghost stories?"

"I'm saying that before Jeremy and the guys went missing the house was normal. I told you it was, and here's the proof. It's like it happened overnight. Maxine always took good care of her things."

Brenda snatched the phone from August. "Cut the bullshit. I don't give a fuck about ghost stories or whatever the town has to say about my mother. My mother is dead. Where is my daughter?"

The officer swallowed. "Gone. At least, she wasn't any of the ones we found inside."

August looked between the two of them. He let out a sigh that turned into a cough. He rubbed his wrinkled knuckles into the corner of his mouth. "Would you be willing to come down to the station with us? Maybe you can help us put some pieces together."

Seconds, then a minute went by before Brenda finally responded. She shook her head, then nodded, trying desperately to keep the tears from falling. "Sure whatever. As long as you find Sorcha," she spat, rising to her feet with stiff poise.

Sorcha wasn't inside, which meant she was alive. The house looked nothing like the one she had sent photos of. *Did she purposefully send me on a wild goose chase?* By the sound of it, the small-town cops didn't know what the hell they were doing either. Mentioning haunts made them sound as nuts as Macky.

Brenda walked swiftly back to the truck, her heart pounding. A flash of white paper fluttered on the ground near her pointed heel. She snatched it up before climbing in, slamming the door behind her. Whatever had happened, Sorcha had nothing to do with. This obviously wasn't the right place. She was taking her time to respond, trying to prove a point to Brenda that she was all grown up.

She was probably throwing some sort of temper tantrum. Sorcha wasn't even here, that's all this was.

She's trying to teach me a lesson. The nerve.

Tires spun as she whipped the car around and sped down the long drive. Perhaps she should have given her information to the officers. But

Bristol was a small town and word traveled quickly. It wouldn't take them long to figure out she was staying at The Bradley.

Brenda swiped her hand across her face; the piece of paper, still pinched between her fingers, slapped her slightly. Her irritation rose as she read the script. She read it again. On the third read, she bared her teeth. She crumpled the piece of paper angrily.

"Superstitious bitch," she said and tossed the ball out the window.

There were once three rules of Glamis Manor, all of which have been broken. A spell of protection, poorly crafted, now failed.

1. Do not look into the mirrors for more than a moment, for they are a gateway to his world.

2. Do not invite guests into the manor, for he shall feast on their blood and bones.

3. Do not leave the shelter of the manor after nightfall, for he is the night that corrupts the light.

Long live the King of the Unseelie, may the gods have mercy on the one that set him free.

ACKNOWLEDGEMENTS

To my editor, Tori, who helped me bring Corban and Sorcha's twisted games to life. To Ariella, for introducing us, and being my hype woman. To Kendall, who is always the first to read my work when it's nothing but bare bones and loving it anyway. To Sam, for braving a real-life moth attack after reading that one scene and still soldiering on to help me polish the first draft. To Tara, for letting me use you to act out scenes even though it meant you had some blood-drenched spoilers.

To my readers, and anyone who's ever craved a happily ever after of a darker kind, thank you for trusting me as I tried something a little different with this one. I hope you enjoyed sinking your teeth into Corban as much as I enjoyed him sinking his teeth into me.

ABOUT THE AUTHOR

ALLISON PAIGE loves traveling with her camera, particularly in the Irish countryside, and has several ongoing projects she writes out of her home in Charleston, South Carolina. She fills her spare time working with animals of all types and is a fervent advocate of bee, ocean, and wildlife conservation.

www.ingramcontent.com/pod-product-compliance
Lightning Source LLC
Chambersburg PA
CBHW032353310726

48973CB00007B/1987